Wild Geese Overhead

NEIL GUNN

Chambers

First published 1939 by
Faber and Faber Ltd

This edition published 1991 by
W & R Chambers Ltd,
43–45 Annandale Street,
Edinburgh EH7 4AZ

The publisher acknowledges the
financial assistance of the Scottish Arts
Council in the publication of
this book

British Library Cataloguing in
Publication Data

*A catalogue record for this book is available
from the British Library*

ISBN 0-550-22520-X

Cover design by Grafik Design Works

Printed and bound by Cox and
Wyman Ltd.

FOREWORD

One of Scotland's most distinguished twentieth-century writers, Neil Gunn, enjoyed a writing career that spanned thirty years, ending in the mid-1950s. The majority of his many novels are set against the backdrop of the Highlands of Scotland; *Wild Geese Overhead* and *The Lost Chart,* the latter also published in the *Scottish Collection,* are exceptions to this syndrome: the action in both books takes place in the biggest and most vital of Scottish cities, Glasgow. Admirers and critics of Gunn affirm that the author is never totally at home in an urban environment, an assertion made with some justification. However, Gunn is no regional author: his quest for a clearer understanding of the human situation transcends boundaries between city and countryside; the ambience is one thing, the search another.

What can be more evocative than a title like *Wild Geese Overhead?* The simple wonder of migratory birds, gloriously free, pursuing their long flights in accordance with the rhythm of the seasons, touches us all. It also begs the question, 'What has this to do with a story of life in Glasgow in 1939?' After all, the birds are flying over a city that is experiencing a period of grave economic depression; the League of Nations has failed and the outbreak of war is more than a possibility. This is the stage on which the principal character in the book, Will, a journalist, plays his part. What then is the relevance of the title?

One spring day while in the country seeking some peace and a breath of fresh air, Will sees a flock of wild geese heading north. 'Watching he was invaded by the feeling that he had seen something which it was hardly right he should see, something out of occult books, out of magic. He should have been better prepared. It was going from him; and he had not got it at all. He had missed something. What he had missed, he wondered over.' This experience works on Will and acts as a catalyst to the development of his thinking on matters social, political and psychological. It also entices him to secure lodgings far away from the hustle and bustle of the city in a farmhouse in its hinterland, and not far from the spot where he had seen the geese. This step does not go unnoticed in the wordly milieu in which he moves and works. The accusation of 'escapism' is the main broadside against which he has to find some form of defence. The accusation comes in various forms and from very different types of people. Family connections and journalism have given him access to a wide spectrum of society. Through the former he moves in the comfortable circle of the Glasgow business community; through the latter he encounters the cut and thrust of debate with his colleagues in journalism and sees at first hand the misery and degradation of many of Glasgow's citizens.

His journalist colleague Mac is his main adversary in debate and the one who taunts him most about his so-called escapism. The debates between the two are in a sense the essence of the book. Mac's negative approach to life is in sharp contrast to Will's positive flights of imagination and his belief in the sanctity of the individual. To him people are not figures or the stuff of averages but real beings with a dignity and importance all of their own. There is something Dostoyevskian in the encounters between Will and the prostitute Ivy that bring out the essential goodness of this woman, a victim of economic circumstances. Will ruminates on the psychological turmoil of city life and the courage of those whom it affects. 'And the overwhelming mass of them are extraordinarily decent; the women caring for their room and kitchen, or even single end . . . putting up a magnificently stoic fight against a real or ever-threatening economic famine that is hellish because it shouldn't be.' And when talking to a girl who loves the country: 'It's that awful greyness, gloom that got me. Their lives are not dramatic. They are grey. But they don't feel the greyness as we would. To them the street noises and the grinding trams are their singing birds.'

There is physical violence, too, to which Will falls a victim and which brings the story to its *dénouement*. His period of recuperation enables him to see all those with whom he had mixed in a new way — and particularly, Jenny Baird, the niece of his landlady at the farm. Her aloofness turns out to be a form of shyness and her inner strength is clearly derived from the rock garden at the farm which she so lovingly tends. Her fascination with the plant kingdom strikes a cord within his own philosophy of life. 'To look at a bunch of grass, a tree, the sky, to feel the wind, the rain, the light . . . ah, light, not only outside, in the air, on the body, but inside, behind the mind . . . to see, to feel, in the final core of oneself, and so to be whole — and therefore all the more game to break the fell clutch of circumstance, individual or social.'

DAIRMID GUNN

For

TOSHON WALSH

CHAPTER ONE

*

I

As he awoke he heard the bird-singing and cunningly tried not to hear it, not to get exasperated by it, so that he could go to sleep again. He did his best; breathed deeply, made his brain dull, let his head fall inert. When his cunning was being defeated, he raised up his will. In the effort of keeping his mind a blank, he became wide awake.

It was very maddening. He needed sleep. Now he would toss and turn and wear himself out before the day started. From the riot of the singing, he knew his watch would show five o'clock. He had been in bed little more than four hours.

How one grew tired and tossed one's legs and turned over—and back, with what increasing torment of anger and bad temper and spasms of violence to coverlet and pillow! So utterly futile the whole affair—particularly the bird-singing. The same things went round and round in the mind; and, behind them, in the most momentary pause—that storm of singing. No good shutting the window with a bang and placing a pillow upon the upper ear. Nothing was any good, for there was nothing he had not tried except tears of vexation, and they had come fairly close to him more than once.

Well, I may as well give in! he thought. Oh, pipe on! he suggested; pipe up your ditties of no tone! Don't mind me. I'll listen. That's precisely, he said, fisting a pillow, what I'm here for.

Then, for the first time, he deliberately listened to the singing that broke out each morning in the grey of the dawn.

And there was truly an astonishing volume of it. The main wood began at the back of the farm steading and the singing receded with it to what seemed an immense distance. It was in fact a sea of multitudinous sound. No individual song emerged. Individual notes—yes, if the ear listened acutely, but in the very act of listening, the individual notes were lost, fell like little jets of water back into the main tumult. It was the whole throbbing vibrant sea that lived, writhing and interwoven. An ecstatic creative sea. . . .

That beginning of symbolic thought revolted him, and in a sudden calm moment it was not a sea at all but a plain, an immense prairie, where the notes of individual songs, previously like tiny fountains, were now grasses, sticking up here and there, and fronded, in the way one might see them when lying flat to the earth as they bow against a remote horizon. This was a perfectly clear image after that vagueness of a sea. Precise, with a fine morning light over the prairie and above the horizon. And cool, too, so that one could look at it and almost smile, feeling the cool morning breath of it on the sticky sweatiness of the body. Besides——

All at once, it was the real sea, advancing upon him with the sounds of its green waters smashing over rocks and boulders, advancing up the valley from the shore which was miles away. For several moments the illusion was absolute, and he caught the crying of the gulls, with the cavernous echoes acquired from cliff walls. The cries were smothered every now and then in the spume of the advancing waters. Advancing upon him . . . up the valley . . . tumbling over, sweeping on, growing louder, near at hand . . . until he suddenly realized that the crying *was* the crying of gulls.

He remembered having seen a company of them on the field below the house the other day. At last, his smile emerged. For the space of five seconds he had completely forgotten himself in wonder—evoked out of the vision of himself as a small city boy on a stormy shore.

The vision had arisen in a magical transparency superimposed like a film. . . .

What was that? The short sharp cries of terns, ripping the air with their narrow beaks, right above him, over the house. . . .

His smile, with its faint irony, faded out and left him listening more acutely than ever.

An iron gate creaked over in the farm steading. Or

was it? Again—and again: *Honk! Honk!* And then suddenly happened the miracle that transformed his life and he felt himself lifting on the wings of wild geese.

2

Just a year ago, he had been here in the spring. An afternoon it was, and, standing not far from this house, he had heard that rusty *honk! honk!* and wondered—and then, strung out in an irregular arc, he had seen the geese. At first he had thought they were swinging to the south, and that had vaguely disturbed him, for he had the notion that they should go north to nest. As they continued to swing round, a deep pleasure and reassurance had flooded in upon him, and when they assumed their arrow formation and headed a little west of north, he had watched them enthralled. One barb of the arrow was much longer than the other and, going away from him, it undulated slowly like a ribbon drawn through the still air. Where had they come from? And whither bound? Watching, he was invaded by the feeling that he was seeing something which it was hardly right he should see, something out of occult books, out of magic. He should have been better prepared. It was going from him; and he had not got it all. He had missed something. What he had missed, he wondered over.

This wonder in one form or another had worked in him through the gritty summer days in the city, and during the winter time he had found himself inclined to a greater conviviality than ever. Not that he was exactly drinking too much, but still he was perhaps drinking more than was good for him, enough anyway to make him swear many a time that he was a fool and that it was high time he chucked it. His thirtieth birthday, falling on the first Sunday in March, he left the city by bus, and, from the bus-stop, set out on foot for the place where he had seen the geese.

It was undulating farming country, lowland country, for when he turned to look northward he saw a remote dark-purple rampart circling slowly against a pale-blue sky, like the contour of a strange land seen from a ship. The sunlight glittered in his eyes, so that they grew smaller and, breaking their stare, glanced hither and thither, as if they had emerged from a winter sleep and were not to be taken unawares. His face was pale and thin, his hair mouse-coloured, and his eyes a flecked brown. His body was thin and tall, but walked with an easy light footfall. He looked at everything near and far with pleasure, yet also with the unconscious air of a nimble animal making sure of its environment, a rather graceful animal, if grace rises from supple joints and sensitive responses.

Touched with a knowingness that was something more than irony, his eyes glimmered, good-naturedly amused. Already his body was feeling the weight of his heavy dark-brown overcoat for it was very susceptible to change of temperature. The narrow country road wandered its way up the slow incline.

He took off his gloves and stuffed them in a coat pocket. A farm steading a hundred yards off the road drew his attention. It was an old steading, badly needing some whitewash, and stood surrounded on three sides by churned-up mud and an uncertain scum of grass that was very green compared with the grass in the pasture fields. Broken-down farm implements and the rusting chassis of an abandoned car gave the whole place, with its begrimed outside walls, a forbidding, even a sordid air. Life could not be comfortable there, but always a little raw, and dirty, and in winter cold to the marrow. Yet it fascinated him. For he was haunted by the notion never to forget the fundamentals. And for the animal part of living, every occupation or preoccupation of man could be dispensed with—except this fundamental one of growing food out of the earth.

His mind, from that simple point, adventured into speculation so that for a hundred yards the country was not within his focus of attention, even though his eyes were continuously alive and might not have been surprised. He removed his dark-grey felt hat and wiped his forehead with an open palm. Then he unbuttoned his overcoat but did not take it off, because there was a cold nip in the air, made all the more treacherous by the thin sunshine, and he had been laid up twice during the winter with feverish chills that he had found difficulty in shaking off. The cool air now penetrated his clothes to his hot skin and he began to cough. When the spasm passed, his face was left with the watery pallor of a plant grown in a cellar or under a stone.

As he began to approach the crest, excitement crept into his skin. Soon he would come in sight of the next valley and see the farm-house with the dark plantation stretching away behind—the house had stuck in his mind with a remarkable visual solidity—and stand on the spot where he had watched the geese head north by west towards regions where, if he listened, he could hear icicles tinkle in vast desolate noondays.

Some such element of faery had hung about the valley itself, which was no more than a fold in the rolling land, and when at last he looked down upon it he found that the element of remembered intimacy had, if anything, increased. This was a pleasant surprise, and it made him hold his breath a little, until he realized that the effect was due to the strong sunlight on the bare lands. Under that light the earth and all it contained lay utterly dead. In December and January the sodden earth is a drowned body, but by the beginning of March it is blown dry as a skeleton. Towards the sun, the bark on the old gnarled trees was not the pale gold of winter but white as bleached bone. Far out over a grey-green pasture field, birds heeled and tumbled, swooped up and fell, like tatters and fragments tossed by a storm. But the farm-house itself, on which his gaze lingered, was more still than the land, and, where the land was strong and austere, it was roofed and lonely.

Bracing and poignant and a little frightening!

Though where this thin harmony of emotion came from, heaven alone knew. From more than a few thousand years back in time, he reckoned. That at least was certain! No childhood memory could evoke this adult shudder of white light and bleached bone. His mind's eye saw the face of a primeval hunter on the edge of a wood, and at once he moved on to the place where he had watched the geese.

But the sky was empty, and the blue, irradiated by light, of a remarkable tenderness. Remote, certainly, and cold if one let oneself be influenced by the moving air—but summer tender in fact and full surely of divine promise. He stood in a chilly trance, till the sound of a footstep fell on his heart and made him start like an animal.

When he saw that it was only a young woman he experienced the spirt of anger that nearly always follows a foolish fright. He stared at her for no more than a second, before turning back again, his heart thudding from the anger.

Yet in that second he had seen her coming walking down upon him with the calm of Primavera, the Lady Spring! Her incurious blue eyes had looked at him as if he were a tree! A calmness remarkable enough to increase his irritation and then to relieve it with swift derision.

He studied her back and knew the type of city girl she was quite well. Her blue-shot-with-grey tweed coat, with its simple sportswoman's collar, was the sort of thing one saw advertised "for country wear" at seven guineas. She exactly suited the fashionable illustration! And her shoes were really sensible—a quiet brown brogue with a single strap; and her hat, a blue felt that covered her head, had a brim outline of cunning simplicity; style, without obtrusive fashion, for the country!

Tall, without being too tall, and slim without being too slim! he thought, as he watched her moving easily down the road and disappearing beyond a belt of trees. Then a cold crepitation went over his skin and he sneezed violently three times and blew his nose. "Blast!" he said, and wiped his eyes. For it was not so much that he was frightened of getting a cold as unutterably weary of the very thought of it. He had got heated coming up the hill and then had stood roo long. He must keep moving. It was too soon to go back, so he went on—with reluctance, because it was the way the girl had gone.

When he came to the belt of trees, he saw the private road going into the farm. It sloped gently down through the narrow belt, mostly thorn on the right, but on the left quite a tongue of deciduous trees, and a few Scots firs. Not a wood so much as a shelter; yet it seemed to withdraw the farm from the main valley road into a measure of privacy. Usually a farm-house, it seemed, was little more than an extension of the steading, one with the mud and the manure and the cold gape, unless, of course, it was big enough to have given the farmer in the old days a tall Sunday hat and a high-stepping horse, to have made of him a little laird; then the farm-house might be separated from the steading by a bank of thorn or privet hedge, and might even come within measurable distance of being as comfortable as a manse, though never with the manse garden.

Would he go and ask for a drink? He was shy of intruding on the privacy of any house even to ask for a glass of water, but still. . . . His feet, however, had begun taking him along the farm road, which was quite dry, if badly rutted by cartwheels. He could see an uprising grazing field through the bank of scrubby blackthorn. On his left, the trees, not very large, were huddling together. Birds flitted across the road, very active little birds, shedding quick notes. Finches or linnets, possibly, for some of them were beautifully coloured. He knew next to nothing about birds, and certainly could not have told a chaffinch from a greenfinch or either from a tit. But he liked their swift ways and bright notes. Notes of coloured sunlight, he thought. Quick-darting little shuttles, weaving their bright invisible threads—about the grey bone! It was warmer in here. He looked about him. Nothing was watching him. He was still alone, could still go back. On his right, the hedge made a small bay, with a wooden gate in the middle giving on the upland pasture. His feet took him a few yards farther before they were suddenly held.

Crocuses, yellow and purple, in hundreds, and clumps of snowdrops with drooping heads. He glanced up swiftly from this unexpected sight to the farm-house. Grey stone, plain front door shut, window each side, two windows above, eaved, out of a blue slate roof. Back to those crocuses, hundreds of yellow and purple lights, all about the grass, running out of sight over the shallow bank, circling round the cherry-tree, moving in single file up the hollows between the grass-covered roots to the very base of the great elm. No garden; just plain grass. And below the bank, a pasture field, with sheep and broken turnips. Straight across, through an iron gate, he saw one side of the steading with its red doors. He could not see the rest of it because up from the gate, separating the house from the steading, ran a stone wall, banked with earth on the near side out of which grew a line of low heavy-foliaged evergreen trees. He went up the gravel path to the door, looked at the black iron knocker, raised it on its stiff hinge, and knocked twice.

"Excuse me," he said to the elderly woman who appeared, "but would you mind giving me a glass of water?"

After a moment's frank pause, she said: "Certainly."

"I have been walking", he explained, "and am very dry."

Her round grey eyes smiled and she nodded. A comfortable, energetic woman, with a kind full face and strong greying hair. "Just wait a minute." But she had no sooner turned away than she turned back. Perhaps it was the way he raised his hat; or perhaps the pallor of his face touched her heart; she asked him: "Would you like a glass of milk?"

"Well——" he paused, his expression deepening, "that would be too much."

"Not at all." She was quite herself now. "Come in."

With a vague word or two of protest, he followed her and was shown into the parlour on the left. She said she was sorry there was no fire, but if he took a chair she would not be a moment, and in a swirl of air she closed the door upon him.

Quick work! He smiled, looking about him. There was a china dolphin on each end of the pitchpine mantelshelf. There was an enlarged solemn photograph of a man in the prime of life, with a heavy moustache, hanging above the small black marble French clock on the centre of the shelf. Other photographs. A wedding group. A young man of to-day. Black hair-bottomed arm-chairs, male and female. An oak table, laden with ornaments and one or two more photographs in upright silver-bright frames. A slightly stuffy smell, preserved by camphor balls. Very clean. And silent—the clock was stopped. Sunday in a Scots farm parlour!

The window drew him and he went and looked out. The brightness of that bare world was even more silent than the room—but how wide and immensely high! And the light on the trunk of the elm-tree picked out its wrinkles. Like an elephant's hide. What a world! And the crocuses, the amazing crocuses, tiny yellow and purple lights for a fête—come up at the wrong time or left over from some wild night revel. The clumps of snowdrops—drooping arc lights with the inner radiance dimmed in the cold daylight. He held his breath and listened, and everything listened with him—until he heard her footsteps and turned towards the door.

She brought the glass on a little tray. A kind-hearted woman, with a warm bustling manner. "Not at all," she said. "It's nothing." He saw the marriage ring and took a mouthful of the milk. Lord, it was cold! He was not used to drinking cold "dead" stuff and had better go canny. "This is delicious milk. I have come out from the city, and the walking, with this heavy coat! . . ."

She understood. "Having a day in the country? Well, it's a pleasant day, but the country is not at its best just now, is it?"

The milk was delicious, but its coldness anaesthetized his gums. In his stomach, he could feel a few alcoholic microbes getting the fright of their lives!

"It's so quiet out here—after the rush of the city. I work in a newspaper office where things keep going."

"Do you?" She obviously had never looked at a pressman before. "You'll be up most of the night?"

"Well, no. As it happens I am on an evening paper, so I don't have to work late."

"Oh?"

"I could wish we had some of this quiet occasionally." He took a mouthful and held it a moment thoughtfully before letting it down, then he turned his face to the window. As he looked out, he felt the sensation of what he was going to say coming over him in an odd hush. "I don't suppose there is any one hereabouts who would take a fellow like myself as a lodger?"

A minute ago the question would have surprised him even more than it now surprised her. His expression, however, was almost casual in its friendly way. "I had a beastly cold this winter—twice, in fact—and I feel some time in the country might do me good. You don't actually know of any one?" And he looked into her eyes.

"No. No, I don't know of any one," she answered slowly, her head tilted upward, thoughtfully. "No. We're all so far away from anywhere."

"Quite." He nodded.

Then there was silence, and she knew he was too polite to put the personal question direct.

"As for myself," she added, in a constrained way, "I'm afraid I had never thought of such a thing."

"You wouldn't care to think about it?"

"Well—no. I—my husband died three years ago. I am keeping the place going for my son. He's in East Lothian, where my husband's brother has two farms. He's learning dairying in particular. He's studying to take his B.Sc. in agriculture. In less than two years he should be home and then he will run this place himself."

But he could see, while she was speaking, that she was really thinking of his offer, that it excited her, that she was tempted.

Her expression caught a self-conscious warmth. "In any case," she concluded, "I don't know anything about keeping a lodger."

"Oh, that's quite easy," he answered, glancing at the table. "A boiled egg in the morning and anything handy you might have for supper at night. I wouldn't be home for lunch except on Sundays. I would pay thirty-five shillings a week—if that wouldn't be too little." His eye was caught by a photograph in a small silver frame. It was the photograph of a girl he had met somewhere.

"I don't know," she replied, agitated by the temptation. It would be "found money". She did not know what to do. "Would you excuse me," she asked, "till I—till I go and see——"

"No, never mind just now," he answered. "I want you to think it over. Here's my card." As he was withdrawing it from his pocket book, he "placed" the photograph as that of the girl he had encountered up the road. "Now I'll come along and see you this day week. That will give you plenty of time to think it over. And please don't feel that I shall be disappointed if you cannot take me. I mean—I will be disappointed—but——" They both smiled.

"All right," she said.

He finished the milk. "That was grand. Thank you very much indeed."

"Would you like——"

"No, thank you. I've been admiring your many photographs. Members of the family?"

"No, just friends—apart from our son there, our only child. And, of course, my husband." The man with the moustache.

He nodded and they were silent a moment. "Well —good-bye. Whatever happens, this has been very pleasant!" They shook hands warmly.

Lord, that was a narrow squeak! he thought, as he went up through the trees. What on earth possessed me? And he had all the relief of having escaped from a trap. The whole incident brightened him up wonderfully.

For the idea of coming and lodging in a place like this had, after all, its exciting side. He could stop lodging in it at a day's notice. It wasn't really a trap. Something bright behind the idea prompted him to laugh; something behind and above the idea, reaching up to the radiant blue sky. His eyelids crinkled in humour as the sky acknowledged his confidence.

And then the sub-editors' room—if he did come and live here! It would almost be worth doing it for the comment. Bulls, cocks, hens' food, rats, and the servant girl—the going would be pretty bawdy now and then! A chuckle came in soft gusts through his nostrils.

He would do it! Even if it would mean a lot of drink. He looked around on the bare lands. A lovely economy in their austere lines. Lovely! lovely! he thought, and his bright humour moved in his head like a song.

3

It meant even more drink than he had imagined. But his wit served him well enough, for there was a sense of freedom in the project that gave him unexpected power. He had thought that he would have to be on the defensive. Whereas he found he could even afford to say nothing and merely look in a certain way, the way that implies a fool's confidence. Or laugh with the laugh against himself.

On the Monday afternoon, between five and six, when the usual three or four of them were having a parting drink, Mac, out of a lengthy silence, nodded. He had got it at last! "It's none of all that," he said, referring to innuendo about "the simple life" on a farm. "After all, that sort of thing requires a certain amount of guts. In this specific instance, they don't apply." His lips pursed tight and he nodded slowly. He was a man of forty-three with a sandy face and a satiric disintegrating manner. As he regarded his glass, his lips moved leftwards into a fleshy opening that exposed three strong upper teeth, and a heavy sniff moved brown hairs in his nostrils. The four of them waited as they generally did for Mac. He looked up. "Remember Tommy Stink?"

Don and Rob burst into laughter.

"Who was Tommy Stink?" asked Jackie, the youngest, a slight nondescript Glasgow boy, full of the bright camaraderie of his native streets.

"He was a man," said Mac, "or at least, he was a sub-editor, who went to the country, to write a book!"

"A book?" said Jackie. "A book! !"

Mac's head went up and then down like the head of an old brown horse. Laughter warmed them.

"If you weren't all so preoccupied with intestinal matters——" began Will.

"Guts got him!" cried Don, a quick-thoughted black Highlander.

Mac nodded.

"——You would have tumbled to that long ago." Will's calm judicious manner was expected of him. "However, you have sure got it now. But of one thing you can be certain: in my book I shall do the decent by you. I'll draw each of you to the life. I'll shirk nothing. Everything will go in—everything. And even you, Jackie, who are so astonished at the thought of a book, will not be forgotten."

"You make me blush," said Jackie with ironic modesty.

"I shall not forget the secret dreams you drew from Rupert Brooke, the verses you made in emulation, and hid, and secretly re-read; the ambition that walked with you at night down quiet streets, from one island lamp-post to another—for we are all lonely dogs after our fashion—the ambition that saw itself in the world-renowned glory of a book, not of verse, but of poetry."

"Oh, dry up!" cried Jackie, boisterously.

Will dipped a forefinger in the spilt beer and began drawing a pattern on the table. "No need to blush, for yours is the ambition that's launched ten thousand subs. Take Mac here. What would you say now is the secret ambition of Mac's soul?"

"You'll know, I suppose?" said Mac.

Will tilted his head and looked at the pattern, then resumed his drawing. "Lost dreams looped out in lewd jest, in the mirthful sarcasms of the damned, bedewed with Scotch, soddened with beer, irrigated with coffee. Looped round and round by this octo-

26

pus till all the blood and juice has oozed out——"

Don tilted Will's mug and drowned the pattern.

"Yes?" said Mac.

"*Slàinte!*" said Will, lifting his mug.

"Clever, what?" Mac looked at him with his ice-blue, unrelenting eyes.

"No," said Will, "merely descriptive. You don't like it?" The way he raised his eyebrows in a casual smile set the others laughing, for they felt that between these two men, so opposed in temperament, there was a latent hostility, and it was as well to keep it within bounds.

They were not wholly right in this, for Will had a curious regard for Mac's strong character. And he was aware that Mac responded to his presence more than to that of any of the others though the response was almost always satiric, as if his was the type of mind that Mac must hunt and worry.

The hunt was on.

By the end of the week, he felt compelled to visit the farm in sheer self-defence.

So on Sunday off he set. There was a touch of dry spite in his going, an uneasiness. It was a fool's business. He was inclined to drift into things in a vague intuitive way. He needed more character, more certainty of aim in life. . . .

He got off the bus. The day was dry but overcast. No radiant blue to herald his approach! The farm steading on the right was more squalid than ever. But as the road rose to the crest he found his spirits

27

rising with it. There was something in a wide expanse that either frightened you or let you take wing.

And if there were no geese, at least there was no city female either! A peewit blew up from the road-side with noisy wings and a sharp crying. He stood and watched it circle and tumble. His new friends!

The crocuses were still alight, but the snowdrops were burning low. The lady of the farm answered the knocker with a welcoming smile. There was a fire in the sitting-room!

"I've been thinking it over," she said. "I don't know, but I thought if you cared to chance it we—we could see in a week or two if we suited each other. I mean I have never done this before and—and I'm not sure if——"

She was nervous over so extraordinary an under-taking! "I'm very glad," he said. "And then if you find in a week or two that it's awkward or difficult, why, I'll perfectly understand. And if I should have to leave for any reason, you'll understand." When he smiled in spontaneous friendliness, his face was very attractive.

"Yes." She nodded. "Yes—that will do fine. I'm glad you understand." She hesitated, then went on: "This will be your sitting-room. Will it be all right?"

"Couldn't be better. Ideal."

"Would you like to see your bedroom?"

"Well, all right." He followed her up the rather narrow steps of the stairs to a brown-linoleumed landing. "It's a bigger house than I thought."

"You don't see this back part from the front. But this would be your room."

It was a clean room, aired, with a slope on the roof in front towards an out-jutting peaked window. There was a faint autumn fragrance of apple that made him involuntarily pause and sniff.

"I had some apples spread out on the floor." she explained. "I thought the smell would have gone by now."

"I think it's exciting," he answered. "I'm trying to remember where I got it before." But he was quite sure he had never got that scent before, not in such a place. Whence this vivid memory? But he turned his face aside to hide his wonder and saw the flat window in the gable wall to his right. He went over to it and exclaimed: "Why, a garden!"

"Yes, the garden is to the side of the house."

"I did not think", he tried to explain, "that you would have much time for a garden. Shows all I know!"

"Well, indeed I don't, but I get one of the men to do the heavy digging, and then my niece comes at the week-ends and looks after it when the time comes."

"Is that the girl in the photograph on the table downstairs?"

She looked at him, astonished. "Yes."

"I just happened to glance at it," he said. "I think she passed me on the road last Sunday. What a bright airy room!"

"I'm glad you like it."

There was a pause.

"Well—is that all right, then?" he asked.

"Yes, I think so."

"I think so, too," he said.

There was a moment's awkward hesitation, then they both laughed and shook hands.

The following Saturday afternoon, he moved in.

4

That was three weeks ago, and he had stuck it out manfully. For the first week there was the novelty of the situation, particularly the incredible quiet of the evening, so that sometimes it made him listen with breath held, caught him out of his chair to walk about and stand and listen again. Once or twice he experienced an almost ominous tension in the quiet, as if space or time were made of an invisible glass about to crash in on him. Occasionally he caught himself all taut by the closed door hearkening for the slightest sound from the kitchen premises. The farm cottages were on the other side of the steading, below the edge of the wood.

His landlady had even improved on acquaintance. A mothering women, with bright greetings and a warm husky laugh. Her eyes would move over the supper table even while she was speaking to him, anxious that everything should be there. He had already developed the habit of bringing home the last edition of his paper and any special tit-bit of city news. She loved this and he knew she looked forward to it. Yet though she would stand talking in the friendliest way, she was never obtrusive and always withdrew at the right moment. She respected his privacy and he hers; and it was as well perhaps to keep that up, for a time anyway. Besides, he wanted to do some reading, quiet reading in which he might gather some ideas to turn over and feed on.

His reviewing for the parent daily often dissatisfied him, because he was conscious of using ready-made, if high, standards. Academic and correct, rather than fresh and pungent. There was a sense in which even the best of his reviews were almost automatic. He knew at once when to apply Aristotle!

He got his deepest interest out of books of literary criticism. They excited him more than any other kind of book, certainly more than the usual modern novel, play, or even poetry. He saw the obvious weakness in this for it implied greater interest in the criticism of a thing than in the thing itself. But the implication was only half true. Great literature did not excite him: it quietened him, gathered all his warring parts into a harmony that was self-illumined. But criticism excited him. A Communist turning the Marxian dialectic on H. G. Wells or on Surrealists or on Ezra Pound was enough to whet his mind to a cunning edge. A point for analysis and challenge on every page! For he abhorred a special or propagandist pleading that blurred exact analysis by inexact or partial definition, and none the less because he might agree with the essayist's main position. For his one birthright that he was not going to sell to any one, or to any cause however he might believe in it, was that ultimate apprehension of truth which brought illumination and, in the complete suspension of disbelief, the spirit's clear freedom. It was a fundamental of the spiritual life of man as a farm was a fundamental of his economic life. If ever he did write a book, it would probably be a long essay with some such title as *Definitions*. And with luck it might show a passion for fineness of thought rather than a pedantic appreciation of lucidity!

Yet though here he was in the right spot, with whole long evenings to himself and a quietness he could feel—surely the perfect environment for careful thinking—he found he could hardly even read! This astonished him. And when he tried to think it out, his mind fumbled. Even simple issues slid away unresolved as if his mind were in fact going vague and woolly. The vacant earth! Or the bovine stare!—out of which he had already wakened himself more than once.

True, in that first week a certain positive value did accrue; the morning walk to the bus-stop, the evening walk back, the regular hours and the quiet living—particularly the cutting down of drink—did have a beneficial effect on his health. Imperceptibly his reservoirs began to fill with energy. The coughing that had troubled him on going to bed had diminished to a few dry hacks quite free of discomfort. (After his first night's performance his landlady, in deep concern, had put a fire in his bedroom. She would lose money on him yet!) More than once when walking to the bus-stop in the morning, he had been invaded by a feeling of physical well-being. It would suddenly come over him, send his eyes happily questing around and his legs in long spanking strides down the road. He had time for a walk in the gloaming, too, and went up through the farm fields, into the wood, and generally explored his immediate environment. Twice, before going to bed, he had had short walks in the moonlight and had heard the owls hooting in the wood.

But the one thing he could not do was concentrate.

The more he recognized the fact, the more restless he became. He could listen, he could "stand and stare", but he got none of the poet's sensation of pleasure or fulfilment. On the contrary he was merely pervaded by a feeling of personal futility that, dwelt upon, rapidly mounted into irritation. He found he could do nothing with his physical well-being in the country. There was no way of spending it. Deep in him he began to realize by the end of that first week that the country was of no use to him—apart of course from the animal matter of physical health. He could now understand the gold-diggers who came back to the nearest town to squander their "dust" in a glorious blow-out. One endured in the country for specific reasons.

Deeper than all that, too, lay this thought—the only one he found no difficulty in sustaining. It was a thought or theory that had begun to divide the whole modern world. It dealt with the conception or nature of freedom. Hitherto we had believed that a man could not be absolutely free until he found himself independent of his fellows, with the power to go where he liked and do what he liked. No one man must have dominion over another. So feudalism was fought and conquered and man became free. But soon it was found that man was not free, that he was still everywhere in chains, and more inhuman chains, because they tied him to machines rather than to other human beings. And the results were certainly more inhuman than the world had yet known, in the form of slums, unemployment, poverty, and wars of a brutality and magnitude beyond any medieval dream.

So there arose in the modern age the new school of thought which said that man does not attain freedom by being able to break away from society, but, on the contrary, attains freedom only in and through society itself. Only in a community working, not for the profit of a few but for the good of the whole, does man really become free. For he is a social animal and without his social inheritance would be no more than a beast of the jungle. The old bourgeois conception of the freedom of the individual apart from society was a pretty myth with a hellish inheritance.

So the opposition went. And Will had to admit to himself that, as far as his little effort to attain solitary freedom in the country was concerned, the new school of thought won hands down!

And the experience of being introduced to the land-lady's niece on his second Sunday on the farm did not disillusion him. He could see by an instinctive withdrawing movement the girl made on his unexpected approach that she would have avoided the introduction if she could. But that was now impossible for she and her aunt were standing on the grass in front of the house regarding the dying crocuses, and Mrs. Armstrong, turning round, greeted him, and could not but present "My niece, Jenny—at least I should say Miss Baird." Her laughing words were a trifle self-conscious, for there was little natural guile in this warm-hearted woman. They bowed without shaking hands, and Mrs. Armstrong to cover her astonishment at such behaviour asked him where he had been and he told her, adding a question or two and being answered. Jenny showed no interest, and looked politely at her crocuses. She was without coat and hat and her hair had deep gold lights in it. There was admittedly a cool distinction in her face. Lifting her eyes unexpectedly, she met his—and did not waver—but calmly regarded him so that he got the impression of the eyes being set wide apart and so clearly blue as to seem translucent. He removed his own as if they had been contemplating her absent-mindedly and had in no way been impressed.

He walked into the house chatting to Mrs. Armstrong and, without turning round to acknowledge Jenny, entered his room.

That should about suit her! he thought.

All the same, something in the encounter excited him and he felt acutely annoyed. He understood her attitude perfectly well. Like himself, she wished to be free of the city; had enough of its contacts during the week; did not want, in particular, to run into the city male type. And here she comes to her small estate in the country and finds it invaded by—of all things—a city lodger! It must be a bit galling to her, obviously. And she must have exercised restraint in not persuading her aunt to refuse him. Yet there again, restraint was palpably her most striking characteristic!

But, above all, what right had she to do the whole thing with so calm and untroubled a face? He could see the face still. Primavera in the picture! Her cool grace did not impress him, and if she was afraid he might claim her acquaintance, either here or in town, she was mistaken, vastly mistaken. The legend of her little country estate was safe enough as far as he was concerned!

Finding himself all worked up, he paused, contemplated himself, and began to chuckle.

His landlady came in to set the supper table. They talked about his walk again, where he had gone and the degree of less cold in the air. There was nothing else to talk about—except the new item, the niece.

"She works in town, but loves to come out here for the week-end. She's been giving me my orders to-day about getting the garden dug and manured! She's daft on flowers."

"Is she?"

"Yes. Every week-end she'll be out, after the next one. It's a craze with her. And she knows every flower there is, I think—Latin names and all!"

"Really!"

36

"Oh, she's a one! And very clever. She works in an office in town. She's the private secretary to a partner in a big firm of exporters."

"Very clever of her."

"She had to know Spanish."

"Oh!"

"Yes. She had to learn it specially."

"She would, I'm sure. I mean you don't usually get it at school."

"No." She was modestly proud of her niece. "Do you like this stew?"

"I think it's delicious."

"You are not difficult to please, I must say."

"You don't give me a chance to grumble. By the way, if I should be late any night getting home, for goodness' sake don't wait for me. If I'm not here at my usual supper time, you'll know I'm eating in town."

She paused. "I hope you're not going to start working late. If you don't mind me saying so, I think you're looking better since you came. And that cough has got less a lot."

He reassured her. It would only be occasionally. And if he was delayed beyond the last bus and didn't turn up at all, she mustn't worry.

When she had gone out he asked himself ironically: Paving the way for return to the fleshpots—already?

He was not blinding himself any more. The whole final truth of his retreat to the country was no more than an elaborate (and rather silly) pretence.

Then one morning, on the way to the bus, a cold morning of sleety rain, he got wet from the thighs down and spent a miserable day with a swelling throat, drank hot whisky toddy in a cosy corner with some of the boys, caught the last bus, and got soaked again on the mile-walk home. That weather kept up for several days. He bought waterproof leggings and a sou'wester.

With blind darkness and rain over the face of the country, Don asked him on the third night: "Honest to God, is it worth it?"

He got up and stretched himself before the fire in the saloon bar. He could not give in to them. That was his trouble now. The argument grew hot.

"All the same, that's what gets you," said Will. "You live in this fetid atmosphere, you crawl home through the streets, like rats through open sewers, and tumble, half-sodden, into your bunks——"

"And what do you do?" interrupted Mac.

"Ah—I stride through the country, wind and rain in my face, exhilarating, like a song. In fact, I often do sing. I arrive in a glow. I strip—and into a bath—and then——"

"You don't sing again?" Jackie raised his eyebrows.

Rob intervened for the first time. He had been watching Will. "You're all wrong. I know what it is. The dam' fellow has got a woman."

Light broke on their faces. There was a clamour.

Will glanced at his watch. "Good heavens! She'll think I've got run over. I'll have to sprint. So long, you bunch of soaks!" and he grabbed his hat.

"You dark horse!" cried Jackie. "So that's why you have never invited us out!"

Now he had not invited them out because he dared not, because there was nothing to show them, nowhere to go. All he could do was to take them to the nearest country pub and that meant a walk of over two miles. He could not ask fellows, bright intelligent fellows, out to his place for the privilege of gazing at trees and hedges—all bare—in a cold wind and expect them to be excited! After the first few minutes, they would feel helpless, awkward, and would begin looking around for some way of escape. All that could possibly be done at such a moment was to put more coal on the fire and produce a bottle. They would then brighten up at once!

In their position he would feel exactly like them and would brighten up at the same moment.

Inside the bus, the damp air made the atmosphere fuggy. Smelling of stale tobacco smoke and sweaty clothes. The bodies swayed and jerked at the same time; then off again in the incessant rumble that seemed to judder the bowels.

His thought continued of its own volition with the queer effect of a cinema inside a moving vacuum. It lifted up a recent book on Iceland by some young London poets that he had been given to review. Entertaining—but not a book on Iceland. Iceland—a new exotic background against which to place Byron, the civilization and culture of London—and themselves. Iceland for them meant death. Their book's real message. Honest in its modern fashion and (had there been anything to fear) fearless. Another young poet of the same school had characterized a fine peasant woman profoundly portrayed by a northland writer as "a primitive creature". Something of pleasant condescension in the phrase had made Will call the poet a pup. But there it was! And if he took his own landlady—well, in the hands of a great writer she might be a remarkable figure, a sort of universal mother or universal provider—she certainly had many admirable human qualities—but as far as interesting or attracting him was concerned she was his particular interpretation of the odious phrase "a primitive creature". It was no good pretending otherwise. The poet's country was an ideal country, "remembered" for the most part within four walls. In direct contact with the real country, a thinker found it full of distracting discomforts, and a poet abstracted from its harsh realities notions for verses, not only according to his gifts but also to suit the sentimental bourgeois illusion of being free, of glorious freedom. Objectively it was impossible, but subjectively quite a lot could be made of it.

That was the game. His colleagues did not need to be thinkers or poets to come to the same conclusion. He must be writing a book, or wenching, or doing something equally daft, before he would hide like this! They knew about it all, they knew!

The bodies swayed back and then jerked forward like corpses. He got up. The bus conductor was a girl with a soft skin and dark eyes, and dark leather straps. She returned his smile of good-night. She had been kissed often, he could see. She would make a lingering kiss. The bus roared away, and the wind and the rain got him. He hoped his landlady was in bed. He was weary and wanted to tumble into sleep.

For there was one thing he could do in the country: he could sleep. If he lost that gift. . . .

And then he lost it.

It happened one night when coming back from the last bus, he found that a small rain had taken all the winter out of the air and he smelt the new life in the earth.

His landlady was in bed and as usual had left a tumbler of milk, with a saucer on top, not far from the fire. The thought of what the boys would say if they saw him now drinking this strange liquor made him smile. He must order it sometime in the Press Club!

The enlivening touch in the atmosphere had freshened and slightly excited his mind. Turning up the wick of the Aladdin lamp, he decided he would try a few minutes' serious reading.

And what could be more apt than an essay on *The Modern Mind*, by T. S. Eliot? For the interesting thing about Mr. Eliot was that, though regarded as the most revolutionary force in modern poetry, yet no man in his essays put up a finer case for orthodoxy and tradition.

Will found himself, for the first time since coming to the country, reading with close attention, indeed with almost a full measure of the excitement fine literary criticism usually raised in him, and this highly pleased him. He could see the author thinking out his subject not pedantically but with wisdom. The inclusiveness and precision of his definitions acted like a stimulant; and when suddenly he came upon Mr. Eliot exhibiting not only, as it seemed to him, a doubtful wisdom but—what he would have betted was quite impossible—a questionable taste, his enjoyment was quickened.

Mr. Eliot was discussing the work of the distinguished scholar and critic, Mr. I. A. Richards, for whom he explicitly entertained a great respect. Mr. Richards had been trying to come to grips with the very difficult matter of how properly to appreciate or respond to poetry, and in this connexion was inclined to believe that "something like a technique or ritual for heightening sincerity might well be worked out". For sometimes after one's best efforts, response to a poem remained uncertain. When that happened, and in order to get the heightening of sincerity necessary to penetrate and dispel the uncertainty, Mr. Richards suggested one should "sit by the fire (with eyes shut and fingers pressed firmly on the eyeballs) and consider with as full 'realization' as possible:

(1) *Man's loneliness (the isolation of the human situation).*"

And promptly underneath it came Mr. Eliot's comment: "Loneliness is a frequent attitude in contemporary lyrics known as 'the blues'. . . ."

Will laughed, as if he could hardly believe it!

Restless, he laid the book aside and lit a cigarette. Was he going to get a slant on Eliot's vulnerability through his blind spot (even if deliberately blind)? . . .

It was two o'clock before he got to bed, and it was his belief that he had never properly fallen asleep, his mind remaining active below a thin skin of sleep, when all at once he found himself wide awake, listening for the first time to that full chorus of bird-singing in the dawn.

For a few moments it was as if he had awoke in another and more innocent world, and he held his breath. The music of the dawn!

Yes, there was the poet's chorus! Marvelling, he continued to listen. . . .

He was glad he had heard it. . . . However, he must get some sleep.

He turned round and snuggled his head and lay still—and found himself thinking. So he turned round the other way.

The chorus continued, grew deeper in power, more compelling. His brain began carrying on last night's debate from *The Modern Mind*. When he shut out any one particular thought, another immediately entered, until his brain was like a seething dormitory inhabited by Mac, Mr. Eliot, Jenny, the office, the staff, the city, the whole blasted world that he had ever seen, thought, hated, craved, or imagined in any form whatsoever!

And all with an etched intensity. It's this cursed mind of mine! he cried. It's lain fallow so long that now it's all naked and white and fierce as ten thousand

devils! He banished them with a stupendous effort—
to discover himself in a moment looking at Mac's
face, Mac's satiric face, now openly sneering and disintegrating. Yes, he knew that face, he knew what it
was after. It was the face of a man, thwarted himself,
warped and thwarted in his spirit, pursuing him, Will,
slowly, remorsely, until he would break his resistance, bit by bit, get him down to his own level and
then dominate him with a devil's satisfaction.

Will turned over and groaned. He hated that picture. It was like treachery. It was filthy. And then
another mind, remorseless in its inescapable insight,
regarded him with still irony: it was his own mind.

The dawn-chorus continued. . . .

He had just fallen, not into sleep so much as into
a state of exhaustion, when his landlady knocked. He
did not answer. She knocked again. He had to make
a real effort to subdue a blind wrath and answer in his
normal voice.

That day he was lunching with his school and
college friend, Philip Manson, already a junior partner
in an old-established shipping concern. They had
packed a few scrums in their time, arms round each
other's neck, and, when they happened to meet, they
would finish up: "What about lunch sometime?"
Philip would consult his diary and a day be fixed.
After lunch and a few drinks, they would agree that
it was a mistake they didn't meet oftener, life was
short and. . . . The intervals grew longer.

"Here, don't you find the roosters troublesome in the morning?" Philip asked.

"No; can't say I have."

"You must be a good sleeper for a townsman. You should thank your stars!"

"I've heard a few birds singing," said Will.

"Oh, that's all right. That would suit your literary tastes! But when a couple of roosters get answering each other—you could twist their necks off. Fearful racket. And then you sort of begin to look for it; waken up at three or four at their clarion shrill!" He smiled reminiscently. "It was an extraordinary spring that. You remember it? I was fourteen."

"You were sent to the country to recover from that spell of diphtheria, wasn't it?"

"Yes. The most remarkable thing I remember—sex *would* impress at that age—were the cows; it must have been late April. They were all mad and bellowed with incredible ferocity. In my .bed, I could hear them being let out into the field in the early morning. And when a cow was well away with it, she would bellow even when she was drawing in her breath. I used to get up and steal to the window and watch the bull go through his mystic rights." He laughed pleasantly. "But of course it's too early in the year for that yet. And you'll miss the day-long racket because you'll be in town. But you'll always have the week-ends—and the early mornings, of course!"

"It's all right pulling my leg—but consider what it's meant to you."

"How do you mean?"

"Well, wouldn't your life have been thinner without that experience?"

"Oh, I see!" He thought for a moment. "Do you know, it would," he confessed. "It's like something that happened very long ago and—and——"

"And not quite in this life."

Philip smiled thoughtfully, then looked at Will. "You don't change much! You are still—you still get that queer slant on things."

"As if I hadn't grown up!"

"Honestly, I don't know. You are the only fellow who ever contrived to make me feel I missed something. And yet at the same time did not arouse envy. It's difficult to explain."

"That sort of thought does tie the mind up in knots."

"It does rather," said Philip, with the characteristic self-assurance that permitted him to continue being interested in his own thought.

His clothes had always been distinguished by quality and personal taste; a tie, a shirt, a new texture or colouring, something that attracted the eye without being obtrusive; a man's clothes. His manners had always been easy and good; the brown note less evident now perhaps in his dark hair; his eyes dark-blue and prepared to remain upon one with the same old candour. From the beginning he had been cut out for a directorship, for he had restraint and tact and inspired a friendly confidence. A managing director, a chairman! Already, at thirty-one, he could afford to look back on the more curious aspects of life with a natural self-possession.

He now wanted to pursue this elusive quality in life which he must have got, he said, that time in the country.

"No, not then," said Will. "You didn't get it then. You never got it until just now."

Philip deliberated. "You think so? But how, then, could I know about it?"

"Let us start at the beginning. What exactly is *it*?"

Philip's brows gathered. "I'm hanged if I know," he said, and laughed candidly. "Let's have another drink. I'd like to get down to this."

Will was still feeling a bit wretched, and now up over him crept a premonition of awful boredom. But he liked Philip. Had always liked him.

The talk went on. But it was Will who had to define; who had to entertain Philip with the thought he did not normally encounter. Will felt himself being drained, and finally said he had to get back to the office.

"I really have enjoyed this." Philip got up. "Couldn't you come out some evening. . . . Not at all. The bill is mine. I asked you. Look here, what about. . . ."

Will spoke to his landlady at supper.

"We did have two roosters," she replied, "but just before you came one killed the other in a fight, and then some one left the door into the old pigsty open and he went in and pecked the bait on a rat-trap.

But I'm getting one on Saturday, I hope, and he'll have to do until our own grow up."

Tired as he was, he took a walk in the dark, stumbling here and there, so that he should sleep soundly. He left all essayists severely alone. Once or twice, after an illness, he had had a spell of sleepless early mornings, and knew the devilish accuracy with which the mind delighted in awaking at the same hour. If such a habit were to be formed here, life would become finally intolerable.

He awoke at the dawn chorus.

The following morning he awoke at the same time.

And now here he was awake again. The habit had been well and truly formed!

5

The making up of his mind deliberately to listen to the singing was something more than a gesture of despair. It was, at the root of his being, a cold and bitter defiance. If he had to listen, then listen he would in a detachment so complete that he would conquer the singing, master it, withdraw from it, and so, as far as he was concerned, annihilate it.

He lay flat on his back, his arms extended by his side, his legs slightly apart and at full stretch. His breathing came evenly and lightly through his nostrils. His mouth and eyes were shut, his head sideways.

He listened.

For a time the underlying hatred kept him from

anything like detachment. But little by little as the dramatic varieties in the presentation of the chorus claimed his attention, the hatred began to sink down, to seep away, and the feeling of exhaustion, freed from emotional enravelment, brought to his body a certain cool ease.

This in itself was a great relief, as if his drained flesh had grown lighter. That thick congestion of the brain, charged with obscuring pulsing blood, that followed the intense visualizations of sleeplessness, was thinning away at the same time; was thus no doubt the real cause of the lightness and ease. So that the vision of the prairie in the thin but clear morning light came not only upon his mind but also upon his body, filtering in a cool air through the bedclothes. As the advancing gulls brought the sea, his body began to lose its corporeal feel altogether and to float in a still wonder. This wonder quickened with the short sharp cries that he thought were the cries of terns. Then all in a moment, before his body could ground again, the wild geese opened the world above his closed eyes and in a movement of sheer enchantment his spirit, his own most intimate self, rose up and experienced such a sensation of freedom as he had never known in his life.

While the enchantment—a convenient word— lasted he was not excited or deeply moved. If the term "moved" may be used at all—and it is heavy— then, in the literal meaning, he was highly moved. It was a still, freed, high-up delight, in the sense that the light and horizons of the morning were about him. The hemisphere over his flat world opened out like a bright fan—though fan implies something opaque, when the experience was essentially and indeed precisely a removal of the opaque. More than that—though this is difficult—he not only experienced this delight in himself, as an intensely personal realization, but also he was part of all that was about him. Was this the final problem of "identification with the object" that so troubled his professor when expounding Hindu thought? Will did not "think" the question. The question and its answer were the one flash of light.

How long the experience lasted he could not tell, though he would be prepared to say not more than a few moments. For here time obviously did not matter, except perhaps in its implication that the nature of his experience was timeless. He let it pass without any desire to hang on to it. In fact when he felt it sinking down with him into sleep, he thought to himself, How delicious this is! drawing out the thought through a lingering lovely triumph that left him breathing lightly in a sleep that might have made curious eyes imagine he was listening somewhere.

CHAPTER TWO

*

I

He slept until his landlady knocked him and then awoke quickly with the feeling that this was a holiday or some "free" occasion of the kind that he could not recollect. As he remembered, a slow humour spread over his face. He looked up at the ceiling. It was just the ceiling. But as he kept looking the ghost of his experience rose in a faraway brightness beyond the house-top. Very visionary indeed! Very flimsy!

It was a good joke! He could not "rise" now if he wanted to. Did he want to? Not he!

He threw the clothes off with a swoop and leapt to his feet. A good sleep was a blessed thing. He hummed a snatch of jazz and chuckled at the dancing movement of his feet. Carry on! he said. But it was fine to have the feeling of life, of being alive in a living world. Yes, a fine day. He stooped and sniffed the air through the bottom half of the window (the top half was permanently fixed). Spring was coming in and no doubt about it.

"You look nice and cheerful this morning!" said Mrs. Armstrong, as she tugged the cosy with the green leaves and pink buds down over the tea-pot. It was a close fit, with a hole for the spout, like an old maid's mitten. Last night he had very nearly told her not to do it, on the principle that stewed tea was an abomination. He must have been pretty low!

How many persons living in town knew what a fresh egg was? White curd and vivid yolk. "I had a grand sleep," he said. "It's a nice morning, too."

"Yes. You can smell the spring in the air to-day. Jenny will be getting quite excited."

"Why?"

"So many of her things coming up. There are two of her special daffodils out to-day. Whenever she arrives she makes a dive for the garden. And then it's look at this and look at that! You would think Santa Claus had brought them."

He laughed so spontaneously that Mrs. Armstong's smile broke into a husky note or two on its own.

Santa Claus! he thought, going up the avenue. The birds were extremely busy. Not one of them rested a moment. A flash—and gone. His sight was so keen that more than once it caught dark-beaded eyes. And one blackbird, wings lowered and tail flicking, suddenly kicked up an extraordinary row. A blacker blackbird swooped swiftly down and up and into the hedge in front without a wing-beat in the loveliest curve he had ever seen. Spring magic! Or just plain love? It sure quickened their pulses! *Green shoots from Santa Claus*: O.K., boys, let it ride—right through to the end.

Here now was the public road. Country faces might poke up and behold his mirth. Or lean over a gate and wonder.

Lean over a gate and wonder!

Words were haunted. Lightning-sketch artists of the haunted chamber. All alive like birds—or dead as a pile of counters.

We're all dead! said Will. And I'll probably be dead again to-night, but what the hell does that matter? To-night will then be now, and unborn to-morrow will be now, and—you can smell the spring in the air. Oh, dear God, you could, but don't smell it too strongly, not too strongly, not this scent of paradisial promise, not this memory of primordial mornings, not this freshness of creation's dawn, not—not too much of it, anyway. Just a little in the by-going, as much as you have a head to carry. Only a fool, who has lost his cunning, gets drunk.

A good sleep did make a difference. It cleansed the sight in so remarkable a way that it caught birds' eyes and unbroken hawthorn buds in a side-glance.

And then the wind—not much of it but soft, soft. He once knew a man—an electrical engineer from Lancashire—who told him he stopped being a spiritualist when he began to see the wind. It had the loveliest curves, he said in a morose tone. So you stopped? . . . I got frightened, he said.

If he had gone on until he was able to see spring's

scent in the wind as well! But probably it was no laughing matter. . . .

The bus—with the girl herself! "Good morning," he greeted her normally, squatting down on the rear seat instead of going forward, as usual. "And how's life?"

She gave him a quick astonished glance (it was the first time he had been personal), then smiled, reassured by his eyes. "Oh, not too bad." A soft friendly honest country girl. "And how's it with yourself?" she ventured.

"Champion!" he said.

She smothered a laugh.

"You don't live in the town?" he asked.

"Why not?"

"Come on, now—I know you don't."

"How do you know?"

"You're real."

"You're fresh, for so early in the morning."

"Because I live in the country—like you."

That fairly amused her, and she turned her back to the interior of the bus.

"Do you like living in the country?" he asked.

"Why shouldn't I?"

"I merely asked. But, look here, I'll tell you something. You wouldn't mind living in the town except for one thing."

"What thing?" She looked at him, and her soft eyes were shrewd enough.

"Because he doesn't live there."

"Are you trying to be personal or what?" But her cheeks caught a slight flush.

"Sorry if I'm personal. Did not mean to be. Say you forgive me."

"I don't think you're so simple as you look."

"Compliments are fairly flying."

"Yes, aren't they?"

He lit a cigarette. "No good offering you one, I suppose—now that you're on duty?"

"No. Thanks all the same."

It was not very easy to out-talk the rumble without raising his voice, and as she swayed expertly with the motion of the bus he sometimes had to lift his face slightly and she to lower her ear. It bred a kind of conspiracy, for they had to watch that the performance was not too obvious to the passengers.

"Tell me," he said. "What does a shy fellow do when he wants—when he doesn't know how to go about it?"

"Wants what? When I want anything I ask for it."

"Do you? That's an idea." he nodded solemnly. "But tell me—who do you ask?"

"Santa Claus," she said.

He laughed abruptly so that several of the passengers turned round. She began to check her tickets. The bus stopped and more passengers came in. . . .

As the bus drew into the terminus he got up and hung on, standing beside her. As the brakes were applied, he swayed and murmured in her ear: "Any good hanging up my stocking?"

"You're daft," she said.

The street itself was a wide grin as he went down it. The chimney pots—had he ever seen the chimney pots of this street before? He felt so friendly to her in the end, so excited by her warm presence, that he could have kissed her!

Though the street went downhill, not one of the endless crowd looked any way but straight ahead on the human level. Bowler hats, neatly rolled umbrellas, felt hats, handbags, all ages, with tweed caps and workmen's dungarees here and there in small coveys. A double stream each side the street flowing on to an endless destination, while in between roared cataracts of traffic.

Was the "endless destination" achieved by the streams going both ways at the same time? Was this an illustration of the mathematician's three-dimensional world moving up a stationary fourth-dimensional block? It probably wouldn't be. It so rarely was! But in heaven's name don't smile on the street to yourself. Smile in a church to yourself, but not on a street. See how solemn these business men are, solemn and correct. And those eyes, myriads of eyes, looking ahead, straight into nothing—concerned, weary, glittering, expressionless, with something vaguely combatant, in their vaguely intolerant reserve.

And all fundamentally concerned with making nests like blackbirds, only bigger and better nests.

And what things to make nests out of in the shop windows! What lovely things, what cunning gadgets, what beauty of line and brilliance of colour! All for making nests. Bedroom suites, evening dresses, marble baths. . . .

But the songs, the tumultuous singing? Here, in

the radio shop, next door to the plumber's shining display of lavatory pans. Everything you want for everything. The civilized man puts it over on the blackbird by turning a knob and getting some one else to do it for him.

It's all been said so often, thought Will, that it means nothing. Beyond the chimney pots the sky was spring's own blue with little angel clouds puffed out in light. Let us sing!

You're daft! she said.

He saw the policeman on the kerb glance at him. Out of curiosity, when he had gone on twenty yards, he looked back—and saw the policeman's face still gazing after him. I must have smiled! I'd better be careful! This is the eternal city.

And here, his own place—with the latest photographs of the international situation in the window, flanked by sporting events and personages. Now for the thick of it, now for the whirling hub of the universe!

Past the long mahogany public counter of births, marriages, deaths and advertisements—and up in the lift. "Fine day, Jim." "Ay, it seems more settled like." Crash of the gate and along the corridor. Before a dark door, on impulse he knocked. "Come in!" He entered, hat in hand. "Could you tell me, please, if Mr. David Macgregor is supposed to work here?"

Mac turned his back. "Jesus, he thinks that a joke," he muttered to no one.

Don gave Will a wink. Mr. David Macgregor was in bad form.

In between the rush hours they managed a bit of fun now and then. Will was the rugby expert, but he knew the soccer lingo inside out. Boxers, footballers, racers—their own personal stories or expert criticisms written while they waited. Don had a native flair for international affairs. His Highland guile! It was in constant demand those days and famous international names were tossed about the room with a freedom of jocose epithet denied to footballers. The soft black pencil cut, shaped, completed—or conjured—marvels to be shouted along the street. Decisive strokes—right, let it go! There were fellows who, though regularly cut to bits, would keep on sending in screeds.

The peak of the forenoon rush was got over. Mac was up in the case-room seeing the first edition through. He was really first-rate at his job; thorough and incisive, from make-up to bill captions.

"He must have been on the skite last night," said Don.

Will nodded. "Fairly late—by the threads in his eyeballs."

There were about a dozen of them in the long room with its long desk. Next door the news phones were trickling the sap from the world tree, main trunk and branches.

The old Ygdrasil for the modern myth.

But Will would not let his mind function all out. Clamp it down. Hang up its receivers. And a fellow could be decently normal, if only his eyes behaved. They were the very devil. For the worst of eyes is that when they see a new thing—or an old thing plain—they look at it. He did not look directly at Don, but smiled as they chatted, tapping the wall behind him with the butt of his pencil. Don's black hair was luxuriant, rising resiliently from the main shed and brushed over into the suavity of an advertisement for hair cream. A slim handsome fellow, his own height. But his skin was a little raw and grey to-day. The city product—the Highlands drained out of him—yet not and never of the city, like the city born. A practical fellow, knowing the right side of a good time. The bleak Highlands behind him, thank God. Reading French and German at night—sporadically, with no method. The foreign correspondent. The adventurer. Destined never to adventure.

You could not look at him—and see his essential ghost.

So he looked at the others and saw the envelopes their minds put around them, saw each moving about in his own, carrying everywhere his invisible balloon!

Nothing could ever break this integument. Like the lens of the human eye, it would thicken with time.

In due course those of them who wanted a drink went out and had it. The majority preferred coffee. Mac wanted a pint whoever else wanted anything. Don and Rob and Will went with him. As dry ground sucks in water, Mac's flesh sucked in the draught beer. It watered him and did him good.

"A thick night?" said Don.

"Oh, so so," said Mac. "What's this stunt on gardening that's biting Tamerlane?"

"Bungaloid growth and popularity of BBC gardening hints," explained Don. "He'll give Lady Burly-Motley the push, and get some one who'll really do it—and spread herself on it."

Mac turned to Will. "Why don't you apply for the job?"

Will looked at him and kept looking, thoughtfully. "That's an idea," he said.

"What the hell you looking at?"

"The idea," said Will. "I wonder if you would be kind enough to put in a good word for me with Tamerlane? You're his white-haired laddie and I might make it worth your while."

Mac exploded in one word and pushed his glass away from him. The others laughed. Then he turned back to Will. "Know what's wrong with you?"

"No?"

"Protracted adolescence."

Rob guffawed. But Will appeared to take it thoughtfully. "I don't think you're right," he said.

"No?" Mac showed the three satiric upper teeth.

Will shook his head. "I think it's protracted childhood."

Mac drew his hand over his face as if Will's eyes were giving it an itch, and wrung his mouth. Then he cleared his throat, and, going to the fire, spat in it.

"You *would* know," he said.

They all laughed at that.

"Yours", continued Mac, looking distastefully at

his empty glass, "is the sort of cheerful morning face that gives a fellow a pain in the guts."

"Perhaps you had a cheerful face last night," Will suggested, "though no one might guess it. Another pint?"

"Where were you last night, Mac?" Rob asked.

"Where wasn't I?"

"Actually, he means," said Don.

"You trying to be clever, too? What a bunch of wits has Tamerlane! You'll be going to London next."

"You're a philosopher, Mac," said Rob.

"That's something higher than a wit," Don explained.

"Oh?" said Mac, looking at him.

"The difficulty about being a philosopher", said Will, "is the difficulty of knowing when you're a philosopher or merely a comic turn."

Rob let out his guffaw. Don glanced quickly at Mac. Will saw the red-eyed weasel in Mac's eyes and continued: "And at least we know you're not a comic turn."

"That's it. Rub it in!" said Rob, laughing huskily. The more one hit off the other, the more Rob enjoyed things.

"You're a bloody——," said Mac directly to Will, using an ugly word.

"Oh come now, Mac," said Don quickly. "Play the old game. That's bordering on the personal. Besides—I think his aunt must have died."

"What aunt?" asked Rob.

"The wealthy one. How could he be so cheerful

else?" Will recognized that Don was giving Mac time to get over his momentary spleen. "You'll be able to touch him for a bit, Mac."

"I would not touch him with the muddy end of a barge pole."

Will smiled sarcastically and presently, as they went out, Don gave him a wink. Will nodded acknowledgment. One must understand the morning after the night before.

But that evening, as Will was leaving the building, he came on Mac buttoning his coat.

"Hurrying home to your farm?" inquired Mac satirically.

"Well—yes, I am."

"Not even time for a small one?"

Will looked at his watch. "It would mean missing the next bus—unless we made it a quick one."

"Come on, then," said Mac grumpily. So they went into the usual office pub, and, when the drinks were served, sat down. Mac had hardly looked at Will and now remarked: "You were trying to be pretty smart this morning."

"Was I? I didn't notice it."

"You were. You can be damned irritating when you are like that."

"Is that so? You used a stinking word yourself."

"Hurt, did it?"

"Not noticeably. Still—if we can't keep things within bounds they've got to stop."

Mac was looking at the glass his fist gripped on the table. Will saw the internal struggle and knew that

Mac had deliberately waylaid him. Mac was sorry now he had used the word but could not bring himself to apologize. He would prefer to jockey Will into the position where an apology would be unnecessary and he would still dominate.

"They've got to stop, have they?" Mac asked.

Will felt himself weakening. He hated to push a man against his nature. "Let us forget it," he said. "Doesn't matter anyway."

"Doesn't matter, doesn't it?"

"No," said Will.

"Oh, all right," said Mac, as if he were being choked off. "So long as you say so."

"Right," said Will. "Same again?"

"Dammit, you can", said Mac, accepting his drink with a softening satire, "be—sort of—complacent or superior or something. It does irritate a fellow before he knows where he is."

"I'm sorry, I'm sure."

"There you go!" said Mac, with a snort of laughter. "Can't help yourself." But the tone was more human. He was becoming friendly, and Will felt himself weakening still more.

"When it comes to being complacent and cocksure, you take a lot of beating yourself," Will said. "The hell of a lot."

"Do I?" wondered Mac.

"You do. Yours is the most destructive annihilating mind I know."

"Is it?" With a vague smile towards his fingers, Mac revolved the glass on the table.

"There's no 'is it?' about it. And I'll tell you some more." And Will went on and told it. For he knew that Mac, in his present mood, was accepting the denunciation like flattery. The more oaths in the language, the better Mac liked it. I'm toadying to him now! thought Will. I hate this language. It's fake; it's weakness. And all to put him right with himself, to warm him. Deeper than that, too: he is dimly aware in his cunning animal part that I am being weak; that I am not strong on my own plain where I could defy him, madly irritate him, but being weak on his plain, and therefore weak all over, and fit, in a final thought, for the snort of contempt that is comforting.

He withdrew his eyes from Mac to his own glass.

"Perhaps you're right," said Mac. "God knows, perhaps you're right."

Will lit a cigarette and said nothing.

"It's all bloody show anyway—this whole nightmare we call civilization. What's it all getting at? God, think of us in our daily round, think of Tamerlane and his cock-eyed stunts. Muck—slush and muck. Each trying to be a bit superior to the other. Each sure in his own rat-infested mind that he is clever enough to put it over on some one else. Toadying to this one, toadying to that, toadying to Tamerlane, toadying to the Lord God Almighty. The whole thing is a vomit."

"I wouldn't say that."

"No? You think you can put it right with your socialism! Or by living in the country! Socialism—

what's that but something to get a kick out of? When some one stands up in a blind alley and spouts like a diarrhetic fountain, why do you think he's doing it? For love of his fellow man? Listen to him. The pure fire-eater. The fighter with his mouth. The hater. Have you ever heard Christ's humility there? He wants to kill half humanity for a kick-off, the half that doesn't agree with him. Love of his fellow man? Jesus! The only man he loves is himself. And when he hears his own voice, he is the most thrilled person in the bunch. You can see it warm him. The warmth the actor gets, the exhibitionist. And then—the sense of power. Power over his fellow men. Not love of them. Power over them, until his bowels move with his own importance—or such tripes as he may have for bowels."

Will gave a soft laugh. "There may be instances, but——"

"I'm not speaking instances. I'm generalizing from experience and an elementary knowledge of normal psychology. Have you ever stood up at a street corner and spoken? No. Why? As a blessed socialist your love of humanity is no less, I assume, than the fellow who does. You don't do it because it doesn't take you that way. You would get no kick out of it. Which is my point. You belong to the crowd who have in them the instinct of escape. So you escape—to a farm in the country."

"And you?"

"I take my stand in the only reality I know—the mud. And be damned! The rest is all sickening egotism and fake."

Will looked with a start at his watch. "Heavens!" he said, getting up. "I'll have to do the escape trick pretty smartly."

"Hey, you're not going?"

"Sorry, Mac, I must. I warned you."

Mac's brows lowered darkly. "What the hell are you going for? Isn't there the whole night?"

"Not to-night. And I've got to run. So long!"

"Here!"

But Will was out the door. He had already missed his bus by ten minutes, he knew, but if he had admitted that to Mac, he would have found it difficult to break away an hour later. Mac was obviously prepared to make a night of it. He was still decidedly under the alcoholic weather, or he would not have spoken at such length. Mac wanted to have him, to take him, step by step, down into the pit of the night. . . .

How furious he would now be, how darkly he would curse and hate him!

Will felt himself drift along the street like a tall leaf. When virtue was taken out of him in this way, his body became light and evasive as his mind. People and objects, the street itself, also became slightly detached from normal reality.

When they had mentioned his aunt, the idea had flashed through his mind that he would visit her, and he had actually been leaving the office with that intention when he had met Mac. But Mac had been too strong for him, and now there would be a smell of whisky off his breath. He could not visit her now.

Did not want to. He had better go and have some tea.

He drifted on, straight ahead, and almost collided with Philip Manson, who was standing gaily chatting to a young woman while consulting his small diary.

"Pardon——" muttered Will, before the two men recognized each other.

"Hal-lo!" Philip all but laughed. "We don't often barge into each other!" He turned to the girl. "Talk about the devil!" he said. "This is the friend of mine I was telling you about who went to live on a farm." Will had already seen that the girl was Jenny. "May I introduce Mr. Will Montgomery—Miss Baird."

"How d'you do?" said Will pleasantly and naturally as if he had never seen her in his life, then turned to Philip. "I must have been coming along half-dreaming——"

"It's his normal condition," Philip explained. She had flushed slightly, for she had involuntarily been about to recognize Will. "He generally has some strange theory or other—and in argument is more slippery than any eel."

"See how cleverly he destroys any argument I might have before I open my mouth? He was always like that."

"Don't believe him!" Philip was in good form. "You know the awful sort of person who says something to you, almost negligently—and you're still wondering about it a week afterwards? That's him."

Miss Baird smiled socially.

"I hope you can imagine him wondering a week afterwards about anything?"

"My dear fellow," Philip said, "if I can remember a remark of yours for a week, I trust you can understand that there are other things which might stick in my mind more strongly and possibly even for a longer time."

"My dear fellow," replied Will in the same amusingly artificial tone, "you have hit the nail completely on the head with, if I may be allowed to say so, your usual gallantry."

Both men laughed, but the last word just managed to touch Philip on the cheek, and with the interchange of eye-flash, Will conveyed an extra small chuckle of triumph for luck.

"But I must be off," Will said. "It's all very well for you townspeople to dawdle about and enjoy the civilized amenities——"

"Quite!" Philip interrupted. "While you go to assume your arduous duties on your farm. By the way, it is only after you left that I remembered. Wait. . . . What is your country address?"

"A note to the office is the surest way of getting me. Good-bye." He smiled to them both, raising his hat; turned and was gone.

I'm escaping all right! Will thought to himself. Nobody is getting me! Then he drifted along thinking no more, but amused in a vague bright way by the chance meeting. Philip and Jenny were of a kind. Her lips and nails had city paint they hadn't had in the country—or hadn't they? She had the brightness in her colouring of—daffodils.

He sat down at his tea table and looked around the

room as if he hadn't seen it when he came in. Then he had a second look because he had missed the faces after all. There was no one he knew. The waitress came beside him and stood still.

"Anything you can suggest?" He glanced up with a smile.

Her face was pale and wearied and her smile was wan. Its waxen frailty stabbed his heart with its long-suffering. He dropped his head over the menu card, shutting his teeth, then glanced up with a still pleasanter smile. "A poached egg, please."

"One poached egg, thank you."

He looked at her dark-clad body as it moved away between the tables. His own body quickened in a spasm of pain.

"Thanks," he said, when she had disposed his food before him. But he did not look at her this time. What right had he to introduce a winning smile, an easy sympathy, a hidden understanding? She asked for nothing. Got it. And kept her head up.

What more to be done?

What a plague of interference with the hidden lives of others! Winning smile? . . . No wonder Mac got the grue!

The poached egg was like her waxen cheek. What in the name of providence had made him ask for an egg? Reflex of the pre-farm era! Its smoothness tickled the roof of his mouth. It smelt faintly. The misbegotten thing was sick. Its pale yellow oozed over the wet toast. The taste was death on a bed of rotting straw. He stretched out knife and fork beside it, quietly shoved the plate aside, and, looking up, encountered the face of Jenny as she entered.

Jenny's face passed over him in search of a vacant table. There was one immediately on his left. But she found another three tables away and went there. She had seen him all right, but had not allowed the smallest flicker of recognition or subsequent self-consciousness to show. Not even a flick of hauteur. Just nothing.

That definitely was something to her credit! He listened for her voice. "Mixed fruit." He couldn't have guessed better!

She would probably be going somewhere this evening with Philip. But why, then, had she not gone home to change? Home? Digs? . . .

What was Philip doing with her anyway? A startling thought came into his mind. Was he the partner in the firm of exporters and she the "private secretary"? Was Philip, to put it normally, running his typist?

Philip would enjoy that quite all right. He always had had some one or other. But he never got embroiled. He was never silly about a thing like that. He always, in course of time, contrived to make it clear with his candid eyes that of course it is up to each individual to look after his or her destiny without encroaching upon the destiny of her or him respectively. That understood, well——!

Jenny had better mind her step! It wouldn't do her any good falling head over heels in love with Philip Manson, however much she thought of herself. For Philip was a man apart and dedicated to the high calling and social suavities of money as power.

However, she could always have her fling!

And she wouldn't have to call—like him—for the bill!

He put something beside his plate for the waitress, got up and into his overcoat, and, about to move out, moved instead to Jenny's table.

"Pardon me," he said quietly. "Mrs. Armstrong asked me to inform you that two special daffodils are out this morning in the garden." He bowed very slightly to this stranger and immediately turned away.

On the street his eyes brightened in still laughter. That's another one who'll think me daft!

But his own girl wasn't on the bus. There were many buses and she would work in a shift anyway.

He checked his laugh, for this daft aspect of life would have to be watched. All it meant was that the ego was enjoying itself to the exclusion of all else and every one else. And every one else didn't like it.

Astonishing how it hurt a fellow like Mac. To be gay and cheerful—not superficially, not in the usual cackling social way, but inwardly and deeply—it was an affront, an insult.

Was life, our modern life, getting like that? Full of such torturing realities and fears that it was disloyal to move outside them, outside their groups and philosophies and strenuous aspirations? Would it yet become a crime to be secretly happy?

Hell's bells and it's beginning to look like it! he thought.

The shades of evening were falling fast. Over the

crest, he paused. A blue dimness was far away upon the land, and in the woods, and purple-dark on the remote mountains. Here and there a bird sang its last song. He was prepared to bet they had had a great day.

Oh God, I don't care what you say, he muttered aloud suddenly, head up, as he strode on. I don't care! I don't care! Life is a lovely thing! Not my life, or your life, but all life interpenetrating on this lovely earth!

A small cold shiver of delight went over his skin.

In the middle of the avenue of trees, he paused. A last few reflective notes fell from the branches. What was this thing the birds had given him, like a jewel in a box?

Should he throw the box away from him now—or hold it tight shut in his fist?

Cunning! for if he threw it away it was in the hope that he might thereby more surely retain it! And if he held it fast and strongly—he would retain it, too!

His hands opened of their own accord and he smiled, listened for a moment, and went on.

2

Next morning he awoke to his chorus at the same time. There it was, waiting for him, creation's dawn! Its urgency, its tempestuous delight, filled all the world, and pervaded his mind in the darkness of his room with a quiet mirth, a darkness growing grey in the window blind, a greyness spreading its presence as he looked, the grey slow-moving cloaked and gentle figure of the deep twilight.

He knew the "technique or ritual" for getting that "heightening effect" all right! But cunningly let it be done, unobtrusively, as if one were not doing it. The gods of the deep twilight are shy gods. Not to be hailed or spoken to.

Slowly he stretched out his legs and his arms, lying over on his back, and let his head fall sideways slightly as if he were going to sleep. All very lightly so that the enchantment might work.

But what was this? Instead of rising, he was sinking, and sinking so deliciously that he knew he was letting go, and that no vision of morning light and freedom could be tempting enough to stop him. Sleep! Sleep had him, sinking him in its soft wool, drowsing him with its warm fume. He knew he was going, letting go, drowning, aware of it as a most exquisite sensuous sensation.

All expression faded from his face leaving it very calm.

When the landlady knocked him into consciousness, he immediately answered. For a few moments his features were very still. He looked at the bedclothes, about the room—and at the window. Then he lay back.

He had an impulse to chuckle, out of a sheer irrational gaiety, as if some one had played a joke on him, some one he cared for.

The joke accompanied him on the way to the bus-stop. For "they" had fairly done it on him in the grey light! If it's sleep you want, why, you'll get it! As easy as that—and as miraculous. For insomnia is no laughing matter. One of hell's more subtle brands of torture, it feeds on itself. How priceless would escape from it be to many!

Had he ever before been so conscious of sheer physical well-being? The mere asking of the question increased the well-being. In a moment, consciousness of it could mount to ecstasy. He actually had to take hold of himself, or he might go dribbling a stone up the roadway, slipping past an opponent, and laughing in glee. His old love of athletics brought an itch to his toes. And once he ran, for about fifty yards. They'll think I'm hurrying for the bus! he reckoned, and then had to pause to keep his laughter in.

Spring madness! Only that? God knows! he thought. And it was a momentarily sobering thought. For all that he knew, the mass of people might often feel as he felt now. He couldn't swear they didn't— however unlikely it was! But he kept his laughter in. Take Jenny—when she would come out to-morrow and see her special daffodils, would she get a thrill? Not a mere surface pleasure, but something deep enough to weaken her joints in wonder?

Why not? Who was he to say she wouldn't? And others, too. But each secretly. There was the point! A little ashamed of it, in this sane world. This sane world of intellectual values, of business, of economics, of politics, of all the real things—unemployment and international crises and bloody wars, *Life is real, life is earnest.* He paused involuntarily and said: What a blasphemy!

Life is not earnest, he cried inwardly: life is delight, life is ecstasy, and when you lose that you lose the whole bag of tricks.

Well, it was worth saying! he concluded, amused again. But with a lingering animosity against those who took life's central purpose of delight and smothered it, out of fear and self-importance and egotism, and the devil's thrill of power over others. Each manifestation a form of perversion of the impulse. Therein lay its blasted cunning and appeal. With a swift penetrating insight, he saw how it worked. Even his animosity felt like a snake-bite.

Don't talk about sobriety to me! he said. I know every tool in your kit-bag and every trick in your hat!

But he smoothed his face gravely as he got into the bus. "Good morning," he greeted his conductress in cold tones. She looked at his eyes as though they surprised her. His left eyelid quivered. "Nice morning, isn't it?"

"Yes," she said, turning half away to smother her amusement.

"You finish in the afternoon?"

"On this shift, yes."

"I thought you must."

"Why?"

"Because I don't see you in the evening."

There was nothing she could say to that.

"Bit of a corker, isn't it?"

"What's that?" She lowered her ear.

"I said you had nothing to say to that."

"To what?"

"To the fact that I don't see you in the evening."

"Oh go on!" she said.

"Go on where? I mean is there a place where . . . ?"

"Come off it!"

"You ask me to go on and then you ask me to come off. You would have to provide me with a bus all to myself where I could practise."

She enjoyed this fooling. It was all in the flash of the eye, the sway of the body, the surprise of the blood in the skin. And the rumbling bus was a chariot.

Soon he would tell her where he lived, and ask her where she lived, and they would talk simply in a friendly way. For they were simple ordinary folk, he felt, glad to be alive and to call the warmth out of each other, and particularly this strange exciting mirth that was more exhilarating than any wine.

"So long!" he said, swinging off the bus. She gave him a smile and his fingers went to his buttonhole as if he were going to wear the smile there.

The streets had not quite the same freshness and wonder they had had yesterday, and in due course Mac paid no attention to him at all. He was aware of a hardening within himself, of a certain cool craftiness. He was not going to be robbed by any one of the jewel smothered in its box!

He had a glass of beer with Don before lunch.

There was a native warmth in that Highlander which he liked. It showed itself at odd moments, particularly when they were together talking.

There was another international crisis on and Will asked him how he thought things were looking.

"Pretty bad," said Don. "It'll pass, of course, but it brings the débâcle just one step nearer."

"Would you be sorry?"

"Sometimes—personally—I think I shouldn't mind. You get worn down by this eternal mess. You begin to feel it would be a change, to do something, anything. Oh, I don't know. The only thing that sticks in my gizzard is the sheer illogicality of the business. It's a sort of mass-hypnosis of all the people in the world, a belief that what they all loathe is yet inevitable. It's a hell of a state."

"Isn't it really implicit in the existing system?"

"Change the system and we'll all be nice fellows? If every country in the world was a true socialist state there would be no war? Quite. But first of all, our country isn't a socialist state. And secondly, the countries likely to win the war will be the best organized countries militarily. The strongest iron hand will rule the peace. What chance do you see of a true socialism emerging from a war between the present alignment of the 'crisis' countries? In our time?"

"Doesn't look too promising."

"Fundamentally again," said Don, "it's the old socialist illustration of the haves and the have-nots and you can't get away from it. The other fellows want a share. We won't give it. Yet socialism demands common access to and ownership of the productive sources."

"But that would mean international socialism first."

"Well, are you working for it—on a realist basis? Isn't socialism in this country running down our potential war enemies more violently than toryism is? When logically what it should be doing is attacking the British Empire as a *have* concern and assuring our brothers, the enemy, that whenever socialism gets power here, the appropriate parts of the British Empire will be available on an equal basis and no exploitation to the have-nots? By thus dissipating haves and have-nots on the international plane, you dissipate war."

"A bit too simple, you think?"

Don smiled, too.

"What I mean——" said Will.

"What you mean is that now we're going to have a slippery argument!"

They shrugged, Don giving a humoured nod. All their arguments finished much in the same way whoever were taking part. An indecision that left a momentary feeling of helplessness, of fatalism; a small dark cloud that had to be grinned away, because one had to live meantime anyhow; while the vague undercurrent of anger against something or some one flowed for a little time longer before it, too, appeared to fade out.

As it was Friday, he had to attend his socialist committee meeting at eight o'clock. His official job was looking after the publicity; which always meant finding out what public meetings were about to be held where heckling, distribution of leaflets, and similar propaganda might usefully be carried on.

It was a damp raw night and the bare dingy room was cold. The chairman had not turned up and without his strong quiet personality there was a feeling of incompleteness. During the quarter of an hour they waited, Will realized how much they depended on the one absent man. Without him there was lack of cohesion, sporadic grouping here and there, a tendency for the emotional extremist to raise his voice and lay down the law. One or two of the women began to chatter in an induced excitement, and under their tweed coats gave little noisy shudders of cold. "I think we'd better start the meeting," he said to the vice-chairman.

So the vice-chairman raised his voice and suggested that they should perhaps get on with the business.

The faces gathered together and the minutes were solemnly read.

The new religious meeting. It took the place of his parents' church; supplied the doctrines of brotherhood and universal peace; made possible the bearing of present economic ills in the certainty of future equality and justice.

He withdrew his eyes from the faces. He did not want to see the rawness of flesh, the bone underneath the sinew, the skeleton. He did not want to look through the glass of the eyes. Wasn't he one with them, of the same flesh and bone and eye—and far less than many who did such unselfish work for the cause?

But this cry of a natural humility made no difference. He saw them better when he was not looking at them. And their voices completed the revelation.

He knew all the words beforehand, all of them, the shibboleths and inane suggestions, the interruptions, the cross talk, the denials, the affirmations, the tiresome eternal repetitions of intolerant certainties.

A pitiless cold insight, that he had warmth in him to hate. Not for a moment could it make him lose faith in the ideal. On the contrary, it could make him more ruthless, make him contemplate revolutionary acts with a steadfast fury, reconcile him to dictatorships through transition eras of indefinite length. Its very bafflement urged him to the drastic and final.

Then the chairman came in and said in his quiet voice that he was sorry he had been held up.

He was a young man, two years younger than Will, tall, broad-shouldered, with a full pale face, blue eyes, and a quiet confident manner. Good looking, with a reserved friendly smile, he must, Will felt, be attractive to women.

They now drew more together as if renewed purpose and direction had been given them, and the meeting proceeded.

It was no good asking the chairman, Joe Wilson, out for a drink. He neither drank nor smoked, but as Will chatted with him after the meeting—for they often worked out difficult points or drew up schemes before bringing them to the committee—Joe asked: "What are you doing?"

"Nothing, except that I've got to get home into the country."

"Of course. I forgot."

"Why?"

"I'm going down to see Jamie Melvin. His wife is expecting a youngster. She was in a pretty bad way and they were talking of taking her to the infirmary. I thought if you had nothing better to do we might look in and cheer him up."

"Oh well," said Will, "all right."

"What about getting home?"

"There's a bus after eleven. It's barely nine. So long as I catch that, I don't mind."

They buttoned their coats up round their throats and set out.

"Jamie's had bad luck," said Joe. "He's a carpenter by trade and about three months ago he lost his right arm. We're fighting his case for compensation, but the circumstances were unusual and the outcome is pretty uncertain. His employer is quite a decent fellow, not in a very big way, but he has to contest the case, because of course the insurance company are not going to stump up unless they have to. The point at issue is: did Jamie lose his arm while genuinely working on his job, or did he lose it in his spare time while working for himself? If for himself, then no workman's compensation automatically. Apparently there was some old rotten scaffolding that the boss told them they could have for firewood and put on the saw merely for the taking down. Now two or three of them set about doing this immediately after they had finished their normal day's work. An apprentice, a nice lad but a daring young devil, began a bit of trapeze work that burst a rotten dook. Jamie rushed in and broke the lad's fall. They say he undoubtedly saved his life, but in the hearing of the case in court the point was ruled out as irrelevant. As it was, of course. Jamie, however, in this irrelevant process of saving the lad's life, was sent spinning round and on to his back. The released beam nose-dived and got him just below the shoulder here, ripping off the flesh and smashing the bone. All they could do in the infirmary was cut the mess away. And then the nice point arose as to whether Jamie had been working for his boss or for himself."

"What happened in court?"

"The sheriff took it to avizandum. The good point is this. The boss stuck to his statements that the scaffolding by his orders had to come down, that there was no particular hurry about it, and that they could have it to themselves. Fortunately the cross-examining solicitor got his goat a bit and the boss stuck doggedly to his statements. He had not mentioned any hour for the job, he had merely said that the scaffolding had to come down. The men were not paid extra time for taking it down. But on the other hand, they were paid by being given the wood. And so on and so forth. Hours and hours of it."

"The human factor doesn't get much of a show."

"Purely irrelevant."

They walked on for a little in silence.

"Must have been a terrible shock for his wife in her condition."

"It was," said Joe. "She's only twenty-one. They got married about a couple of years ago and have a little girl about a year old. This is the second. He's no more than twenty-four himself. A harum-scarum warm-hearted fellow, who completely reformed when he got married. Used to drink, and get into a scrape now and then. But he put all that away when he married Ettie. She's a pretty, pale, dark-haired girl; but rather simple, soft, affectionate type; feckless a bit perhaps, but attractive in her way. Anyhow, she was all that Jamie wanted. And then this happened to him. They hadn't saved a halfpenny, of course, and now here's a new youngster. Ettie is anything but strong—and they've been on short commons. I hope they take her to the infirmary."

Joe spoke quite dispassionately, as if this were no more than a typical case. Will felt the solid confident bulk of this young man walking beside him. A strong presence, something hidden and fine in it, assured, austere.

They turned a corner and, all in a moment, were shut off from the town he knew. The change was dramatic, and Will experienced a sensitive half-shrinking fear, as if he were intruding into a region, another dimension of life, where he had no right to be. The gusts of wind blew bits of paper and refuse along the pavement, into the street, about his feet.

The men were undersized and thin, and, with hunched shoulders, seemed to move along on stealthy business; the women were blowzy, with slumped bodies, and stared at them from close-entrance or other point of gossip. Will could not look directly at them, could not give them more than a glance, lest his prying should justly provoke them.

The bright lights of the great thoroughfares were gone. Here was only a darkling light; and presently, as they passed a street entrance on their left and Will looked down it, his heart constricted. The electric globes went into the distance, one after another, balls of bluish light, suspended in impenetrable gloom. The balls hardly lit the air about them. No traffic. No headlights. Involuntarily Will stopped, but went on again at once.

"I had thought I had visualized the thoroughfare to the underworld," he said to Joe, with an effort at light irony, "but I was wrong."

Joe glanced at him. "You mean?"

"The classical conception provided a certain measure of drama. That was not drama. The gloom of a terrifying nihilism, hung with balls of incandescent steel."

The streets they traversed had more light and a number of little shops. Children seemed to be everywhere, ragged urchins, holding a moment in groups, before darting away. They paid no attention whatsoever to the two men. When they disappeared, Will got the impression that they went underground and not into the tall tenement walls with their scatter of window lights.

He had seen all this before, but never for long enough at any one time to get used to it, to dissipate the feeling of unease, of half-nightmare. And the smell, the pervasive smell that dried up the back of the nostrils, held something more than squalor, something vaguely threatening. The whole body went on the defensive, sensitive to the atmosphere, as the ear-drum to a threatened sound.

And *there* was one well-defined smell: fish and chip shop! Dogfish. Dogfish from the Arctic. . . . Trawler-men, working like galley-slaves, in tem-pestuous icy seas. The dogfish that fishermen loathe.

Some children had their noses glued to the window pane. A man in a greasy apron came to the door to see about custom or take a breath of the night. He told the children to run away. The glass might be less strong than their noses. They shouted at him and ran.

To them the smell would be delicious, exciting. They would burrow into the long-dead dogfish like eels. Grab from one another, fight.

A covey of them suddenly alighted at their feet in a whirling rough-and-tumble. There was a blow, and a challenging voice whipping out a mouthful of sexual filth. The game little orator couldn't be more than ten.

"Now boys!" said Joe.

The little orator swung round on him, his ginger hair over his eyes. "You go and . . . . yourself, mister."

Joe looked at him and then took a step forward. They scattered like rats.

Will would not have interfered; knew he could not have dominated them so completely. Joe gave a quiet laugh. Will experienced the sensation of a wild outward humour but inwardly he shrank.

"It's perhaps not so depraved as it sounds," said Joe, "though actually there is an alarming amount of precocious sex about. But then—where isn't there? Here you merely hear it, one remove from the drunkard's mouth. We go in here."

It was the usual narrow close to a "backland" house—a house built on the small back green of an earlier house. All the back greens here were now slum tenements. The area was extremely congested.

They went up the close and into the narrow back court where children were playing a wild rushing game with pieces of burning newspaper. Smoke with an acrid smell belched from the midden. The sight of the children in the gloom, weaving their whirling fantastic patterns of fire, affected Will strongly. It was pagan, the response of their young hearts to the spring, the same response that at this very time was moving country boys to burn whins and heather. The small darting black bodies, like tiny demons, ecstatic in their fire worship, paid no slightest attention to the two tall men who moved through their whirling circles.

The stone stair wound upward, like a turret stair in an ancient keep. At each landing the stair opened into the night, the orifice in the outside wall being protected by a grille of pointed rusty iron spikes. At the second landing they paused, while Will stared

86

between and over the spikes at the great back wall of another tenement beyond the yard. One or two un-blinded windows were so near that he could see intimately what was going on and felt he was prying. He sniffed. "What door is this?" he asked Joe.

"It's the common lavatory," said Joe.

Jamie's door was on the third landing, and as they ascended Joe said: "Jamie had a better place than this but of course he couldn't keep it. That embittered him a bit. However, he's all right. So long as Ettie needs him he'll be all right."

Presently Joe knocked and in a little while the door was opened by a young woman.

"That you, Mary? How's Ettie?"

"You didn't hear?"

"No."

"She's dead."

"Christ!" said Joe.

They all stood still for a moment, then Mary said: "Come in."

For one wild instant Will wondered if he could mutter an excuse and turn and fly. But Joe had for-gotten him and was following Mary. Will shut the door and the still inside atmosphere pressed against him like a wall. He walked into it, his nostrils—as always at such a moment—intolerably sensitive. The oppressiveness blinded him. He could smell death. Sheer animal fear and horror of death assailed him. The atmosphere of the room was thick with the damp scorched fug from a man's shirt and underclothes drying before a small dull fire. It was a smell that in

87

any circumstances brought upon him the tremor of sickness. He stood behind Joe, knowing the bed was to the left. Joe turned slowly round and Will had to do the same. The bed was empty.

Mary was clearing two wooden chairs for them, and Will was glad to sit down. She looked a woman over thirty, though she was no more than twenty-four. Her face had the pallor of a face drained of blood, wrung dry. Her eyes accordingly seemed enlarged and dark and tragic. But there was a stubborn meeting-place between her black eyebrows, a furrow of dull endurance. She was the dead girl's sister.

Will looked away from her to the wall. The small gaunt room was half-clothed in a tawdry way. The cheap discoloured paper had unframed calendar prints stuck here and there upon it. Two great horses drawing a plough over the crest of a field against the sky, gulls wheeling and the ploughman taking the pressure with his right shoulder. Full of vigour. Photographs of women film stars, in a group, covering a black splotch. A sheer note of colour, like a cry, from a print of gentians, intensely blue. Cut out of an American magazine probably, by the dead girl. Joe's previous description of her now brought her into the room and Will felt he knew her as well as he had ever known anybody in his life. If not better, for he knew her now with a strange intolerable ache of the spirit.

"They took her to the infirmary the day before yesterday. She was not strong enough to give birth herself, the doctor said, so they took her away," Mary

88

was explaining to Joe in a voice pale and dry as her face.

"We were expecting that," said Joe.

"Yes," said Mary. "She was not strong enough. She was not strong enough to do it herself, so they did an operation on her and took it out through her side."

"What they call a Caesarean operation," said Joe.

"Yes, that was the name. The young surgeon was nice. Every one was kind. And the operation was successful. It was quite successful, they said. Everything looked as if it was going to be all right. The child was fine. It's a girl. Still fine and going on. I saw Ettie myself."

"Did you?"

"Yes. She was glad to see me but——"

"Of course she would be pretty weak," Joe helped her.

"She was. Yes. Only I did not like the look of her. It's not that her colour was—oh I don't know what it was. She smiled sort of faraway—as though—as though she had no interest." She started slowly pressing and chafing her fingers as if to warm them. Joe said nothing.

"Then she began to weaken. She never picked up. They sent for Jamie early this morning, but she was dead before he got there." Without any movement, she began to weep in dry sniffs that left her face staring and solemn. Every now and then she took deep breaths. Finally she filled her lungs to the full, held the pressure, and let it go. After that she breathed quickly for a little, and then became quiescent as before.

"What went wrong?" asked Joe, who had made no effort to comfort Mary. His tone was gentle, but matter-of-fact.

"I saw the matron this afternoon. She was quite kind. I asked her. She said Ettie had let her strength down by not taking enough nourishing food. You needn't tell Jamie that. She said the best skill in the world couldn't have done anything for her. She had no strength to help herself. Her strength was all drained away." She added dully again: "Don't tell Jamie that."

"Where is he?"

"When he came back, he sat over the fire all morning. He was terrible hard hit. He asked the matron if Ettie left any message for him or said anything before she died. The matron told him no. She did not ask for any one. She told him that the last words Ettie said were: 'I am very tired.' After that, she died."

They sat quite still.

"You haven't seen Jamie since?" Joe asked at last.

"No. He hasn't come back."

"You don't know where he'll be?"

"No. I couldn't go out because of the bairn here."

Joe looked round, and Will now saw the low crib in the dark shadows by the head of the bed.

"Are you staying the night?"

"Yes," said Mary. "I'll have to. Some one must. Who else is there?"

There was silence for a few moments. "You're not afraid?" Joe asked.

"No," she said. Then a dry hopeless expression came over her face. "It would hardly matter whether I was or not anyway."

Joe got up. "We'll have a look round to see if we can find Jamie. I'll look in again to see you, Mary, before I go home."

"Thank you," said Mary. "It's very kind of you. I'm glad you came in."

Will could feel Joe's quiet strength; could see Mary heartened by it.

"This is a friend of mine," Joe explained, as she followed them to the door.

"Ay," she said indifferently.

When they were out of the darkness of the close, Joe said: "She's stunned a bit."

"Not much more in the way of misery for her to find out." Will was beginning to feel drained and arid himself. *I am very tired!* It had pierced him to the quick of the heart, where the last impulse lives before it shoots in agony and dies.

Joe paused. "I wonder where Jamie has gone?"

"Drink?"

"If it is, he's sunk. This finishes him. Only, I don't think he'd likely go to the pubs where he'd be known. However, we'll try one or two round about first."

"Just the one room they have?"

"Single end. Yes." As they came to a pub door, Joe said: "You needn't come in."

Will understood Joe and waited. Two of them

going in and searching around might rouse attention.

After the third pub, Joe started out for a fourth. "I met a pal of his in there. Jamie used to frequent, he said, the Red House."

But the Red House and two more pubs held no trace of Jamie. Will could see that Joe was now getting alarmed. They walked along the river, but they could not see it. Why shouldn't they be able to see it? Why should it be banked in, shut away? Why should there not be boulevards along it? He was going to ask Joe, but had not the energy, and also he suspected that Joe would blame a capitalism that cared nothing for the well-being of the folk and less for the beauty of their town; and at the moment Will did not care even about capitalism. The night was damp and raw, with gusts of wind that set misery creeping along the bone. A figure started away in front of them. Joe increased his pace. The figure broke into a run, head down. Joe stopped. "He has two arms, that fellow." He stood quite still. "I hope to God he hasn't gone and done anything desperate."

He started walking purposefully. After some time, he turned off a wide thoroughfare, and all at once they were in a place of spacious peace, with a great steamer's black and red hull towering above them. The city of contrasts! Will half turned, glanced upward at the city, and saw the vast dark wall, burrowed with lights, of a tenement slum. Between him and that gaunt wall, a tramcar, tall as a ship and all a mass of light, went gliding swiftly and noiselessly by.

What an animal was man! How brilliant in his gifts, how ruthless in his greed!

Not a soul moved about the dock. Will read the name on the steamer; read the name on a large signboard of a famous shipping firm. There were other steamers beyond. And cranes, queer-shaped cranes, like giants with bandy legs thrusting an arm at the sky. And peace; and strength.

Joe went and spoke to a policeman standing in the open doorway of a vast shed.

Will looked at the black water, which glittered here and there, and thought of Jamie. Beyond the dock, the river slid past. Will imagined its slow, drowning, rat-coloured swirls, its choking smoothness.

Down past the building yards, where carpenters and riveters, dockers and dredgers, worked, where his comrades worked, where all the men worked whose forefathers had made the river, the river of sea-borne traffic, the wonder river, bearing Jamie's body, the one arm turning over, not in salute, not in underwater farewell, not in bitter irony, but in filth and grime. Food for the eels.

"Come on!" Joe called.

He had not noticed that Joe had gone on.

"I was feeling a bit romantic," he explained, "thinking of the river."

Joe glanced at him but said nothing.

They left the dock and came to a street, a cul-de-sac, and in the mouth of it was a meeting. "He certainly won't be here," said Joe, "but we'll have a look."

The speaker stood in the middle of the deep ring of listeners. He had a walking-stick and used it like a sabre, holding them spellbound. When he took a stride or two, he limped. He was a man of about fifty, squat, wearing an old bowler hat over a full bluish face. Will involuntarily stopped and watched him, his height giving him a clear view.

"Take your river here. Two yards out of every three idle—and the third yard busy on what? Warships! War! Most of you are unemployed, some of you have never been employed—but all of you will be employed in war. Don't worry about that. You'll get your bellyful of employment then. They'll employ you all right. For however they've warped your bodies, however they've underfed you, whatever pitiful C3 specimens of humanity they've made you, you'll do all right as bomb and cannon fodder. You've still got a modicum of guts and blood to be scattered about. Or have you?" He paused. He limped a couple of steps and turned round swiftly. "Or have you?" he shouted. Then quietly: "Honest to God, men, forgive me, but I sometimes wonder if you and I have blood and guts. For if we had, how could we endure this nightmare they call civilization? Think of the wealth of the world, the brimming bursting wealth of the world, wealth created by the workers of the world—yet wealth which you can't touch, wealth which is destroyed; fish dumped into the sea, wheat burnt as fuel, tea and coffee and rubber and cotton—all the things you need, that you and your wives and your children could have in abundance, all kept from you, for the profit of the few. Your hands are idle. Your hands could build ships, not death ships, but merchant ships, ships to carry the goods the workers need to all the ports of the world. Your hands are eager to build them, proud to build them, your hands—the finest craftsmen's hands in the world—are unemployed, are idle, are rotting. How long——"

Joe plucked Will's sleeve. "Come on. He's not here."

"Do you know him?" Will nodded back towards the speaker.

"Oh yes," said Joe, as they moved off. "Bill Beaton—sometimes called Bill Bailey. An extraordinary fellow. Has had an incredible life. I'll tell you about him sometime." Joe stopped, looked to left and right, then stared straight towards the river. He obviously did not know where to go next.

"Let's go on this way," said Will.

Joe went with him, but with the air of disliking doing a vague thing, as though time must always mean something, have a purpose.

"If he's in a pub," said Will, "it's unlikely we'll find him until the pubs close. We might then run into him coming back."

"Something in that."

"Tell me this," said Will. "Does that sort of stuff have any effect on these men?"

"I used to worry about that. If it had an effect, you think they'd have risen in revolution long ago?"

"Yes."

"And they haven't. So what? I know. It's difficult. You can only have a theory about it. My own is that it is having an effect, a delayed effect. There just is no doubt in my mind that it will tell in the end. In its simplest elements, it's a form of education in economics and sociology—the only form these men are directly taught. Now it's extremely complicated, the whole thing, because of human nature. And the human nature of these down-and-outs is more intricate than yours or mine. You believe, for example, that the world is a fine and simple place when things are going well with you. Birds singing and flowers growing and music and art and books and pretty women and good food and so on. But when things are not going well with you, when you are a down-and-out and live in one room, then life is not a lovely thing. You become suspicious. You trust no one. You are like a cornered animal. You don't even trust Bill Bailey. He's getting money, you suspect, from some source to come and do his stuff. You listen to him—if you haven't the money to be in the pub. You agree with him. And the more your hatred grows, and your rancour, and your madness—the more oh what the hell's the good of spouting? You have heard all that before. You have heard all about the bursting wealth of the world. You have heard it, and your fathers have heard it, and your sons are hearing it." Joe paused. "Think of yourself as Jamie Melvin listening to that. Look through Jamie's eyes at Bill Bailey doing his dramatic stuff. It does not help that Bill Bailey's stuff may be right. The rightness is merely an added poison. You don't say, Yes, I'll help to organize. You hate. You could act, you could throw bombs, but you're not allowed to act *now*. What'll we do? you cry to Bill Bailey. Join the socialist party, answers Bill. Jesus! So you laugh and hate. They have lost faith." Joe added after a moment, "Not all of them. There's the continuous trickle that join up and work. But many of these become so ruthless in their logic that they lose their common humanity. They gather the irreconcilables around them. But the great bulk want kindness and decency and humour—the old human nature—and when they don't get it, they go sour."

They found themselves by the river again.

"Let's get back," said Joe.

Will saw the illuminated sign of a pub up a street. "Come on and have a drink."

"Feel you need one?"

"Yes." Will looked at the glowing red and gold sign in the street's dark tunnel. "Underground to Fairyland."

Joe followed him in.

There was a crush of men standing deep round a curving mahogany counter, with two young barmen serving, and one older man serving also but quiet and watchful. After the misery of the night outside, the place was a gabble of sound, a crush of warmth, a thick stench of tobacco smoke, beer, and old clothes. Will began to cough, and coughed till the tears came into his eyes. "Damnation!" he said, his face holding its pallor, his eyes glittering. "What's yours?"

"A lemon squash," said Joe.

"A lemon squash and a large whisky."

Joe began quietly to look around. Will also saw the faces but he couldn't look at them, couldn't think about them. They hurt him. Each lineament, the look in an eye, the twist of a mouth, discoloured teeth, a snigger, a laugh, a strong vindictive face, a furtive face, a lost face—instantaneously conveyed the inner story. He did not want the story. His mind felt skinned, sensitive as a raw wound. He knew their lives, how the weaklings amongst them shuffled and slept; even their secret incontinences came at him. It was too much. "Here's how!" he said to Joe, and drank his whisky in a gulp.

"He's not here," said Joe.

The general topic of conversation was football. Different teams, different views, different sides. He knew the whole lingo. Hit and come again. But the talk here had an aim, an object. For here was the real home of the football coupon. The penny, the tuppenny bet. Normally he might have seen this as the poor man's gamble, his pennyworth of fun.

To-night, Friday night, it had a heat, an earnestness, a wild sarcasm, a lust. Hunger and greed at the core of it.

They were drinking draught beer with thin frothy bubbles on top. But just behind his right shoulder were three or four fellows drinking wine. Will blew out a long stream of smoke from his newly lit cigarette and gave them a side glance.

Dark heavy Empire wine, full of alcohol, four-

98

pence a large glass. The stuff that, with a dash of meth., was called Red Biddy. One of these, with a chaser of beer, and a fellow could be well on. They were not having chasers. They were sticking to the wine. Taking it in little mouthfuls, and discussing —film stars. Will could not believe his ears. Not young lads. Men of over thirty, over forty. Yes, they were discussing a film that had been, a film that was coming, and the stars concerned. "Ay, she's grand." "I'll tell you what I thought was awful good. Remember that time when he came in and she was——" Pale-faced, bright-eyed film-addicts, living a dream-life on the dole, with sixpence twice a week for the pictures and a little more for Empire wine.

A buzzing of blood went into Will's ears. Never in his life had he been assailed by the pathetic in this frightening way. In comparison, Bill Bailey and his listeners were he-men.

"Want another?" Joe asked.

"One minute," said Will and he looked around. "Where's the lavatory?" he asked the barman.

"Through that way."

Will edged his way through, was involuntarily stopped by his nostrils on the threshold, held his breath, and went into the latrine. Men's backs and shoulders; one or two swaying in their drink. The fellow next to him was leaning forward, supported by the forehead which pressed against the flagstone wall. All at once the horizontal pipe a few inches above the man's head noisily gushed out water through its small perforations. The water descended upon his cap, soaked it, and trickled down his face. His whole body convulsed and his mouth ejected a violent gush of vomit, which hit the flagstone and spat back upon Will's clothes. Will let out a harsh grunt of disgust and began wildly brushing the stuff off with his naked hand. Slowly the face twisted round at him. Black burning eyes. The eyes held him, torture drawn to fine points. The face drew back from the wall, slowly, and steadied, concentrating on Will in a demoniacal satire and hatred. Only as the body squared up did Will notice that the right arm was missing.

Before he could be assaulted, Will turned away, re-entered the bar, and went up to Joe. "He's in there," he said.

"Who? Jamie?"

"Yes."

Joe looked at him. "Feeling sick?"

"Yes." Will kept wiping his left side. "Must get some fresh air." He turned abruptly and pushed his way out. The cold raw night hit him in the face. Two policemen were standing on the opposite pavement a few yards down. It was near closing time. He turned up the side street hurriedly. One policeman slowly moved up after him. He strove to keep his sickness down, going on blindly. He could not keep it down. He moaned aloud in agony and the sickness came in a spate through his teeth. He groped for the wall and steadied himself. His legs began to tremble; his head went icy cold. A hand with metal fingers gripped his shoulder. "What's this?" But he could not get breath. His legs were giving way. He got breath and moaned:

"Leave me." The policeman shook him and said roughly: "Come on!" He did not mind the policeman, because now the fainting sensation was ebbing, casting the thing that was himself high and dry again.

He slowly straightened up. "Sorry, constable." He gasped, for some bitter stuff had got into his windpipe.

The policeman stooped and looked into his face. "Who are you?" The voice was gruff and suspicious.

Will did not answer. Deeper than his human sense of shame, than his hatred of the animal mess, was this feeling that he was coming all right. For there had been one terrible drawn-out moment when he had felt himself shooting into a black abyss. The policeman shook him. His strong fingers bit the shoulder bone. Will lost his balance, but the policeman held him upright. "Come on!" The policeman began to drag him away.

"One minute," said Will. "For God's sake, listen."

"What's that?"

"I'm not drunk. There's something wrong. Listen to me."

The policeman was all attention now and looked shrewdly into Will's face.

"Give me a minute," said Will. "Let me lean against the wall." The policeman helped him to the wall. Will shut his teeth against an overpowering desire to sit down. "It happened in there. I have only had one drink to-night. You know I'm quite sober." Any one could see he was sober. "Only one drink. I was in there. The atmosphere—cut it with a knife. I went into the lavatory. A fellow spewed over me. It turned my stomach."

"What were you doing in there?"

"My job. I'm a journalist."

"Oh, a journalist, are you?"

"Yes. I work on the *Evening Star*. Special articles—social conditions. You know. God, I'm feeling sick yet."

"So you're a journalist?"

"Yes. Give you my card." A weak smile came to his face. "I thought I was tougher. It was the way the stuff—oh heavens!" Will had brought his hand up to open his coat and now began brushing the breast of it with sickening distaste.

"It isn't a very nice thing to do on the street," said the constable in a mollified tone.

"Don't rub it in! I'll make a contribution—to the scavenging department." The weary humour was a friendly effort.

"How would you like, if you were living here, and came out in the morning, and slid on that?"

"Hush—or I'll do it again."

"You better not," said the constable.

Will felt assailed by a humour wild and fantastic as the night, the black convoluting horror of the night. Something in the policeman's voice was faintly reminiscent of Don, too. The Highland accent! The tangle of the Isles! The cheek-bones protruded like stem or sternpost of a small boat. Smashing green seas and white spray.

He had got hold of his pocket-book, when an

uproar arose from the pub. "Come along," said the policeman, taking Will in tow.

As they reached the spot, Joe and Jamie came clattering through the doors, as if they had been forcibly ejected. Some men followed, but when they saw the policemen they backed away. Joe seemed to be doing his best to hold a one-armed maniac, whose language was foul. It was a strange, terrifying, agonizing foulness. Some youngsters, who had been following Will and the policeman, listened to it with frightened faces. Normally they would have listened like connoisseurs, with the general assessment: "Jesus, hasn't he got a—skinful!" But now they were silent, the eyes in the pale faces glistening with a queer dread. Nothing on the normal plane of social horror was strange to them; but this was pushed off that plane into the abyss where there is no footing, only the cry coming back.

Joe had said a few hurried words to the policeman, who was now helping him, and both of them began dragging Jamie away. The constable, who was with Will, strode forward, had a word or two with his colleague, and turned back, meeting Will.

"Good night, constable—and thanks," said Will.

Their eyes met. In a slow grim way the policeman nodded. "Good night."

But Jamie wasn't beaten yet. For he wanted back. He wanted back to the warmth of the pub; to the light and the warmth, to the obliterating crush of bodies, drinking, drinking, all drinking. He wanted back. The children at a little distance heard him cry:

"For Christ's sake, let me back! Let me back! Let me back!" his voice rising to a roar, then choking in his throat as he dug his heels in. It looked as if his captors were taking him to torture, not ordinary bodily torture, but some other hellish and unthinkable torture. It was this note that troubled the children.

Will followed a few yards behind, as if he were leading the children. After a time, unable to stand this isolation, he quickened his pace and came beside Joe. "Can I help?"

"No," said Joe. "It's all right." Every now and then Jamie roared aloud and struggled, fighting drunk. But Joe and the policeman had him firmly. The children were darting about now in their excitement. They were getting used to the underlying terror, as they would get used to the sight of a mad young bull, roped, being led to the shambles. Their instinctive fear made them more active than birds. Grownups, back against the walls, stood and stared.

When they came to the corner of the street where his home was, Jamie made his great struggle. The policeman, losing patience, told him to shut up or he would bash him. He manhandled him a little and a thin screaming note pierced through Jamie's harsh throat.

"It's no use," said the policeman, who apparently knew Joe. "I'll have to lock him up."

"We can't do that," said Joe. "It'll ruin him for good."

"Not a bit of it. It's what he damned well needs."

"But, man, can't you see——"

"All I can see is he's dangerous. I can't take the responsibility of letting a man in his condition near a woman or a child. He's capable of anything. Can't you see he's fighting mad?" The Highland accent was very strong.

But Jamie had gone suddenly still and silent. He was staring at Will. Hatred focused to torture points. He let out a low throaty growl and, if the policeman had not had a lock on his arm, he would have broken free.

The impetus of Jamie's rush started them up the street. Will fell behind, his heart beating in a suffocating way. A deep bitter shame, a self-shame, overcame him, a conviction of worthlessness drawn out and lost in the outer dark of the night.

Opposite the close leading to Jamie's home, Joe paused and made his desperate appeal. But Jamie did not listen, and it became very clear that this close was for him the gangway to his final torture.

Joe could do no more, and actually as they went up the street Jamie grew much quieter. By the time they reached the police office, he was walking silently between them. Will saw him enter without offering any resistance. The three of them disappeared, and he was standing alone on the street.

Not a soul on the street but himself, no darting children here or staring men and women, as if all the world avoided this office. A profound sensation of the emptiness of the world, of life, of himself, came upon Will. Like a plague street in a dim-dark foreign town under an empty sky. All dead—except for that office, where Jamie was being charged. He moved slowly down the street, turned, and came back. A tall dark helmeted figure came out of the police office, looked at him with slow deliberation, and walked quietly away.

Will went along the pavement again, saw a tall dark figure coming towards him, and turned back. The figure came up behind. Will could feel it looking at him. It did look at him, slowly round and into his face, as it passed on, with quiet strides, and entered under the solitary light above the doorway.

The dark upright watchers of night in the underworld. Islesmen, cheek-bones like blunt timber-ends, straight-stemmed, unyielding, going out into the dark, returning from the dark's dark fishing with catches of strange tragedies. How fantastic the drama of destiny!

Will felt a cold bodiless fantasy getting hold of him. This touched him with fear, as though his normal mind were slipping. At last Joe came out.

"Still here?" he said, in his usual voice. But there was a quietness about him now, and he stood silent for a little while. "It's a pity," he added, "but there seemed nothing else for it."

"No."

"I couldn't take him home. And, anyway, he wouldn't have come."

"No. He wouldn't want to be with friends."

"Suppose not."

They were silent again. In view of the accomplished fact of Jamie's imprisonment, there was nothing to say. The weight of it pressed down on them. Nothing to say—or too much; too much, in anger and bitterness and defeat.

"What about your bus?"

Will tried to read his watch.

"About a quarter to eleven," said Joe.

"I could just make it."

"Right. I'll go back and have a few words with Mary." He spoke quietly.

"Don't suppose I could be of any use?"

"No. You get home. I told the sergeant I'd be here before eight in the morning. I'll see then how Jamie is taking things. We'll straighten him up somehow. Well, thanks for your company. Good night."

"Good night, Joe."

They parted, but after twenty yards, Will swung round and called: "Joe!" Joe came to meet him.

"What about ready cash? Will Mary have anything?"

"She can't have much," said Joe.

From his pocket-book, Will took out a pound note. "Would that be any use?"

"It's far too much."

"Good," said Will, handing it to him.

"Thanks very much," said Joe.

"Needn't say it's from me."

"All right. Sometimes you have to make an excuse or other. I can honestly say it's not mine!" He smiled in friendly weary irony.

Will smiled back, and they said good night again. Joe always made Will think of the brotherhood of man. In his large strong body, in his forbearance, his capable handling of any event, his quiet understanding, his tendency always to act rather than to talk, Joe *was* the brotherhood of man. And to-night, too, in this matter of feeling, of sympathy, Joe had been subtle. It was as if he had learned the need for feeling with his head. Having work to do, he could not let anything touch him too closely. He thereby not only kept action intact but assisted those who had lost hold on action.

A deep admiration for him flowed over Will, and he felt Joe walking back . . . through the streets of the ages . . . forward into streets with the dawn breaking. Joe—the figure that has never failed to appear, the solitary figure—here, there—down the streets of time, down the streets of men—the figure that bears all the tragedy, the sorrows that are beauty's inverted dreams, the bitter anguish. . . .

Will had to move his head from side to side to get a proper feel of his body. The Figure had come before him very distinctly. Not the face, not the expression, but the body, with its grey coat or cloak about it, standing a little way off, solitary.

This tendency to fantasy—he must watch it. But in a moment he cried against himself: It's not fantasy, it's truth, and you know it! Don't be a coward. You know it!

Had he let his voice escape then? Had it cried sharply in the street? He looked from side to side with furtive eyes.

As he passed one close-entrance, Will was pierced

by terror exactly as if he had been stabbed by a knife. It was something that came out of the close. He did not see or imagine anything. The intense sensation of an act of horror being committed clung to him.

The streets were menacingly empty, and when two or three figures suddenly appeared and disappeared, he stiffened all over. Once a young woman's voice screamed out, screamed again and again; then there was a gabble of voices, followed by complete silence.

He was reacting too vividly, of course. And actually the vast majority must be law-abiding folk, tolerant and obviously slow to wrath. Decent people, like those he had met, Mary and——

He shuddered and began to hurry. He would have to hurry, anyway, if he was going to catch his bus. But he was frightened to run. That turn in the pub had given his muscles an odd jumpiness. They felt weak. He felt extremely weak, too, about the pit of the stomach. Afflicted the whole body with a sensation of unreality.

Ah, but here were bright lights again and here a taxi! Empty, too!

The taxi sped upward swiftly through the thoroughfares he knew. The theatre crowds were fading out. He lay back and looked out of the windows at the lights, the figures, the tramcars. Bright lights and gleaming rails. Well-dressed people, the lifting of hats, laughter and good-bye. Two women wrapped in furs, their thin dresses about their ankles, and two men, getting into a car. Home! A drink, or a cup of something hot? Whisky, or sherry—there's beer if you really want a drink?

Will closed his eyes, exhausted, and felt himself being borne backward. It's back I should go, he thought. Back there. I should live it out there, live it into and out of my system, so that, like Joe——

The taxi delivered him at the bus terminus only just in time. "You cut that fine," said the driver. "Thank you, sir. Thank you."

The bus moved off as he sat down. He hadn't minded really whether he caught the bus or not. If he had missed it—he would have wandered back—perhaps met Joe again—or Bill Bailey. It would be an experience, dossing with Bill Bailey! Sleep was a thousand miles away from him, but he was very weary.

The cold dampness of the night was working up into a spitting rain out here in the country. For a little while after leaving the bus, Will had to search for the side of his road with his foot. But after a time, its brown surface became vaguely discernible. There seemed to be neither stars nor moon about. But he did not search for either because he had not the energy, he did not care.

He went long distances without much thought or feeling of any kind. Then he came to the place where he had seen the wild geese. This moment had been waiting for him. He knew that.

His knees got a little out of control and he staggered. Blast it! he said, and sat down by the roadside on the wet grass. Oh God, I'm ashamed! He rested his forehead on his palms.

He was ashamed of the wild geese incident, of the bird-singing, and of all the easy emotion that had been born from them. Bitterly ashamed, so that he would hide from the memory of it, if he could; from its weakness and egotism and poetic echoes. He pressed his palms into his forehead like a man driving out the memory of an uneasy sin. No wonder Mac had got the grue! That glory, that elation, that appalling self-hypnosis. Talk of narcissism! The individual, with his holy-glory little heaven all about him. Not that the miserable little affection would have mattered, in a world where things were humanly decent. *For Christ's sake, let me back!* Will crushed his forehead between his palms.

Jamie had seen the wild geese in his eyes—and hated and loathed him. He had seen the self-assurance, the superiority, all the stronger for being instinctive, unconscious. . . .

He got up and went on. The key was under the grey stone. The lamp was turned low down and he left it as it was, lying slumped in his chair.

As thought got at him, he moved uneasily. His face in the dim light was pale as death. Suddenly his eyes opened wide and black, with intense pin-points of light.

Malnutrition. Nothing else had killed Ettie.

He got up. All along, it was Ettie he had been frightened to think of. He did not want to think about her now. He could not trust his mind. Whether the bird experiences were to blame or not, something had thinned inside him somewhere so that he could be more easily pierced. The exposed skin of the mind felt the slightest impact, felt it coming.

He blew out the lamp suddenly, before he could think of stopping himself. Slowly he began to unlace his shoes, staring at the red flameless crumbling fire. His slippers were ready for him on the hearthrug; the glass of milk with the saucer on top he ignored. He took his shoes off without removing his eyes from the fire. His hands fell idle.

The wind blew in the elm-tree beyond the window. Right in the core of the sound the wind made, there was a separate and very thin sound, like the whine of a spirit.

He deliberately concentrated on the fire, on the red core of warmth; without physically doing it, he slid to the hearthrug and spread his hands. This is what man had done through the ages; their hands to the fire, in little earth houses, in snow houses, in tents, in open desert places, in beehive huts, in forest clearings—spreading their hands to life, with death in the shadows around. Now and then looking over a shoulder. . . .

He looked towards the blinded window. The bare branches and thin twigs of the elm made a great harp for the wind which was rising. He turned his head to the door behind him.

The small tick of the French clock grew noisy and rapid. *Tik-tik-tik-tik* . . . very swift. Speeding up; the mechanization of time! It went straight on, on and out—out into the night, into the void beyond the night. . . .

Illusion, for it was ticking inside the brain, its tiny hammer beating a taut surface. *Tik-tik-tik-tik*—on a ganglion centre. With French precision.

He got up and shoved his feet into his slippers. Things could get the better of you, even though you were watching them and could command them. When you stare, your defences are open.

As he had blown out the lamp, so he turned for the door, before thought could question or order him. He was going to bed. Hurriedly he fumbled in his pockets for matches, struck one, and made for the stairs, concentrating on lighting one match to another and causing no noise. A lit match stung him and he dropped it with a whispered oath before the candle caught fire in his bedroom. The candle seemed malignant, as if it did not want a flame; and when he forced it to accept the match, it died down and took a long time to come up again.

But now here was the flame, showing him his face in the mirror, his disembodied face. He turned away and began to undress. As he slipped his braces over his shoulders he sat down heavily on the bed. Lord, I am tired! he muttered. And like an echo, from the outer void: *I am very tired*!

In his pyjamas, he brought the candle to the small table by his bedside, placed his wound watch beside it, saw the box of matches was handy, and blew out the flame. He tucked the bedclothes round him snugly and disposed himself for immediate sleep. A man could only do his best and then prepare to sleep.

And for a little while the flame in his mind kept

dying down. Down, down—it was going softly, warmly out—divinely smothering itself. He kept his thought from it, kept everything from it, so that he would fade with it into its sweet death. It got so low that it was no more than pin-point bright . . . like the pin-points in Jamie's eyes. . . . That extraordinary concentration, that dark electrical charge, ready to leap across at him. Immediate destruction in it. Murder or killing would not be enough; it would have to rend asunder; to tear him bit from bit. . . . It was not the wild geese in his eyes that Jamie had seen. What Jamie had seen was his disgust. But any one would have shown it. Yes—but not in my way, not that instinctive, that fierce disgust, that awful sickening horror, that recoil from him as from a leper. . . .

The flame inside had now got a grip and was beginning to burn up. Will groaned and, turning over, smothered his mouth in the pillow. The pillow, pressing into his eyes, induced an extra darkness. He might evade the light and slip into forgetfulness through the dark. This darkness had faint spangles in it like a memory of dim lights in a dark street. . . .

Tall dark tenement walls. . . . Cliffs, canyon walls. Bodies appearing and disappearing, in a furtive inimical secrecy. A long street, blue-dark, lit by blue globes. . . .

A besieged, a beleaguered town, seen from above, like a Cretan maze.

They would never find their way out.

Even if they wanted to find their way out.

Did they? Did they?

Why should they? What was there outside? What, in very fact, was there outside but the nothingness of outside, the void?

But that word void was the one word Will wanted to evade. As he had come down the road, the wind with its cold spitting rain, with its ravening cry in the branches, had made him think of it as hurrying into the void, as if the void were the space behind the rushing sphere of the earth, the final lost place, the outer darkness. He had immediately shut off the thought.

He shut it off now, but an extra blast of wind in the elm startled him into listening. There was the inner thin cry, like the whine of a spirit, rising, holding, but not able to hold, falling back, falling away behind the rush of the earth, into the outer darkness.

The *outer* darkness. Its appalling meaning had never even touched him before. The rush of wind—the void, cold and sleet-bitten, and the spirit-face trying to keep up but being defeated, Ettie's face, lost in the icy winds of the formless abyss of the outer darkness.

Jesus Christ! moaned Will. But no invocation could now smother the horror that was come upon him.

It was the horror of the *outer* loneliness, a fear so intense that it curdled away the flesh from the cold bone. He felt himself disintegrating, and fought to keep the strands of his body together. He spoke to himself with cunning. He deflected his thought from Ettie and Jamie so that they became apparitions for which he no longer had any feeling. He held himself still, very very still—and was succeeding, until his head began to go round. Round, slowly round, sickeningly. . . .

He gripped the bedclothes, the bed, and pushed himself up. He saw for the first time that he might be beaten, that the forces of the outer darkness might in very fact destroy him.

As he made for the ewer of water, he staggered, hitting into the chair that held his clothes and upsetting it. But he now did not care about the noise. He would not have cared if his landlady had come in, or Mac, or the whole world. His fear had to be kept down, his panic conquered, the wild desire to shout defiance had to be smothered. He sluiced water on to his face, drank the ewer water; and at last stood back panting on the floor. Breathing heavily but with the giddiness gone, he found and lit his candle. His legs now started trembling so violently that he had to get back into bed. There was a real sickness at the pit of his stomach. But he was not going to lie down. So he put the pillow behind his back and sat upright, leaving the candle burning. As he began to shiver, he pulled the clothes up around his shoulders. The breast of his pyjama jacket was wet. He stared into the room, commanding it, a relentless expression on his drawn face. He would fight the cruelty, the evil, of the outer darkness, until the last shred of will was sucked in by death.

His head leaned back, and his eyes closed; then leaned forward and the eyes looked slowly about the room. His breath presently grew stertorous. His head sagged against the wooden back of the bed. The candle made skeleton hollows in his face. Outside the wind in its rhythm rose to the shrill whine, the defeated wild cry, in the heart of the elm. Will looked like a dead man keeping watch.

3

On the way to the bus the following morning, he thought: Dammit, there's that girl I'll have to chaff! There was no reason why he need do it, of course. He could just simply pass up to a forward seat as he used to do. It was at a moment like this that one saw how silly it was to form warm human relations. The thought of it made him tired, and if he could have taken the next bus he would, just to save bother. But this was Saturday, his busiest day of the week. He looked at his watch. He would have to step out. As he increased his pace, his heart began to beat. That strange orgy of feeling last night had taken it out of him. God, what a night! he thought, with a humour dry rather than bitter, for he felt himself curiously detached from life this morning. Even the bird-singing when he had wakened to it, shivering with cold, had not affected him much. He had thought it might have been an irritation, a renewed agony. But he had not cared very much really, and for the most part had dozed through it in a sort of half-drunken stupor.

The bus drew up. "Good morning," she said, with a smile.

"Good morning," he answered and passed up to a vacant seat.

She did not follow him at once, and he sat conscious of the back of his head being towards her. She came at last and, before punching his ticket, looked at him. He nodded. She punched and he paid. Then she retired without a word.

This is silly, he thought, but I haven't the energy. He began to feel vaguely miserable and resented it. But the touch of emotion passed quickly.

As the bus drew up at the terminus, he swayed, standing beside her, and gave her a vague smile. "I had bad news last night."

He saw her brown eyes darken with feeling as they looked at him frankly and yet as it were from under their lashes. "I'm sorry to hear that," she said.

He nodded, looking away. "We'll get over it," and he swung down from the bus, turning to give her a wry glance and meeting her eyes once more. She smiled with a curious, steady, shy tenderness.

The streets or the people or the chimney pots had no slightest interest for him, and the thought of the office held no concern. Mac's obvious back he ignored, and when the rush of the first edition was over Don and he had a drink.

"Looking somewhat grey about the gills this morning."

"Had a bit of a night," Will confessed. "Nothing deadly."

"Up to some mysterious game in the country—or what?" Don's eyes tried to penetrate.

"Mysterious is the word." Will's mind was just as subtle as the black Highlander's.

"Oh, all right," said Don.

"Have another?" said Will.

"Don't think so."

"Well, I'd like one. Better join me."

"You'll be going like Mac, if you don't watch."

Out of a speculative humour, Will said: "I wonder. I wonder exactly what put Mac off on that tack of his. It's a thought!" He ordered two drinks. "Some strange twist of defeatism—in love, or religion, or ambition, or vanity, or—fear? What do you think?"

"I'm sure I don't know," said Don indifferently, because he was vaguely uneasy.

"An extraordinary thing to think that it may be religion, inverted religion; that Mac is haunted by the hounds of hell; that he has made the great denial, and into the empty place of the denial has brought home nothing. Stranger still—that he does not know it is that; that he thinks it is the state of the world, the worthlessness of the ambitions of the world; even that it is Tamerlane."

"I don't think Mac is the religious type. I should say he is the very opposite. Obviously. My God, yes." Don gave a small harsh laugh.

"Perhaps you're right," said Will.

"But you don't think so?"

Will looked into his eyes. "I don't know."

Don lifted his glass and drank, checking his haste midway.

"You see," said Will lazily, "it's an extraordinary thing, the mind. I don't mean in neurotic or psychopathic manifestations, but in the case of the most normal of us. There are moments when it becomes skinned, becomes superbly sensitive. When it is attacked in that condition—and it has to be attacked to be in that condition. . . ." He went on talking for quite a time, with a slow but fluent certainty, that was quite flawless and slightly inhuman. Don felt himself more than once being got at, but Will's apparent innocence, his good nature, was too profound a mask to penetrate.

"This is an extraordinary way", said Don, "to suffer from a hangover."

Will laughed softly.

"Come on!" said Don. "We must go."

"Why all the hurry? Time enough."

"You want to go on talking?"

"You've said it." Will nodded. "But I don't know why. To indulge in arabesques of talk, arabesques that have no beginning and no end, that go on coiling on themselves like slow snakes, too tired to bite, too weary for poison, but loving the slither of their skins and the beauty of the patterns they make without conscious effort, and so——"

"Look here," interrupted Don abruptly. "Have you been taking drugs?"

Will's eyes concentrated and gleamed.

"Oh, very well," said Don, "keep it to yourself. I

don't give a damn, I'm sure. Come on." He set down his glass with a firm bang and got up and walked out.

Will followed him. The drink had done him good. How fine it would be now to lie back in a deep chair in the dim lounge of some luxurious hotel and talk and drink till physical life was trussed hand and foot in arabesques of gleaming wire and dropped discreetly out of sight!

In the height of the afternoon rush, with the football results streaming in, he felt light-headed and gay. As a rugby player, he had always, out of some odd sympathy for the amateur, been a supporter of Queen's Park, who were struggling as usual to retain their position in the first division. And Queen's Park won. He saluted them, and Mac turned so dark and satiric a glance upon him that he sat down abruptly on his stool and began weakly to laugh.

But he was glad when at last the strenuous day was over. It was food he needed, yet he had no great inclination to eat. He should take Don out and stand him one and be humanly reasonable, to make up for that egotistic interlude of the forenoon. However, he allowed himself to drift out of the building without being embroiled by any one and in a near-by pub stood himself a large whisky.

For all day he knew that some time he must see Joe Wilson. All day the figures of last night were at the back of his mind, visibly or invisibly, like phantoms. They did not touch him at all. But they were there, and he must speak to them before the day was dead,

He sat for a long time with himself, staring at the people who came in and out. For the most part the sheer fleshiness of the faces was a revelation. He had never before seen the outside of faces so vividly. He did not look inside them at all, had no desire to, did not care what was inside. A face here and there was so extraordinarily gross that it fascinated him. The bulge of a neck, the lumps of a forehead, the acuteness of small eyes, the glass at the mouth, the dribble at the corner of the lips that pursed in a swinish way as the back of the red hand wiped them. Not surely because the man was merely fat. Fat men were jolly men. There was quite a lot of jollity, of whisperings and leanings-back, and tilting of bowler hats.

Will lowered his eyes to his own thin hand on the table and stared at it. Flesh is opaque; it lets no light through. And when no light comes through, outside flesh slithers against outside flesh in a dreadful promiscuity.

He got up and moved along the street to an eating-place. When the waitress came along and raised her eyebrows, he suddenly thought: If I don't go immediately to Joe's home he'll have eaten and gone out for the night. So with a smile he excused himself to the waitress, who smelt the whisky in his breath, and put on his coat. At the door, as he half-swung round, he saw that she was looking after him. She immediately turned her head away.

That strange penetrating human thing, a woman's sympathy! However gross a woman was—and heavens! women could be gross enough—she never lost the capacity for an eyeflash in which there was light, good or evil!

Joe's folk lived in a real petty bourgeois street. The sight of its trim little decencies made Will smile. This was the sort of street poor but aspiring women put up as a barricade against the drunken horrors of early industrialism. Back here they hauled their men from the promiscuity of the gross all-levelling pubs, whose promise was a fiery freedom, and whose fulfilment was a vomit. Here in this quiet, rather dirty, rather mean little street, with its lack of spaciousness, its suggestions of faint smells, its ardent respectabilities, its flowers behind closed windows and its sunning cats, the great drama that Joe knew so well had been fought—and was still being fought. The new public school poet-communists did not understand that. The petty bourgeoisie to them was anathema. They wanted in their imaginations to be warmed by the great army of the toilers. Quite! quite! said Will.

He paused and, as he lit a cigarette, treated himself to a husky laugh. For he was now trying to banish the smell of whisky from his breath, lest Joe's mother come to the door! The ritual and the discipline.

Lord, what a history was behind that! What realism and tragedy and horror and aspiration and courage, indomitable courage! Did any city in the world ever put up such a fight for workers' rights as this city did? Perhaps, but surely never with so prolonged and bitter an intensity, with so much fury, that strange historic fury of the Scots.

Will felt this fury far back in his mind, like an echo of trumpets. He drew in a last deep breath of smoke, slowly let it out through mouth and nostrils, and climbed the three steps to the door.

Mrs. Wilson herself answered his ring and, after greetings, for they knew each other quite well, said that Joe had gone out after his tea, half an hour ago. She had at once a sweet and a hard face, her smile being slight but very attractive. The smile centred in the eyes, filling them with a light that was, however, steady and penetrating, so that a sensitive person felt measured by the smile. Her smooth hair, though greying, was still predominantly dark. She stood quite still and asked Will if he would care to come in.

Will thanked her and said no. Turning his face over his shoulder thoughtfully (but actually so that she might not smell his breath), he said that he had been with Joe last night and wanted to get certain information from him. "You don't know where he has gone?"

"He has gone to some meeting or other, but where I can't say."

"All right, thank you. I may run into him. I have an idea where I might find him." He was backing away and smiled to her. She smiled, with a small nod, and closed the door slowly upon their good-byes.

He breathed heavily for a little, feeling quite weak again, and when at last he got to an eating-house, ordered an underdone fillet steak with chips.

Joe, in physical appearance, took to his father rather than his mother, but the mother was the power behind him. During the ten minutes required to grill the steak, Will sat vaguely dreaming of that very distinctive phenomenon, the Scots mother. Scotland herself, known as The Auld Mither. On the surface sentimental, but beneath—was there something powerful and enduring, fantastic and strong, poverty and the barricades, eldritch and wise, steady, steady, steady—and unyielding? Or was this just the blood speaking, speaking out of an old myth?

When they brought home Joe's father dead, he was smelling of whisky. Nothing more dramatic than a Saturday night street accident which, had he been quite sober, he was almost bound to have avoided. Joe was a little lad then.

If it was fillet steak it wasn't very tender, though it was bloody enough. That fresh thirsty taste of blood. He had got this carnivorous flavour before. Somebody had told him that it did not matter really whether you chewed meat or not, because the juices of the mouth did not help the digestion of meat. So he left the matter largely to the appropriate juices in the stomach.

All the same, it was really difficult for him to have a sound opinion on this mother business, because he could not recollect his own mother. He did have a fairly distinct picture, embodying a sensation of warmth and a madonna face over him, but suspected that it was a later growth or construction of the imagination, for she had died when he was three.

His father had died eight years ago, actually at the moment during the graduation ceremony when Will was being capped.

So he was an orphan, and, as he sat on, drinking coffee, he felt glad that in this world of human relations he was quite free.

Some time during the night, in a stupor of turmoil and nightmare, a moment had come when all was stilled and before him appeared a figure. And the figure raised his face and looked at him, and the figure was himself.

That terrible clairvoyant moment, that light of understanding, of pity, in the eyes, that look of sad unearthly humour, committing them both irrevocably.

"Will that be all, sir?"

He looked at the waiter for a moment. "Yes," he answered.

Joe wasn't in the Labour rooms, and Will turned his steps through the gathering dark towards the lower part of the town.

It was the elfin time of innocence and the old poet's lamplighter. A quiet still evening, overcast but not gloomy. The steak and coffee gave Will a centre knot of stability, dissipated the physical tremors that flush the brain. He walked with a slow quiet pleasure, observing without being touched; observing consciously the twilight within the streets.

A rare detachment came to him—from somewhere, he felt, immensely remote; as remote as this grey light that came from springtimes in the beginning of the world. The grey magic half-light that haunted the poets.

Fashions change and magic comes under the ban.

But dear God, this grey light smiles! A transitory, evanescent smile, down the streets and round the corners. So it played down forest clearings and alleyways of standing stones, seashores and the shadows of mountains on moors. The meeting of light and darkness, love's exquisite foreplay, its delicious fun.

The children were playing not now like rats but like sparrows. And here and there a grown-up face carried a faintly reflected light. But mostly the faces were without light, were dead. And now and then, Will saw faces that wanted this light to pass into the covering comfort of darkness and coloured electric signs. Folk in the sitting-rooms or kitchens of streets immediately switched on their lamps as the twilight entered.

He remembered the Sunday twilight at the farm when he could not bring himself to put the light on. But that had been rather uncanny, and he would not let himself think it out even now.

As he penetrated deeper into the lower parts of the town, this calm assurance began to be invaded by the gathering darkness, by the gloom of the steel-blue lights, by the tenement squalor, the dim entrances to closes, and, above all, by that faint pervasive smell to which his nostrils were so sensitive. A carry-over from the evolutionary process? Stags sniffing the air, wild dogs on the trail. . . .

Did the nostrils convey to the wary brain the warnings of danger and disease and brutality and all evil? Irrational, as he knew. Who could know better? for it was his political concern to produce at a moment's notice exact figures regarding unemployment, housing, and overcrowding in the very area through which he was passing. More than that, he could tell of the occasional single room inhabited by father, mother, adolescent son and daughter into which a total wage of eight pounds came weekly, yet without son or daughter making any effort to clear out of the stifling den. He could tell of the kindness of the poor to the poor, of self-sacrifice, of household decencies and social conventions more rigid than might be encountered in many houses of the rich quarter of the town. Yet though he could have filled pamphlets with exact knowledge, that fact in no way interfered with his nostrils now. His reaction was completely instinctive, and on that reaction he knew it was necessary that he should act until he died.

He knew approximately where the close was in which Jamie lived and he wanted to pass it but not to go in. He had a quite certain feeling that he was going to run into Joe soon. But he could not find the close and presently entered a pub. He had difficulty in pushing his way to the counter, but ultimately managed to get a small whisky. There were far more people about to-night, and more gaiety and boisterous fun. There would be an odd fight later on and some drunken jollity. Great leg-pulling about busted coupons. And arguments over Jimmy or Bobby, over centre forwards and inside rights and referees; with a virulent discussion going on just behind him about "a pure bloody offside goal if ever there was one". This opinion was equally strongly resisted. The language became more pointed. The two favourite sexual words were used with increasing directness and with a penetrating rhythm. Overwork did not dull their variety or scatter their strength. On the contrary, all other oaths were sucked into them. And to bear witness to so strange a fecundity the protagonists called upon Jesus Christ.

"Now! now!" cried the barman. "You just chuck that stuff, will you?"

"Chuck my bloody backside. Were you there?"

"I'll chuck your backside outside pretty smart," said the barman, "if you come any more of that." Then he smiled slowly, if with a glint, and they all got back to the argument again.

A good-natured crowd, except for the occasional thin weedy type that could only make itself important by working up to a clamour. There was more money about to-night, more of the real workmen out for their couple of well-earned pints. Saturday night and the missus away shopping.

Will became aware of a fellow beside him of perhaps his own age. He could see at a glance that he had never worked. He was a head smaller, thin, with nondescript hair growing raggedly down past the ears, and a twist to the body as if it had got used to hunching itself against its own clothes for warmth. He had been struck by the pallor of this type. But now he saw that the fellow was not pale but grey, with the greyness of lice. There would be lice on his shirt. The hunching movement of the shoulders was not altogether an effort to gather warmth.

There was a shifty acuteness in the face as Will accidently met it.

"Were ye at the match th'-day, mister?"

"No," said Will. "Were you?"

"Na. Ah coudny manage to ge' awa'," The sing-song rhythm of the district was strong in his voice. "They say it wis a great match." There was an inch of thin beer left in his glass. He was obviously saving it.

Will finished his whisky. "Have a pint?"

The eyes gleamed and glanced at Will's glass. "Could ye make it a wee hauf?"

Will ordered two small whiskies and offered his companion a cigarette. There were others like him in the pub. In fact humanity was graded in virility right up to an Irishman with a tongue of fair hair sweeping across his forehead from under a tilted sweat-stained felt hat; a big untidy man, with a throaty brogue and rather small blue eyes that seemed in their wary steadiness to listen to remarks behind him while he himself was speaking; a large, good-hearted, rather vain countryman, obviously very fond of hearing himself talk. Will liked him. He had strength and warmth and all a countryman's simple cunning.

Warmth, life warmth: that's what the grey men craved. That's why they were here. Freedom from the burden of creeping misery. Warmth and light and a man speaking out of his own breast; a man uttering blasphemies in the certainty of himself; a man challenging, face to face, spitting oaths, and ready with the liberating blow. Close the pubs and you'll have a revolution.

"So long!" said Will, as he gulped his drink and pushed his way out.

In the next pub he came to, he had only one drink. In the third, he had two drinks and a football argument. From the fourth pub, he wandered down by the river. He would meet Joe, but not just yet. As he lit a cigarette he smiled. "I'm beginning to feel at home," he muttered, and a sensation of ease slowly pervaded him, as if in some queer unaccountable way he had come home to some one or something.

He saw the river through an iron railing, with gleams on its dark surface as if it were a dreaming forest pool. How remote from last night's image of Jamie's one-armed body and its convoy of eels! As he gazed upward, finding no star, he heard Ettie's voice say from so far off that it was suddenly thin and near: *I am very tired.*

He stood quite still, and, instead of fear and rebellion, there came about his spirit an infinite pity.

It may be the whisky! he thought, as he turned his eyes away. But though he could still joke with a wry mouth, he knew that for these still moments he had penetrated near to the core of understanding. So near, that perhaps he had to break the contact. . . . Was it a real voice? He turned round. "I beg your pardon?"

"Hallo, dearie?"

His reaction was instinctive flight from being trapped, the first real personal anxiety he had felt

that night. It died down in a moment. He stood looking at her, and, taking this as invitation, she came
close up.

In the rather dim light, with her make-up, she
looked about eighteen. As she spoke again to him
endearingly, he shook his head. "I'm no use to you
to-night."

She began to exercise her art upon him, with the
appropriate notes of endearment and gaiety.

He shook his head: "No use."

"Ah, come on! Just for a little while. I know a
place. If you don't want to walk with me—you can
follow me."

That silenced him for a moment.

"A girl like you—surely you can get a fellow any
time?"

"Yes, but—not one like you."

"Why aren't you in a better part of the town?"

"Now you're asking, aren't you?"

"I beg your pardon."

She laughed, teasingly.

"I'm not feeling that way," he persisted.

She tried to show him that he might change his
mind, but he held her off. She was afraid of his detached manner and overacted.

"Have you nothing but questions? Besides," she
added lightly, "what's half a dollar to you?"

"It wouldn't break me. Still—that's not the point."

She was going to produce a witticism, but hesitated
and went on another tack.

"What a lovely smell off your breath! You're lucky!"

"Like me to stand you one?"

"You're asking me!" Her eyes assessed him glitter-ingly.

"Well, I'll stand you one. But remember that's all there is to it. If you agree to that, then all right. Do you agree?"

"Sure," she said.

"Well, where'll we go?"

"This way."

What astonished Will was the complete absence of any awkwardness in himself as he walked along with her. Had this happened a month ago, he would have been all conflicting emotions and furtive eyes. Now he felt a curious freedom, as if he were being liberated from a past self.

But he made no effort to understand this or even to wonder why. What he was wondering about was the girl herself, and now he felt that he had no right even to ask her personal questions. After all, the assumption that this girl was a social problem rather than a human being was a rather terrible comment on middle-class complacency. That he should get her "story" and "pass it on", whether by way of ribaldry or an awful example—or, dear heaven, as a politico-economic illustration—seemed to him now so appalling an intrusion on that lonely entity called the human soul that it affected him with a sense of monstrous humour.

She was telling him about the place they were going to and he was interested because he wondered just where—short of the expensive lounges of the great hotels—in this holy city a fellow could take a girl like this. It turned out to be a quiet, rather dingy saloon bar down a side street, and as he passed the policeman at the corner, Will looked at the man and then smiled to himself.

"Does he know you?" the girl asked, with a quick note of mistrust.

"Yes. I met him last night. He obviously knows you, too."

"Only by seeing me now and then."

"Good. I feel as if we had gone up and duly registered."

She did not know how to take him, but here was the door and she led him in.

The atmosphere of secret assignations struck Will so strongly that the undigested whisky turned over in his stomach. Two or three here plying their ancient trade; and a few men, too, committed and not yet committed. Meantime there were drinks anyhow. "What's yours?" asked Will.

"Gin," she said.

"A large gin," said Will, "and a large whisky." He turned to her. "A tonic?"

"All right."

It was not a very big room and the corner tables were occupied, so Will accepted the small round vacant table in the middle of the floor and waved his companion to a chair. Raising his glass to her with a quiet smile, he drank.

"Ivy is my name," she said in an undertone as the glass touched her lips.

He saw now that she was older than eighteen; probably twenty-five. She had quite good bone in her face but the features were thin. Her hair and eyebrows were naturally dark, and the colour on her cheeks and lips and the artificial glitter in her brown eyes consorted well enough with this darkness. She was quite good-looking, if in a rather hard way. Even though he did not regard her very directly, she knew he was appraising her.

"Your first to-day?" she asked, with an effort at humour.

"Not exactly," he said. "Yours?"

"Actually, yes." Her eyes were wondering what impression she made.

"Can you stand much of that stuff?"

"Why? Feel like trying me out?"

They chatted until they were accepted by the room and forgotten—except for a woman's occasional straying eyes.

With her elbows on the little table, she murmured: "Why won't you come?"

"I'm meeting a man down here to-night." He smiled to her lifted eyes. "You think that's an old one?"

"No, I believe you."

"Don't be personal," he said. "Don't soften me."

"I wish I could."

He looked at her thoughtfully, with a considering smile. She met his look, giving him her eyes. Her skin, he thought, judging perhaps from her mouth, had a curious elastic quality, as if it could be readily stretched. The colour was laid on with a thin fresh bloom. Her anxiety to get hold of him was palpable. And in this anxiety Will felt there was something more than cash, more than sex—of which, often enough, she must surely get sick—and he wondered vaguely if he were deluding himself.

"I have a room," she said.

"Have you?"

She nodded.

"Share it with some one, or have it all to yourself?"

"Lily and me—we arrange that—when——"

"Quite." He nodded. "And where does Lily go then, poor thing?"

"That's all right," she said.

"Tell me," he asked. "Why exactly did you mention that just now?"

"Because you are the kind ... who wants time. ..."

He suddenly laughed, then begged her pardon. "I understand you." He added: "Would you really like to spend the rest of the night with me?"

"Yes, of course!"

He shrugged, as if she had missed his meaning.

"You know I would," she said, on a lower tone.

"I'm hanged if I can understand that—apart from the cash. Is that brutal?"

She considered him. "You're queer."

"For God's sake, don't say a thing like that."

"I can't make you out."

"I'm too simple for you."

She still looked at him, through the glitter of her trade and her hard mistrust, afraid to trust herself. He could see she had a considerable amount of experience and not a great deal of intellect. Her choice of profession, after an "accident" or two, had probably been deliberate. Not that that explained much, for inevitably such a choice must have been deliberate rebellion—against what?

She shook her head and said nothing.

"That's clever of you," he remarked of her silent gesture.

"What is?"

"Tell me this, Ivy. I want to be quite friendly with you. I do feel friendly, to tell the truth. You couldn't forget yourself and just be friendly with me? As you know quite well already, I am not in the right mood for the lusts of the flesh. I could spend a few hours with you—but what am I saying? Have another drink?"

She nodded, watching him, the dark in her eyes flooding.

She took her drink but did not speak. He was silent, too.

"I would like that," she said, looking at her glass.

"Sure?"

"Yes." She rather spoilt the effect with the glitter of a quick professional glance, for she was anything but certain of him. She saw, too, that his own mind was rather startled, for he tended to stare.

"You needn't be frightened of coming," she suggested. "I'll make you comfortable."

"Will you?"

"Yes."

"Of course I mightn't", he said slowly, "be such a saint as all that."

Automatically she smiled her small knowing smile. He didn't like it.

"There's one thing," she murmured.

"Yes?"

"I'm quite clean. I see to that." This time her low voice went through his heart.

He nodded. "I had not thought of that."

"Do come," she said. Her darkness had gone into her voice and made it moody.

"All right, Ivy," he said slowly, staring dreamily past her, "I'll come."

Mind and instinct concentrated in her eyes, but they could not read him. It was not desire, not despair, not sorrow, not any need for sympathy, it was nothing in all the world she knew. And she wondered if this slim good-looking educated fellow knew himself. He had such attractive eyes and a smile, when it came, that drowned the heart in a queer warmth.

His eyes came upon her face. "Will we go now?"

"Yes."

He looked at her for a moment. "Come, then."

"You haven't finished your drink."

"Oh, haven't I?" He settled down again, and appeared to smile at himself as he emptied his glass. But it was a good-natured smile, and as he set down his glass he looked at her humanly. "I warned you, of course, that I might meet my friend, and if we do —well, I'll have to go with him."

"Where were you to meet him?"

"We had no fixed appointment. I just came here to find him."

She saw that he was speaking the truth and vaguely regretted having told him he hadn't finished his drink.

"But—weren't you to meet him some place?"

"No." Her puzzled expression seemed to amuse him.

"Does he know you were coming here?"

"How could he, when I didn't know myself? I should say he doesn't even know of the existence of this place. And yet—he probably does. He knows most things—about how folk live."

"Who is he?"

"I think—perhaps—he's God."

She couldn't make a joke of it by asking him if he was loopy, because of the humour with which he watched her expression. So she tried to smile in the way he did. Her smile was not a success, for she was uncertain of herself, a little on edge.

"Are you trying to pull my leg?"

"No, Ivy. Not really. I just have the odd sort of feeling that he may be standing outside, talking to the policeman."

She stared at him, a glint of fear in her eyes.

"Sorry, Ivy," he said. He put his hand out over one of hers and pressed it. "You need have no fear of me. I am a wanderer, like yourself." Fear of the trap vanished from her eyes in a restless confusion. She swallowed, and picked up her cheap gloves.

"Ready, then?" he asked.

She nodded and got up.

As they reached the door, a female voice cried: "Cheero, Ivy."

By the little start which Ivy gave, it was clear that in these last minutes she had forgotten where she was. Will raised his hat and called: "Good night," in a friendly voice, then followed Ivy through the doorway.

Across the narrow street, directly opposite, Joe was standing with the policeman.

"There he is," said Will to Ivy. He saluted Joe and called: "Just a minute." Then he walked on a few paces with Ivy.

"I told you it might happen like this," he said.

"You knew!" she accused him in a low voice.

He shook his head. "You know I didn't know. I just had a hunch. Sorry, but there it is."

"But will you not come? Please. What has he got to do with it? . . ." The pleading note was deep in her voice. And it was genuine enough to affect her breathing.

From his pocket-book he took a pound note. "A small present for you."

She kept looking at him. He shoved the note into her left hand which was against her breast. "You need it more than me. And I've enjoyed our talk."

Her whole woman's nature rose to him. There was no artifice now. There was something in him she did not want to lose, something she suddenly and desperately craved. And she had no words for it.

"Good night, Ivy," he said tenderly, as he took

her right hand and shook it; then, lifting his hat, he stooped and kissed her. Her lips remained quiet and cold.

But she clutched his hand. "You will come for me again?"

He looked at her and said slowly: "I think I will. Please go now."

"Remember—you'll come." Her eyes glittered deeply, then like a woman betrayed into a burning exposure of herself she turned and walked away. He watched her for a little while, then strolled back to Joe and the policeman.

"Where have you been all night?" he asked Joe.

"I should say it's much more to the point to ask where you have been. Don't you think so?" and Joe turned to the constable. His voice was hard and brittle.

"I agree with you fully," said the constable.

Will laughed lightly. "I have had a very pleasant evening."

"Manifestly," said Joe. "Though socially it is not considered *de rigueur* to kiss a prostitute in a public thoroughfare. Ranald here has official instructions on the point."

"If you were gentlemen, you wouldn't have seen it."

"Will you answer me if it is necessary", inquired Ranald, "for the purpose of your 'copy', that you should go to such dubious lengths?"

"In my profession," said Will, "the sky's the limit."

"Indeed, I would have thought it was the other place," said Ranald. "At least—it was looking that

141

way." It was a dry and friendly humour. "However, as they go, Ivy is not the worst of them. Though she has a temper when she's roused. She has that."

"Really?" Will looked at him.

Ranald nodded. "It's my colleague was telling me. It was in another pub farther east there. There was a regular shindy. And do you know what her excuse was?"

"No."

" 'He insulted me,' she said, pointing to a fellow."

"Perhaps he had," said Will.

Ranald laughed thickly. "I wouldn't put it past him."

They all began to laugh, but Will took out his cigarette case, because in a moment, in the middle of laughing, last night's loneliness began to come at him. He shouldn't have looked at Ivy walking away. Suddenly he heard the inner sound of laughter, its hard obliterating cruelty.

"Did he lock her up?" he asked, to kill the sound.

"No, as it happened, he didn't. To tell the truth he didn't know what to do because there was a lot of them. But he had to do something, so he lifted the fellow who insulted her, and fortunately that fellow struck my colleague and that made things easy for him."

Will began to laugh again. The effect of all the drinks he had had was beginning to take the disconcerting form of a cold sobriety. He felt the coldness on his brow. He did not want to lose the mood he had been in all night.

As Joe and he walked away, a certain restraint at once became manifest and Will tried to defeat it by commenting on the human decency of the policeman they had just left (the man who had marched Jamie to the cells last night). Joe agreed.

Will went on to tell how he had called at Joe's home. "I wanted to see you to find out what had happened to Jamie. It would have dogged me in the country over the week-end."

"I think he'll come all right," said Joe in cool practical tones. "I bailed him out this morning. He'll plead drunk and disorderly and be fined five bob—or perhaps merely be given a warning, because Ranald will put in a good word for him. A clean record and exceptional circumstances. That's not the real worry."

"Having been locked up, you mean, won't do him any harm?"

"I hope not."

"I can understand that. It will probably do him good."

"You mean?"

"The humiliation may be a certain payment on account."

"I don't—quite see—what you mean?" Joe's tone was precise and cool.

"A bit fanciful, probably, but the punishment, the abasement, the suffering—a form of tribute to the dead Ettie for her tragedy. His recognition."

Joe walked on steadily and said nothing.

"You think that a bit highfalutin; that a fellow like Jamie could not come near the conception of sacrifice?"

"I couldn't say, I'm sure," Joe answered. "But it seems to me a bit vague. It certainly would never dawn on him that being imprisoned was a spiritual sacrifice."

"Naturally," said Will.

They walked on in silence, and now Will felt quite certain that Joe had been deeply upset by the recent scene before the pub. There, the very foundation of their friendship had been struck at. Joe had kept face before Ranald and supported the idea of "copy". But now they were alone, and he knew that "copy" was a myth. To Joe it would not merely be drink and immorality of the lowest because most calculated kind; but, deeper than that, a betrayal of the proletarian faith that was Joe's religion and his life. Will now understood the hard note in Joe's voice. The understanding so appalled him, that a slow smile twisted his face.

"However," Will went on, "as you suggest, these rather mystical conceptions probably don't matter. You said that was not the main worry. What is the worry, then?"

"The difficulty of getting him to settle down again."

"Why?"

"Well, naturally, he's going to be upset for a bit."

"Of course. But you think he'll settle down?"

"I hope so."

"Was he at home to-day?"

"For a time, yes."

"You've seen Mary?"

"Yes. Fortunately she has sense."

"She'll give him rope. Are you going back to-night again?"

"No, I'm going home. I've done what I could."

"That's wise," said Will. "It'll come all right."

"You think so?" There was a harsh dryness in Joe's voice now.

"I think so," Will answered. Then prompted by a queer malice out of the cold white world of his unnatural sobriety, he went on in a conversational voice: "That close, that room of his, is to Jamie just now what a slaughter-house is to a young bull. He cannot face it. It cries out against him. He could roar when he comes near it. But he knows he has to face it. He can turn and twist on himself as he likes, strain at the halter madly, but face it he must, and he knows it. And to-night, or to-morrow night, or the next night, he'll drag himself back. And Mary will be there. And she'll give him food in silence. And time will go on. The minutes will group together, and the hours, and they'll break him. He'll weep. And for a time she will listen and do nothing; but then, moved, she will go to him and comfort him; and that will soften the hard core of bitterness, and he will cling to her and find comfort in her; self-pity will be upon him now and will deepen his emotions; and he will ask much comfort from her; and in the strange frenzy of life that comes upon a man then, under the absolving hands of a woman, he will ask from her the ultimate comfort her body can give—and she will give him that."

Joe stopped abruptly.

"In this way," Will concluded, standing still also, "they will begin to build a new life relation on the tragedy of the dead Ettie. For days, months, it may go on, but how far into the future, will depend—on circumstance, yes, but, more inscrutably, on the stuff their souls are made of."

Joe looked at him coldly. "You believe that?"

"It is probable. Already in her heart Mary knows it's highly probable. She can look after herself, as you say. And she knows she can. She knows nothing can defeat her—until she defeats herself. But things will happen, in that room between them, so and so. They are not bourgeois. With them artifice or social law will go down before reality, particularly the sweeping force of emotional reality. It may be the greatness of your proletariat that in that desperate hour they will defeat sterile suffering in the deepest mutual warmth. I cannot judge those things. I can only feel their impact."

"You seem to have a deep knowledge of those things."

"Do you mean experience?" asked Will.

Joe walked on. Will glanced sideways at him and saw his face staring straight ahead. He was hurt, he was angry, he was bitterly disillusioned, but deeper than all that, Will saw that he suffered.

But he could not help him; and, in his strange mood of detachment, he had no desire to help him. They were drawing near the wheels of the trams and the brighter lights of the centre of the city. At the end of the street, they were now walking up, they would part.

"I have no wish to intrude on your private life," Joe said at last, "and you do not need to answer. Were you going home with that girl—when you saw me?"

"Yes," said Will.

"I see. I just didn't know you were like that."

Then out of a final perversity, that yet seemed implicit in the need of this bitter moment, Will added almost casually: "I had had a few drinks by myself. There didn't seem much else to do."

They came to the corner of the street. "Well, I suppose we part here," Joe said in his quiet matter-of-fact voice. "Good night."

"Good night," said Will.

Joe swung across the street, his tall broad figure powerful and undeviating. Will looked after him until he had disappeared, then turned the corner to a tram-stop.

CHAPTER THREE

*

His bedroom was full of light when he awoke. Against the pale blind, the shadows of twigs of the elm-tree moved slightly. All was quietude and slow bright ease.

He listened for noises in the house, but heard nothing except the faint sigh of the wind and here and there the singing of a bird through a nearer chattering of sparrows.

What a sleep I have had! he thought. Gratitude touched his heart with the gaiety that stills itself in wonder; so that he kept on listening as if he might hear something that would explain more closely the world beyond his window; catch the unheard note; detect the hidden movement.

Such a listening brings an exquisite panic, that resolves itself in a moment into a delicious sense of security and well-being.

He had been so tired last night that when his foot struck a stone or lump in the road, the percussion had been soft, as if the sole were padded. He had been beyond all feeling, and staggered lightly and not unpleasantly. Even the intricate problems of Joe and Ivy and the strange evening he had spent in the slums had become an abstract play, to which he attributed qualities that were clear but without emotion.

And now here was the morning—and his mind washed and refreshed. Was it not something to thank whatever gods? Not to think, not to become embroiled in thought, in emotion, not to let human relations take hold of you with their sticky sweaty fingers, but simply to open the mind to thankfulness, as the wise old elm to sun and wind?

But stop! he would be thinking in a moment, if he wasn't careful!

He smiled and closed his eyes. What time was it? But he had left his watch on the dressing-table, and at once he got up. Half-past eight! He nearly laughed aloud. Over eight solid hours! He drew up the blind, faced a far blue sky with white clouds sailing, felt a cool but soft wind from the open window, and saw the wide bright world.

The beauty touched him for a moment too closely, but also so deeply that he could hardly let it go. Dear God, he thought, how lovely! and his hands moved as if they would take it and offer it. He stood and stared until the sharpness of the emotion would pass, together with its burden, and leave only its sunny memory behind.

Jenny came walking across the lawn below, the sun in her hair. She was looking about the grass and stooped to a bunch of heavily budded daffodils, two of which were breaking—he could see the touch of yellow against the pale fingers that so gently lifted the heads—then let them drop, while the round golden head above considered them.

Golden head and green dress and the figure of Primavera! Jenny grew her own flowers; sowed the seeds or split up the bulb clusters; dug the earth and stamped it.

Tribute to her for that!

As he looked down on her, he smiled, knowing, because of Philip, that she was completely detached from him—which meant that he was from her! A woman is an oddly incalculable animal, until she is fixed in that way! It was a humour that he wouldn't have minded trying to share with her! But she wouldn't look up. If she had even been capable of looking up, he would at once have mistrusted her. She had other concerns and wandered after them round the house towards the garden.

He went back to bed and lay dreamily gazing at the twigs that moved with so slow and lovely a grace, sometimes remaining quite still, then stirring again, as if the heart of the tree were intermittently touched by half-formed memories.

The old tag was wrong. It was art that was short and life long. Art was momentary, evanescent. The pattern of the twigs moved and grace was born and passed away like the notes of a thrush. He could see the bright blue sky through and beyond the twigs and the white clouds swelling like sails.

The cawing of rooks came nearer; they crossed the window of his vision at some distance; a few tattered old fellows, full of a grotesque humour.

Keep hold of the outside lovely things. Don't get embroiled. Don't interfere. He began to study the effect of the light on articles on his dressing-table, the mirror, the roses on the wall, until he fell into a state that was mostly sleep, but also a something which, when his landlady knocked, he could not remember but knew it had been utterly delightful.

When he had bathed and dressed, chatted with Mrs. Armstrong and eaten his breakfast, he felt fit for the country. He wondered whether he would stay away the whole day, but decided not to. If this sun kept up he might find a sheltered spot in which to lie and read in the afternoon. It would be a way of breaking himself into reading again. There was that column on T. S. Eliot he must do soon.

He started off in good style, until he came to the spot where he had seen the wild geese, and at once the brightness of his morning began to pass. His cunning inner mind put up a fight for the brightness, but, however he tried to think or not to think, it dimmed.

He grew vaguely resentful, resentful of figures like Joe or Jamie, of slums, of economic conditions. After all, he was an ordinary fellow who did what he could. They were not going to suck his whole life away. Within an hour, he felt depressed and in the grip of misery.

It was annoying, maddening; he rebelled, but it was of no use.

This was really an extraordinary state of affairs! He wasn't an emotional person, a moody person. Never had been; in any case, not beyond the normal.

What was happening to him now?

And his eyes—his damned eyes saw the hard machinery of the sunlight on the bare earth, a real Sunday sunlight, too! He grew satiric about it, and in the process all life became satire. In fact, hardly even that; little more than stones and earth and sap that sucked itself up to buds and fungoid growths all with a dull stupid terrifying endurance.

He walked miles and then lay down on his coat.

No doubt life was an affair of ups and downs. And he had experienced so much so swiftly lately that he must expect disillusion to tread on the heels of illusion. For everything was illusion, the illusion the personal eye puts about the stones and the sap and the buds—and what *they* were it was heaven alone knew.

Extraordinary, all the same, the lengths to which this illusion would go, how it would guy a fellow into abysmal fatuities. There was last night—he had to face it—what did it all boil down to?

Mystical! There was no other word.

It had all been a form of mystical communion with the downtrodden or outcast section of society. This communion had in some esoteric way become necessary in order that he might find freedom within himself. And while the process had lasted—there was no good blinking the fact—he had found this freedom; not only freedom within himself but freedom from himself.

And the amazing thing was that in the whole process the mystical was not something vague and woolly, dimly poetic, but, on the contrary, so precise and factual, that it was in the most practical sense more real than any normal state. It had been accompanied, for example, by a penetrating insight and an absence of all those trumpery irritations and moods that so frequently obscure a face, a living issue, a simple scene. He had felt a real access of good nature, a deeper humour, a wider understanding. It had not been solemn. Solemnity or self-importance could not live in its simple air. It had—let the word come!—been rather divine.

Even that parting with Ivy, when he had suddenly stooped and kissed her, had been an impulse from the heart. No one, seeing it, could be expected to understand it. It was not even a kiss to a prostitute out of divine pity! Nothing grandiose in the real mysticism! It was a simple—ah God, it was one of the simplest and sweetest things he had ever done, and that's all about it.

And you can take it or lump it, Joe!

Ivy understood, too. All her soul came up into her eyes, all her defeated craving for completion and peace. It did her good. Just as it did him good. Whatever should follow after.

Strange, too, that Joe would have every sympathy for Ivy in her profession, would befriend her and help her, just as he had helped Jamie, if circumstances so decreed, and yet have this unrelenting attitude to Will's action that evening. It was perhaps not altogether an incapacity in Joe to understand. It went deeper than that.

He, Will, was moved by the personal experience only. Joe was moved by the personal experience as an element in the greater social experience. Joe was the saviour of society, and to be a saviour you must have your code of behaviour, your system of ethics.

Joe was a force gathering things and humans together towards a higher integration. And Joe's fundamental quarrel with Will was that he, Will, should at least be an assistant saviour, not one of the irresponsible humans, one of the waifs. Ah, more than that. For in Joe's eyes, whereas Ivy was the waif of circumstance, Will was, could only be—the deliberate destroyer.

And to think how calmly I did it! How casually, as if it were an everynight affair! No wonder Ranald only half believed I was after "copy"!

Will lit a cigarette. The smoke had a bitter flavour in his mouth. Once or twice before he had noticed this bitter flavour. He suddenly threw the cigarette away, turned over on his hip, and then lay on his face.

There came into his mind that aerial picture he had had of the city the other night—that sensation of flying over it and seeing it below him like a maze. It was more like a model of the city than the city itself, and as a model it seemed to have walls and ramparts. A deep-dark clay model, sinking in a curve from its suburban hills with their wash of space and light to the intricate walled gloom by the river. The inhabitants were not seen but imagined like minute specks; in processional movement over the suburban hills;

grouping and scurrying in the endless bolt-hole corridors by the river. Whenever the eye settled on any portion, that portion swelled to life size, gathering light as from an immense lens.

He saw this light in the slums, and in Ivy's bedroom, a dry sabbatical light along the dead streets, where dustbins still stood about, haunted by mangy cats and sniffing dogs. The Sunday morning of the living dead.

He got up and went on and lit a cigarette again. Even if he turned back now, he would not be in time for lunch. That, anyway, was a relief! He drew a deep breath of smoke. It had the dry bitter taste of sickness in his mouth and scorched the membranes.

Nothing like a touch of Joe's discipline.

For he saw, with an equally dry bitter humour, that "the Scots metaphysical twist" had failed. The cunning inner mind, in its effort at analysis and explanation, had not only failed to free him but bogged him deeper than ever. That's probably where it put one over on the Slav, who wandered in his maze of gloom with the unreasoning apprehension of destiny that gave drama its high unconditional quality! Will called to his irony, in a sudden physical spasm, to shut up, and so blasted it out of his mind.

What he needed was a drink. He took his bearings and reckoned he could reach a certain pub that lay on the main road into town in less than an hour. Certainly no one there that day would have a greater right to register as a *bona fide* traveller!

Having an objective, his mind became easier. That's where Joe—oh damn Joe! He would have a small whisky and a long chaser of beer. Perhaps two chasers, and with the second one, the cigarette might taste better.

He sat for an hour over the drinks, with a plate of biscuits and cheese, of which he ate sparingly. His mind seemed to have become quite normal. Ordinary, rather, was the word. This ordinariness he hung on to. It accompanied him on foot for the next few hours. Until it, too, became a burden. As he repassed the spot where he had seen the wild geese, he said with a last spirt of weary humour, You've had your revenge!

From that point his mind became blank until he stood in the avenue of trees by the little bay with its gate giving on the upland pasture field. Round the corner was the house. He knew he could not speak to any one, could not waken out of this stupor of physical tiredness and brain weariness to greet Mrs. Armstrong, much less to encounter Jenny.

He looked vaguely about him and saw a step in the grassy bank by the gate post. Beside it, two primroses were out—the first of the year. He sat down on the step and leaned back. Lord, I'm tired! he thought, as he closed his eyes. He hardly heard the echo, *I'm very tired*, just as he could hardly think about the primroses —and did not care about them anyway.

It was a relief to let go, to let the mind fade out and the body slump into the bank. Remarkable how comfortable a seat like this could be, how cool the grass to warm limp hands.

As his mind slowly cleared of the congestion of its tiredness, the fingers of his left hand moved lightly over soft flat leaves, tender stalks, buds that the slightest pressure would crush, and—two open flowers. A faint smile came to his face.

There is a strange ringing quality in a thrush's song when heard at a little distance, particularly if the eyes are closed. An ardency that goes out over the world. The most wonderful manifestation of this Will had ever heard was on a cold day last month, with the ground wet and everything bare and uncomfortable, the sort of day when the purest snowdrops look bedraggled and cold, and crocuses a pathetic joke. The thrush's song had risen out of the miry background, out of the wintry twigs, with so fearless a challenge, that the very notes themselves seemed to glisten. But also—and this was so much more difficult to understand—with a power that went out over the world, and not merely in space but in time, so that they awoke past springs, remote springs, and stirred within the listening heart the subtle excitement of eternal promise or eternal youth.

It must be the same thrush that was singing now.

The urgent force of the song was more than strong enough to lift the mind on its cleaving wings. Don't hold the mind; don't let it feel this song is marvellous or magical; don't let it *feel* at all. Just let it go. Let the passionate wings bear the calm mind, as the throbbing aeroplane bears the calm body.

Pleasant to muse with oneself in a divine ease! And when the song ceased, his eyes opened. They directly focused on a small brownish bird—a willow warbler? he wondered, for he had bought his coloured bird book. Even while listening to the thrush, he had heard the small bird intermittently—though only now was he really conscious he had heard it. For in that sustained onrushing passion of the thrush, its little song had been like something left behind, left behind in a small, familiar and loved place.

The wind blew and parted the feathers below its neck. It turned the other way, about to fly off, and the wind parted the body feathers as if they were fur. Quite suddenly, it sang; and the notes were not ardent, they were reflective, thoughtful, except that no thought or reflection touched them. They tumbled down, a little sideways, round perfect bubbles of sound, that burst on the heart not with sadness but with wonder.

A gladness came flooding Will's mind more softly than a summer air. Before his staring eyes, the invisible sheath slowly parted and his mind began to rise up.

A feeling of complete freedom, in a gladness that was calm, an ecstasy that was still as light. His body was in such perfect harmony that it was forgotten. Strangely enough this feeling was intimate, as if it were recaptured. It was not a new experience: it was an entering into an old. This was what he had lost; this was what he had been searching for. And it was not grandiose or mystical or marvellous, but friendly and familiar and utterly utterly certain.

A man living all his life in pain will get used to it, but should the pain suddenly cease....

The normal conception of time or duration perhaps hardly applies here when it comes to asking how long the experience lasted. But when Will felt its perfect moment passing, his whole body stiffened slightly, then subsided in a long deep sigh.

Reverie, in which he forgot to breathe, held him for a little longer, then he got up and looked slowly about him. His eyes were full of a quiet love. The buds, about to burst, were like notes of music about to be struck. The bird had gone. His mouth opened slightly and he appeared to listen for something. The love was a gladness that brimmed in a tender humour.

He moved away, then turned round, as if taking farewell of that little bay that for ever now would be part of his mind.

There was no thought in his mind; only a lingering brightness; as sun and wind linger in the cheeks when one has come inside.

He suddenly remembered himself as a small boy looking through a stereoscope at a photograph of a certain scene (a garden with two figures and background of hedge). The flat surface of the photograph, which had hitherto been accepted as a true representation, suddenly vanished and everything came rounded and alive, with depth and, above all, an extraordinary amount of light. The effect had been that of pure magic, so that he had, after a moment, looked to see if the photograph were still in front of him. He had cried out with delight, that the scene could be as *real* as this. . . .

There was no one about the house and he entered his own room quietly. A month or two ago he had been doing a review of a book dealing with early Scottish literary sources and had picked up in a bookshop a cheap copy of Adamnan's *Life of St. Columba*. He had wondered uneasily about certain passages, unable to dismiss them along with the usual miraculous stories. In the end, he had ignored them. Now he opened the book and in no time found the passages, for they must have troubled him sufficiently for him to mark them.

". . . in some contemplations of divine grace he (St. Columba) beheld even the whole world as if gathered together in one ray of the sun gazing on it as it was manifested before him, while his inmost soul was enlarged in a wonderful manner." Again, also in Iona, the saint's face "lighted up with a certain wondrous and joyous cheerfulness, and . . . he was intensely gladdened."

Intensely gladdened . . . enlarged in a wonderful manner . . . cheerfulness.

Cheerfulness. *He* knew!

Will lifted his face and stood looking out of the window. Written some thirteen hundred years ago, not by Columba, but by another man (his successor on Iona) about Columba—which was more wonderful. And no knowledge here of Indian religions and philosophies. . . .

"Well, well—here you are!" Mrs. Armstrong stood smiling upon him. "You *are* a fine one!"

"I really am sorry!" He shut the book with a laugh. "I got lost and——"

"Did you have any dinner?"

"Yes. I landed in a wayside pub and they took pity on me."

"As long as you have had something to eat, I don't mind. But I was growing quite alarmed—though Jenny suggested you probably would be able to look after yourself."

He laughed again. "She knows! Trust a city person to look after himself—or even herself. All the same, I hope I didn't——"

"Not a bit. I kept it warm for two hours, but then gave up. How do you feel about food now?"

"To tell the truth, I'm ravenous. I walked—and walked——"

She looked at him. "Would you like a plate of soup first?"

He gave in. "I would."

"Ah," she said, "I don't believe you've had any dinner at all." She began to bustle and sent the air about her in cheerful swirls.

He got his lunch, all except the potatoes which were "clean ruined". And then she tried to give him "his tea" on top of it. He loved her, the dear woman, and regretted that his whims should have given her so much trouble.

Jenny's sarcasm about his probably knowing how to look after himself would have had such a dry flavour! He began to laugh softly to himself, as he picked up the book of essays he was looking for in his bedroom. Suddenly he went to the side window. Yes, there she was, trying to divide a great clump of earthy stuff with a spade. And she was game! He laughed when she staggered and returned to the conflict with what dangerously looked like venom. What about going out and talking to her—and observing how a haughty frigidity might consort with the minimum of correct politeness? The clump was severed. And now she was digging a hole.

He went downstairs. His table had been cleared of dishes. Throwing his book on it, he lit a cigarette and sauntered out the front door, round the house, and up into the garden. The wind had completely died. The twilight was coming.

She did not look at him, and he stood silent beside her until she straightened up.

"Seeing we are living in the same house, I thought I might take the liberty of introducing myself. My name is Will Montgomery. And you, I believe, are Miss Baird?"

"Yes?" she said, cool wide eyes full upon him.

"That's all," he said solemnly.

"Oh," she answered. "Doesn't seem very much, does it?"

"No, perhaps not," he admitted.

"I am busy, as I hope you can see. Perhaps we could discuss your business some other time."

"As you will." He bowed. "Unless, of course, I could be of any material assistance to you now?"

She hesitated for one second. "I'm afraid not."

"Sure?" Deep in his eyes came a gleam of tentative humour.

"No," she said suddenly. "I don't want you. Thanks." It was final and abrupt. She picked up her spade.

Quickly, genuinely, he said: "I am so sorry," and walked away.

That was a slap in the eye! he thought in his room again. She really had an unusual face. One of those still faces that covers something rather distinguished. It would never evade an issue: it would encounter it. He had thought she might have been capable of playing a light-hearted game, a friendly game. But apparently not. And anyway why should she, with him? He liked her for that. Her clear decision, like her clear face, was refreshing. And her eyes had quite an aristocratic candour—so very clear in their blue. Trust Philip to know a good thing!

He lay in his chair, enjoying that short encounter, and saw the twilight coming upon the world. It touched him like a secret conspiracy and brought him to his feet. All right, he answered, I'll go out. His legs were stiff and the small of his back had a soft ache. He stretched himself with an animal satisfaction and smiled.

This habit of smiling to himself—or to his thought —or (and his eyelids quivered) to invisible things— was becoming so curious an idiosyncracy that he had better watch it. He would be speaking to himself next!

When he had gone far up the valley, he sat down. The sky was now almost completely clear of cloud and was the loveliest blue he had ever seen. Evening blue, but irradiated with light—particularly in the east. The colour fascinated him. A cloud on the eastern horizon began to gather light, to fill with it. And he saw a pale disk slowly emerge and charge the cloud with glory; and the disk grew, and grew rounder, and became the full moon rising out of the cloud. It was the largest moon he had ever seen, and he stared at it until his heart ached.

When he had left the main road and turned down the short avenue of trees near to the little bay, he saw Jenny coming towards him. His heart gave a quick beat. So she too had decided to go for a walk! Unless she recognized him, he would, of course, not see her.

And he thought she was going to pass him, but suddenly she turned at his side. "I am sorry," she said, "if I appeared to be rude in the garden."

"But you weren't. Not at all."

"It was kind of you to offer to help, but—I—just didn't want it."

"I perfectly understood."

"Thank you."

"One word more, if I may," said Will. "You may rely on me not making any further effort to intrude—here or elsewhere." His voice was clear, almost gentle, in its desire to help her.

She stood quite still, looking up the avenue.

"Thank you," she said again, and walked on.

Involuntarily he remained looking after her, a catch in his breath. Then he turned slowly towards the house.

He went on past the house, through the gate, and up by the steading.

Amazement still flooded his mind. For he saw that it had not been altogether a question of *his* intrusion but rather of *her* state of mind. She naturally did not want him to intrude, but obviously now—or she would never have been driven to apologies—she would not have been abruptly rude in the garden about a thing like that. She would have put him in his place equally well but with a little more suavity. Looked as if he had intruded—on top of some other intrusion —to exasperate her suddenly.

Was Philip getting at her?

That final way she had said "Thank you", with an uncertain expression (rather than smile), and walked on, had gone right to the quick.

So she was having her own problem, was she? Bound to—if Philip was putting it to her. He would do it so well, so clearly, leaving her, at the critical moment, to say yes or no—of her own free will— apparently.

Oh, a very clever game! He paused. It's a damned shame! he muttered—and smiled drily.

A pretty handsome mistress she would make. And, being of the independent kind who accepted responsibility for her actions, she could be relied upon to— well, not to whine or beg. Very very nice. Uhm.

He kicked a rotting turnip into the ditch as he went

up the farm road with its traceries of moon shadows from the hedge of small trees.

What was he making the fuss about? It had nothing to do with him.

Obviously. Still, it was a pity to see any one intruded upon—too far; that is, when she was clearly not too sure of herself. The garden and the flowers—coming between her and them—it was a bit thick.

Or was all this the wildest fantasy? Born of the moon? That round white moon—that seemed to have grown smaller a little as it ascended the sky. What a serene night! Not immediately behind the moon, but around it at a little distance, the blue of the sky was the colour he had seen more than once in a Madonna's mantle: deep and luminous and full of—he did not know what.

Perhaps Jenny knew!

A grave calm girl. Twenty-six—and possibly twenty-seven. At that age—when the troubling thought arises that even to have experience itself. . . . Not to miss too much. . . .

She suddenly touched him on the quick again, and he felt tender towards her, and a little sorry. This withdrew her from him as far as the moon, and his own peace came back with some of the moon's weird magic added.

Life was a lovely thing—and perhaps a little unearthly.

CHAPTER FOUR

*

It was his half day off, and towards four o'clock—
the correct hour for the purpose—Will decided to
call on his aunt. He took a tram and as it wound
its way out of the busy part of the town towards
the wealthy residential suburb where his aunt lived,
he was continuously interested in the changing scene.
He was looking on something familiar in an oddly
double way: the actual scene itself and the same scene
as part of the aerial vision of the city which would
always now slightly obsess him. His vision gave the
actual scene more reality, deepened his interest in a
detached, impersonal way.

Several of the ladies wore furs, elderly women
whose faces looked clean and fresh through invisible
powdering. The characteristic verbal rhythm of the
Scots city was not quite lost in the clear enunciation
of their words. They would have their private cars,
but the tram was handy, and their exercise of economy
was an art. Sound sensible women, giving to their
completely genteel attitude to life almost an austere
warrant. And one of them was gracious, with kind

eyes, and a soft attractive voice—that clearly came long ago out of the Highlands.

He turned his face away, lest his eyes betray him, for this was the society in which he had been born and brought up. He could see it more clearly now than ever before—and with an odd sort of warmth. Even its rigid limitations—and these women would fight for their social rights and distinctions more unyieldingly than their men—no longer affected him as they used to do. How they had affected him in those early days when he had first studied the social doctrines of the brotherhood of man! He had wanted to get away from them—away—where and why?

That was a curious thing, now he came to think of it—he had had no definite ambition, or at least no personal urge to become a leader or a reformer or anything of that sort. He had just wanted to get away into the world of men, to be one of the mass who worked and toiled. In that brotherhood he would be freed.

The youthful form of mysticism—and about as ancient as the world's most ancient religion!

He walked along a quiet street of fine houses, and then round into a crescent where the houses were large and detached, with hedges and a tree or two and the gravelled path going down past the side windows of the basement, where the servants worked and cooked, to the back door and vegetable garden.

He mounted the two broad steps, and rang. The maid appeared, opening the tall wide door as if she were guardian to a temple where quiet and orderliness always reigned.

"William!" His aunt got up slowly.

Quickly he moved towards her and shook her hand. "How are you, Aunt Marion?"

"I am fairly well, thank you. Not too much to complain about—apart from your desertion of me and the awful state of the world. What *has* happened to you this long while?"

"Blame the state of the world and all those crises. Have pity on the poor life of a journalist." He made his excuses with an easy assurance.

Her interest in him concentrated. "The newspapers will have to get all the news, day and night." She nodded. "Have you to sit listening *all* the time?"

"Some one has to," he said lightly.

Her face, with its two baby-pink chins, was solemn. Her hair was very white and a little thin in front, showing the pink scalp. She was dressed, as always, in black silk.

"Poor boy!" she said. "I hope you do try to get a little sleep. It is such a terrible time the world has been going through. Does your landlady look after you properly? I think you are thinner than you were. Are you?"

"No, I don't think so. I am really feeling very well."

She settled into her chair. "We'll have tea now—it's just the time. I do hope no one comes. I don't expect any one. It's not my day. Will you please ring that bell? Thank you. Now, tell me: what do you think is going to happen?"

He saw that her interest in the European situation was almost morbid. This was a relief to him, because

normally when he called on her she was full of personal complaints and an egotistic gloom that depressed him, or, in any case, made conversation very
difficult. He had always felt awkward in her presence
before. But to-day—and he had been prepared for it
—he knew that he could have dealt with her complaints like her family doctor. The European situation
was, so to speak, a gift!

His business was, of course, to reassure her, and to
begin with he adopted the wrong tactic of being too
sweepingly reassuring. It was too much for her. And
then he became genuinely interested, for he saw that
she had constructed an extraordinary myth, almost
medieval in its grotesque pictures and assumptions.

The Germans were the Vandals and Goths of a
schoolgirl's imagination, strong ruthless fighters who
captured and laid waste the Eternal City. Again they
were on the march, this time to sweep on to the
destruction of the new Eternal City (London) and
the conquest of all the world. One could hear the
crash of their tanks and their terrifying laughter.

Russia was half-lit and frightful and unholy. Things
happened there in cellars and dark woods. The awful
thing was that you could not know what was going
to happen next; what would come out of the darkness
and destroy you—as fire might leap out of a black
hole and catch your clothes and burn you to death
while you shrieked. Something fiendish in Russia.
Will tried here—for the talk went on in anything but
a logical way—to discover some realist basis for her
fear in the possible loss of her income (dividends and

house property), but could not do so directly or in so many words. Possibly, he reflected, the parallel was to the religious woman who desperately feared the victory of anti-Christ, without feeling for a moment that she herself would lose her own belief.

Aunt Marion's attitude to the Italians was perhaps most interesting of all. She feared the Germans and Russians, but she only disliked the Italians. They had to be watched. You never knew what they would be up to. They were sly—and shameless "with all those bare little statues and pictures and things. To tell the truth, I never cared very much for them at the best of times. It's a mistake to trust them."

The muffins were toasted and buttered and delicious; the tea rich and excellent; plates of little home-made scones and crumpets; two cakes; black-currant jam. A few years off her head and in charge of a Soviet institution, wouldn't she make the dust fly! They'd have to wipe their feet at the door! He helped himself copiously to the jam.

The way the mythology rose in his head from her simple language, he could hardly explain. It was all really intuitive—the reference, for example, to the bare little statues and nude paintings (not that she used the word nude), brought before him her whole girlhood, its schooldays and art lessons and trooping academy visits, its prudish suppressed little shames— inevitable then—and its elaborate system of reticence. How *could* she forgive the Italians, now that she *really* knew there was so much vice in the world?

His reassurance was conveyed in delicate ways. He

saw her having a picture of him sitting with his ear to the world. She was not going to give up her myth, of course. Her pictures could not be altered. But though things were in fact so—yet they need not sweep on to the débâcle; they need not fulfil themselves; they, so to speak, could be stayed—by the enchantment of our increasing strength. And that's what was happening.

She nodded. She saw. She agreed.

"I feel I am making a beast of myself by eating so much," he said.

"If only I had known you were coming, I would have had your special cake, with the cream and nuts. I am so glad you came. I was longing for a real talk with some one. So few understand."

A suggestion of her more normal gloom, that softly religious personal gloom, touched her mood now. She was all alone in the world and life inhabited places and corridors that went back into the past. Contemplation of it brought a sigh, a sweet sadness, a sad luxury, always of course with a consciousness of rectitude, a certainty that only "the good impulse" had prevailed. What may have been her own small sins were long washed out, forgotten.

He played up here, too, indulging her a little. She had mentioned something that had happened in "the old house", and he said:

"Curious your mentioning that. I suddenly remembered the garden the other day. It was an incident that you will have forgotten, but it came back to me very clearly. I remembered the thrill I got when

172

Uncle James handed me that stereoscope thing—you know?—that you put a photograph in? It was a photograph of Uncle James bending forward to a child in a go-cart. There was a plot of flowers—tall cups like tulips, and behind there was a hedge——"

She got up, deeply moved, and went to a walnut escritoire. After fumbling with a little bunch of keys, she unlocked a drawer; then she came back and put the photograph in his hands.

He had quite forgotten that it was a double photograph, and the surprise of this held his mind for a moment. But it was the old scene right enough, yellowish now with age, the facial features faded (except perhaps for Uncle James's heavy black moustache). Will did not look up at her. He knew her eyes were damp. The little figure in the go-cart had been their only child and had died a year or two afterwards.

He had not thought of this tragedy when he had mentioned the photograph, and a month ago the realization of what he had done would have appalled him. But not now. He felt the sorrow fall on her like small rain on arid ground. In fact he had time to think privately of the astounding difference between the faded photographic double-print and the single picture of depth and sun-brightness that had been conjured up in his mind not so long ago. Then he handed it back. "How vividly I remember!"

"Yes. You were seven at the time." And she went on to detail the family scene and occasion. "We had hoped that you would have a new playmate and companion through life, for your dear mother. . . . It was not to be."

He was silent.

The silence caught them both for what seemed a long time. Its awkwardness, that would formerly have been an agony, hardly touched him. He lifted his eyes to the window and passed out into the light. As the one sigh broke itself twice going in with her breath to the fat recesses of her body, he stirred. He was afraid he would have to go, he said, and looked at her candidly and kindly. Then he quickly heaved himself to his feet.

"It was good of you to come."

"It was good of you to entertain me, you mean. But I shan't be so long in coming again—if I can possibly help it," he added.

"I wish you would. It is so seldom that I hear any one talk intelligently, who really knows, that——"

"Don't you worry about that, Aunt Marion. I'll make a bargain with you. So long as you don't hear from me, you can take it that there's no need for worry. Should the international situation throw up any really menacing feature, I'll communicate with you at once—I'll come and see you. You needn't ring. I can find my way out."

She rang automatically, but ignored the maid, while she herself accompanied him to the door and helped him on with his coat. He could almost feel her lean on him. He was the male head of her tribe (her husband had died many years ago), moving out to the power and mystery of business. "Good-bye,

Aunt Marion." Calmly, as if he had been in the habit of doing it, he kissed her on the forehead.

As he went along the street he turned the involuntary smile into a grimace by putting his hand inside his coat and tugging down the back of his jacket. He heard the tram coming, made a dash for it, and caught it moving. It seemed to bring him back into the heart of the city much more quickly than it had brought him out.

Poor Aunt Marion! Was it weakness to feel a little soft to her? She had at least £50,000. And he realized, as he strolled along the busy thoroughfare, that with very little attention on his part he could hardly help inheriting the greater part of it. Positively too easy.

His thought steadied for a moment. Did he want to? The answer came quite involuntarily: "By God, no!"

It startled him a little, so that he glanced to either side. His mind had cocked its ears like a frightened hare!

What was he afraid of? Dividends and property—that tainted source? Or afraid of losing this freedom which left his shoulders light? Afraid of being caught in the trap?

But he could always give the stuff away. Could hand it to Joe, for example!

Would you? said the cunning inner mind. That's an old one! I know two better than that!

It had a primordial humour, this inner mind, slyly penetrative, dead and eternally right!

He turned his eyes on the street sights to distract

his attention and regain a proper gravity. Offices were emptying.

There was a girl in front of him, in her twenties. Her shoes, with their stylish heels, and her stockings, sheathing up under her smartly cut skirt, came right out of a fashion plate. Her walk was restricted to that merest suggestion of a hobble, with its hardly perceptible stoop forward of the torso, that was nature using the artificial to produce the last word in chic. Her silken legs—very perfect legs—were pure suavity, mannered a trifle. Clever hands had pulled the cloth over shoulders and hips and drawn pins from the mouth to keep the seams together. The hat, an odd little affair, was perched on top of the lot—actually, for his eye was keen, on top of a head of hair that was too rich in golden shadows, he reckoned, to have been artificially coloured.

The whole was taken in at a glance, and before he could stop himself he had the shoes off her and the stockings and the rest—but no, she wouldn't quite straighten up from her bare heels. She merely became uncomfortably naked. He didn't pursue the thought. Had no desire to pursue anything. For of all that had happened to him, perhaps the most astonishing thing was that he could enjoy thus walking along a street that he had so often deemed as drab as hell.

It was almost exciting. He did not want to look at things long, particularly not at people, did not want to look too closely; but, that apart, the people and the bustle and the ringing bells of the trams were exhilarating. And why should he look closely? Sheer bad manners. For each must carry his or her integument of concern or fear or hidden disease or hope or lust or what-not—and make the best of it. But only—oh, if only—there was the slightest chance, the remotest possibility, that one day, all of them, would burst their balloons!

Queer, this detached and friendly liking one could get for humanity. Sly dog that he was! for he was all the time keeping the same distance behind the girl in front. The fair neck, disappearing under the simple, fashionable curls, was ravishingly cool. What a boon her very existence conferred on humanity in general! What a distinguished privilege, what a gift from life, to be able to look at her as he was looking, with an inexplicable, amused, lustless, detached, and yet intimate delight!

All he had got to do, of course, was to quicken his step and glance at her face and find that the impersonal body was too gracious for the personal face. She simply couldn't have a face that would naturally crown that body. So why do it and dispel the illusion? So he did it, and when with a side glance he caught the face, he dropped behind at once, swerving towards what happened to be the window of a book-seller's shop. "Well, I'm damned!" he muttered, under his breath. He stared at the books without seeing them, his heart in a race.

The girl was Jenny.

And now for the first time in years he deliberately evaded a personal question. He began to concentrate on the books, while this completely absurd and irra-

tional action of the muscle in his breast slowly subsided. Amusing, too, that he should find himself
staring at a book on *How to Make a Rock Garden*.
That brought back his normal good humour and he
thought suddenly, Why not? and entered the shop
before he could think any more.

Last night he had been up in the garden, looking
at what was to be seen. To him came his landlady,
asking the time. Her clock which usually gained only
ten minutes a day had "gone off its rocker altogether"
and gained an hour. The little black French clock—as
he knew himself—had a quite ungallic habit of suddenly becoming silent. They got chatting about
Jenny's work in the garden. A bank in the top corner
was the despair of Jenny's life, she declared. She
really must get one of the farm men to dig it up.
"But this is their busy time. It's bishopweed it is. It
invades her, she says, like an army! What she really
wants to do, I know fine, is not only to have the
place cleaned up, but also to have some stones put in
and turn it into a rockery. It's her secret passion just
now!" She laughed. "Oh, I know fine, but I appear
not to let on!"

As Will came out of the bookshop he looked along
the street. Obviously Jenny had been heading for an
appointment and, judging from the pains she must
have taken with her outfit, the appointment was with
Philip. She knew him! And my word, wouldn't Philip
say just the right thing! Not really say it, not anyway
until he had first said it silently with his eyes and acted his
admiration, in slight little offhand yet intimate ways!

He didn't want to run into them. Anything but that! A small ironic gleam shot from his eyes. And there they were, at the corner of the street, waiting to cross! He turned his face to the shop windows. He paused opposite a watchmaker's shop. She had been facing his way; must have seen him. He went into the shop. Five minutes later, when he came out, they were gone. From their office, they would have come different ways, of course!

When at last he shoved his head round the door of the small back saloon where the boys were gathered, he was greeted variously:

"Come on! What's kept you? Where you been? What is it?"

"A small one," said Will against their quizzing eyes. "The Scots are a satiric, ruthless, rowdy crowd of grotesques," and he sat down.

They shouted the warmest hah-haws—all except Mac, who grinned. Don, Rob, Jackie, and Jackie's friend Harry from another evening paper—they had consumed their pies and beer, and were now drinking in the merriest mood. The evening was before them, and fun, the warm arguments and entanglements of sheer fun—oh, full of the most profound thought concerning the nature of God, Tamerlane, political ideology or—oh, shut up!

That was the atmosphere and he liked it. It was honest, and no club in the city could provide such complete male freedom, free in its essence, charged with mirth and irony and ribaldry, swift convictions hotly maintained, good-naturedly shied at, hit and counter-hit and come again. Nothing finally mattered but the jet of life that spirted up out of a fellow's head, with its tumbling coloured ball, and when the ball was knocked off its jet, they tumbled with it into laughter.

"Don't let any one in here, Dan," they said to the barman.

"No? Why?" asked satiric Dan.

"Because this is the moment", said Will solemnly, "in which we burst our balloons."

It was going to be a good night! For Will was obviously in a serene mood, and that was enough for Mac at any time.

The personal hunt started over a reference by Jackie to original innocence when he meant original sin. Mac, *via* a farm that he called the Garden of Allah, came down heavily on the side of sin.

"I disagree," said Will. "For example, most of our present entertaining discourse would be unprintable, but fundamentally it's innocent; and the natures of most—not all—of those taking part in it are moved to the fun like sportive lambs."

"So you have started leading yourself up the garden path of wisdom? Huh?"

"That's clever of you, Mac," said Will. "Only, tell me—how could you know—unless the garden path is in your own mind? You cannot leave my farm alone. Why? Am I doing what you had not the courage to do? If not, what exactly are you trying to define?"

"Does one require to be a lunatic to define lunacy?"

"No. But one requires to be a poet to define poetry. And the trouble with you would appear to be that you can't leave poetry alone?"

"As a terrier can't leave a rat?"

"Or a child its rattle."

"Hurrah!" cried Jackie. "Here, Don——"

"You're getting drunk," said Harry, a slim youth like himself. "Better put on your bowler," and he stuck Rob's bowler down over his eyes.

"Very good," said Jackie, raising the headgear with difficulty to all present. "Mac: you have caught my eye."

But Mac was not amused; not nearly so amused as he was by Will, whom he now began to hunt with a vindictive malice, laughing harshly when he felt he had scored a point.

Until Don interfered, with the tone of a referee. "Mac, you're offside. That's personal."

"Personal bedamned. Aren't we all personal? Are you afraid to be personal? Beyond the personal— what is there?"

"Mathematically," said Don, "everything, every blessed sweet thing, except the personal, thank heaven."

"You're merely frightened of the mud," said Mac, "while all the time it's obvious to the meanest intelligence that what some of you need is a mud bath. Cakes of it to suck your lovey-dovey clogged pores open. Your so-called innocence is unclean, stinks. There is an innocence that is offensive, that is rank, like a skunk's smell."

181

"I presume you mean it is to you?" said Will. "And if so—quite. But it is a considerable assumption to assume that you hold the governing condition for everybody."

"You think I don't?"

"I am quite sure you don't."

"Oh?"

"Yes. You don't hold it for me, for example."

They were all listening now, awaiting the explosion.

"By God, you're a cocksure bastard, aren't you?"

"Stick to the argument," said Will. "Don't run away."

"Run away!" cried Mac. "Who? From you?"

"No, not from me."

"You said run away."

"I said don't run away."

"He said you ran away from the argument," explained Rob.

"We ran and they ran and we a' ran awa' man—or how goes it?" asked Jackie.

"Do you mean", said Mac, with a loose thrust of his lips, "*only* that I ran away from the argument?"

"I admit", Will answered quietly, "that I meant more than that."

"Well?" demanded Mac.

Will met his eyes in a silence that affected them all with a keen discomfort, and yet that none of them could break. There was something new in Will's quiet penetrating look. And when the words came they were slow and distinct, more penetrating than the eyes, and charged with incredible meaning:

"I fled Him, down the nights and down the days;
I fled Him, down the arches of the years;
I fled Him, down the labyrinthine ways
    Of my own mind. . . ."

Mac suddenly threw his head back and gave way to raucous laughter. The strings of his throat whipped taut. They had never seen him give way so completely.

Will took up his glass with a slow smile. "I knew that would get him," he said.

The others were at once released, and Jackie and Harry went noisily to their coats for more cigarettes.

At last Mac gasped, wiping his eyes. "Holy God—kindergarten!" He would have started laughing again if Jackie hadn't whistled. "Boys, will you look at this?" for he had gone into one of Will's pockets by mistake and produced a book with a paper jacket and the title, *How to Make a Rock Garden*. The jacket was a brilliant show of colour supported at one side by the gable end of a cottage with tall hollyhocks.

"Here——" began Will.

"So it's yours?" said Jackie.

"I move", said Harry, "that this document lies on the table."

This was carried, and Mac got hold of it. "Flowers!" he cried. "Hollyhocks! Sweet peas!" His voice was a riot of malice. "She moves amid the hollyhocks and peas." He could hardly open the book. "Kindergarten, did I say? Infantile bloody paralysis!"

"Please give me that book."

Mac ignored him. Mac had a demoniac account to settle. But Jackie was now crying to them to shut up. They screwed themselves round to look at him. He was standing, swaying very slightly, and apparently listening.

In an appalled voice, Harry said: "He's got 'em." He went to Jackie and asked gently: "What is it, Jackie?"

"Shut up," said Jackie, "and listen. Do you hear that sort of ticking sound?"

Harry could genuinely hear nothing. "Feeling queer a bit, are you?"

Jackie swiped him with an arm and Harry grabbed at Will's coat as he was going down and brought it with him. Winded, he sat, head over it; until his head jerked up as if it had been stung. He looked at the coat. "The damthing's beating," he said. "It's alive." He began to push it from him. Then, overcoming the instinctive serpent fear, he inserted his hand into a pocket and produced a ball of brown paper, with prongs sticking through. "Hell," he cried, in real panic, "it's a time bomb!" He dropped it on the coat and retreated in a rush.

"If you're quite finished with my coat," Will began, getting up, when Jackie to cover his own instinctive recoil stooped and lifted a small blue-enamelled alarm-clock from the brown paper that had merely been loosely wrapped round it.

"Please leave that alone," said Will.

"But, look here——" began Jackie.

Will advanced upon him, and now Harry, anxious

184

to avoid comment on his panic, neatly fielded the clock from Jackie and brought it to the table before Will could grab him.

Mac immediately took possession of it. "Exhibit number two."

"Give me that clock!" Will demanded.

"Sit down," ordered Mac.

"Give me that clock!"

"Hold the prisoner at the bar."

The two boys held him, with Rob ready. "And they brought him", said Jackie, "before Pontius Pilate."

"Will you explain", asked the judge, "why you bought this clock?" and he set it on the table before him.

"I bought it", said Will, standing calm and straight, "in the hope that it might explain the meaning of time."

"Haven't you a landlady?"

"I have."

"Well?"

"I will tell the whole truth. I have recently attempted to awake in the grey of the dawn to hear the birds sing, but without success. Hence the need for an alarm—to awaken me at that timeless hour."

They laughed thickly, for they were tired of laughing. Will *had* a fantastic touch. Lately he had developed the habit of saying impromptu the wildest nonsense with the probability in it of the fairy-story. And they liked it. It appealed to something ungoverned or grotesque in themselves or in their tradition,

But Mac was looking at him, trying to fathom him.

And Will, looking back at Mac with a gentle expression, shook his head. "It's no use, Mac."

"What's no use?"

"Trying to escape."

"Escape?"

"The poet, who fled God down the arches of the years——"

"Christ and him crucified!" cried Mac. He lifted the book and brought it down with such violence on the table that it slid forward and shot the little blue clock on to the floor. The glass face smashed and the small bell tinkled.

There was a startled silence. But Will, the gentle expression on his face, stooped and lifted the clock and listened to it.

"It's still going," he said, and placed it carefully on the table. Then he picked up the book. The coloured wrapper was sopping with beer. He dropped it on the floor and wiped the covers of the book with his handkerchief. "She'll never know", he said, "that it knocked time sideways."

They cheered him for his good nature. And at that instant the alarm bell of the little clock joined in with such a ringing triumphant loudness that they lost their balance completely and Dan came in to see what was wrong.

Later, after parting, Will turned and looked back and saw Mac pursuing his solitary way down the arches of the streets.

Where am I now? he asked as he pursued his own country road, and whither am I going? The arch of the dark was lit by the stars. One cannot look long at stars, he decided. Not too long.

Laughter was inside him, and occasionally it came out to have a look around.

This liberation that came with the drug of drink! This irresponsibility! This starry freedom!

The drunkenness that was not drunk; that was sober as the lidless stars—that winked at him!

Let the mole come and the owl, the weasel and the bat. . . .

The cool night air washed fantasy from his mind in a shiver of clarity.

For there was a tremendous difference between the abandon of the old drunken Dionysian revel and this strange exquisite abandon of his "vision". True, there was kinship; up to a point, there was bodily warmth, fusion; but ah how profound, how unbridgeable, the essential difference! For in the Dionysian revel, the self, the ego, whirled unrestricted in its desires into a state of frenzy; but in the "vision" the ego was lost in the calm uprising of the second self, the deeper self, into conscious freedom.

Extraordinary to think there had been times that night when he had got not only an extreme detachment from his fellows but an affection for them, an understanding that had something akin to the understanding of saints! What possibilities of complacency are there! Shut up! he said, poked in the ribs by himself.

He sat down. What was time anyway?

For there was one happy circumstance, he felt, fixed now fairly securely in his mind, helping him at the difficult moment, giving him an odd resiliency and power. He knew he could not command this "vision" —what an appalling word for so simple a reality!— but it did induce its own aftermath; just as a body that has been sunbathing feels the sun-warmth on its skin—even along the bones, in the marrow—long after it has been dressed, so that it seems to walk in airy naked freedom under its clothes.

Presumably there must be the penalty of the old polarity: where there is height there is depth; where there is ecstasy there must be despair. And, by degree, despair that becomes that terrible "dark night of the soul". . . .

Well, a fellow must pay all due penalties. That was adventure. Meantime he had not got quite that length, thank God!

He looked about him. Even Jenny and Philip were detached from him. He could admire their physical beauty and aptitude one for the other. More than that, he could feel an affection for them.

His thought stopped abruptly.

He took out his book, smoothed it with his palms, smiled, and laid it on the grass. Then very carefully he took out the clock, whose glass was broken, and felt for the hands with his finger-tips. Bare, but intact! He nodded. Only our glass face is broken.

Tik–tik–tik–tik . . . it went. He listened to it as to

a magic toy. Talk of overtones in meanings! and he glanced conspiratorially at the stars.

But this time the stars remained aloof and, embarrassed, he became a cheapjack at a fair. Now there is the book of the flowers, he said. See? There. Her book of the flowers. Very well, I will place it under the circle of eternal time and we'll see what happens. Watch!

Immediately he placed the short metal legs of the little clock on the hard cover of the book, the *tik-tik-tik-tik* . . . became much louder and firmer.

Now I wonder, he said, forgetting the people at the fair, what that means? He was prepared to challenge the stars, who had withdrawn from him at the moment of the abrupt stop in his thoughts. But there seemed a greater radiance in the heavens, coming surely from behind him. He turned his head. The moon had risen above the horizon, but now one side of it was half eaten away. The gibbous moon. He stared at it, then his head drooped.

After a time, the impatient little clock drew his eyes.

"Very well," he said slowly, "let's all go home together."

CHAPTER FIVE

*

Forenoon in the office and the telephone asking for him. It was Philip. "Are you engaged for to-morrow night?"

"Well, yes, I am. I have a meeting on. Why?"

"Listen. We're having a show—usual reunion family affair and all that. Quite a crowd. Dancing and what-not. There will be a particular old friend of yours there. You can put off your meeting, surely?"

"I don't know," said Will. "I really feel——"

"What about a spot of lunch to-day?"

"Well—yes."

"I'll be a bit rushed, for I'm in the throes—but the same place same time. Right?"

"Right."

His meeting was the usual committee one and Will wanted to see Joe. He did not want to go to the family reunion affair—which was a collection of the Mansons' friends, a cross section of the influential business and professional life of the city. He remembered it from of old. Tails and all the rest and pleasant enough, but he would rather be with Joe many times over. Moreover, it was obvious that this invitation was very much an afterthought. Some late-comer—obviously a woman—had blown up unexpectedly. . . .

And this proved to be the case. Philip was quite frank about it. "I know you don't care for those things. But when this girl blew in, full of Paris and Communism, and asked for you, I thought you might enjoy the joke. You can guess?"

"No."

"Felicity."

Will laughed. "Félice," he murmured, and his cheeks grew warm.

"Sounds French!"

"No, just Swinburne."

"Like that, was it?"

"No, just poetry. Remarkable thing, poetry, Philip. It's a pity you didn't go in for poetry. Or no—it's just as well. It would have made your technique too overpowering. And it's pretty successful as it is."

Philip gave his easy laugh. "Getting at anything?"

"No. Just remembering from of old. Though I did see you yesterday afternoon again, now that I think of it! It really was amusing, too. I had been walking behind the lady and thought to myself—Jove, there's a beauty. I was wondering whether her face was equal to the rest of her, when you both met."

"And your conclusion?"

"Oh, more so. Trust Philip for that! I thought."

He smiled. "She is pretty good, isn't she." It was

not a question, for on such a matter he never required an opinion. He looked pleased, all the same; a trifle too pleased, Will thought; for there is a male smile of certainty that in its suggestion of modesty almost achieves the unctuous.

"Official?" Will asked, deciding to add a flick of butter to his roll.

"No," said Philip.

"Not that I'm curious or would wish to intrude. I suppose I'm really trying to find out if she'll be there to-morrow night." He smiled as if unaware he had been too direct.

"Actually, she won't," said Philip coolly.

"Pity," said Will. "Not, of course," he added, "that I could have hoped to—ah—have interfered with your eye."

Then Philip smiled. "Would you have had a try?"

"I might, you know."

Philip was lingeringly amused. "All the same, it's a subject we need not mention—there. By the way, of course we'll put you up. You'll have to bring your things from your country residence. You have the necessary gear?"

"If the moths haven't been at 'em."

"Good." And he settled time and place.

As Will walked back to the office, he knew that Philip had rather enjoyed the lunch. Dark blue suit to-day, perfectly cut, and pale blue shirt and tie, giving the cool air of the morning bath to his graceful form. Real man's man—men liked him—and yet with those little intimacies of manner that were so friendly. Almost feminine apprehension he had of the personal relationship; could take you into his confidence and flatter you with a glance, a careless remark. And almost at the same time was reserved and cool. His very best feature was his reserve over a girl like Jenny. It was his private affair—and no one else's. Will liked that in him. It was just one of those little interludes in his life: it would come and it would go. He would manage it perfectly—and would no more unnecessarily expose it than he would his own body.

Part of the enjoyment he got from lunch was talking to Will with a perfect equality, an extra careless friendliness, seeing him not so well dressed, not so well off, doing his unimportant job. That Will had fallen from the realm of social importance merely made it all the more interesting in a way. . . .

Therefore with Jenny, where the cleavage was so vast, with what perfection of "equality" the cavalier in him would act! How considerate he would be of her virgin innocence while he—well. . . .

One naturally helped the thought out with a shrug. And a small laugh for luck.

He managed to get Joe on the telephone.

"I'm sorry I can't come to the meeting, and I wondered if there was anything special on."

"No, nothing special," Joe replied. "So it doesn't matter."

"All right," said Will. Then after waiting in silence for a moment: "Doing anything in particular tonight?"

"Nothing much. There's an outdoor meeting on. I may look round."

"Could you meet me in town?"

"Well—I'm afraid I'll have to go home for tea."

"Oh, well, never mind."

"If there is anything special——"

"No, nothing. So long!" He took the silent receiver slowly from his ear—and hung it up.

Joe must make up his mind a bit quicker than that! Something cool in Joe's tone had hurt him. If he continued to take things like that, well—let him!

It would be pleasant, anyhow, to have the evening all to himself in the country. He really had far too few evenings there. And the quiet of the country was a thing you had to get used to in order to enjoy it properly. Breaking it up too often left you restless, not at peace. For it happened to be a true saying that "peace comes dropping slow".

He shut off the personal mind, his work getting his whole attention. This gave news an individual value, brought it to life more in the round—as the stereoscope did. Murder those days did not have the old selling value, because of the possibility of international mass murder, but women were born individualists and details of personal passion and violence held for them still a morbid fascination. . . . That slick word, morbid! Were the women instinctively right—as you would expect them to be? For women were grounded in the emotions, the individual, the personal —except the few who had intellectualized themselves into a half-neuter state, who had approached apprehension of the strange mad idealisms—now called ideologies—of men. For men were the mass murderers, the gargantuan theorists, the beehive builders, the robots: to make a perfect thing, an ideal state, they were prepared to kill and be killed, they were ready to put a match to the time fuse (what else were armaments?) that would blow up the world.

This undercurrent of comment, flowing like a deep stream under his sub-editor's craft, affected the use of his pencil. It trimmed the murder story to its essential course; it selected his headings and general display. Slowly the story itself took on a living reality. The character-types (through long use, all these murder stories consisted, for the office journalist, in varying mixtures of types) became human and the scene a real scene. It was set in the slums. As he worked, it came into focus, and the whole *crime passionnel* (he would risk the bourgeois dignity of the epithet) was enacted before him quite vividly. Out of the court evidence, the figures emerged and were cast back—as in the familiar trick of the movies—not to re-enact the scene but to perform the original scene itself. This scene had a familiarity that presently began vaguely to disturb him. Had he read about it before—or seen... ? It was actually like something that he remembered ... and then he understood. There was the prostitute, the unemployed man, the youth with the razor ... he had seen them all against the given background, and the youth with the razor (though new) was the most vivid of the lot. To the journalist, and perhaps therefore to the sociologist, to the normal reader, that youth was the "vicious type". As almost certainly he was. But the others. . . . The girl's name was not Ivy. . . .

He made a very attractive story of it. At moments, he was actually excited, inwardly. The murderer (the "vicious type") was quite unrepentant."As he stood in the dock," the reporter wrote, "his face was grey, showing no emotion." It was the only spot where Will stuck for a little, under the urge to shove in a sentence suggesting why he had shown none.

At the thought of committing so heinous a journalistic offence (for his paper had the sound "old tradition" in such matters), he smiled. And as he paused, staring before him for a moment, the whole scene took on a subtly different aspect. It was the same scene, enacted, however, not in the past but, somehow, in the future. Involuntary understanding of "the vicious type" had brought this about doubtless; the momentary substitution (of himself for the murderer) which must be at the basis of understanding, not to mention sympathy. Yet even the grey light of the scene was a *future* light, and it was not exactly the same scene. . . . He shut off the disturbing evocation abruptly, and an eyelid flickered down in a rather ironic humour. Those theories about the fourth dimension and being able to see a thing before it happened were getting rather popular. He drew a deep breath—and accepted the personal call to the telephone.

It was Joe.

"You must have cut me off. I was going to say that

after having tea at home, I could be in town before seven."

"Oh. Righto, Joe. Sorry if I cut you off—but I did not feel I had. You merely sounded as if the matter did not interest you! Actually, though, I don't know that there's anything much to discuss, as you said; and I thought of pushing off home to the farm."

"Very well," said Joe. "That's all right."

But now there was a reluctant note in his voice and Will hesitated. "Unless there's anything you want to discuss yourself?"

"No—not particularly. Never mind. I'm sorry if I appeared——"

"Oh, come and have a lemon squash. Nothing like going the whole hog!"

There was a pause for a moment. "All right," said Joe quietly.

And now we're for it! thought Will. He had a deep reluctance to undergo any sort of questioning, to explain himself or his actions to any one, an intolerance that was instinctive and aristocratic and he did not mind who knew it!

So he met Joe in the most agreeable humour and soon put him at his ease—though not entirely, for Joe's sheer bulk of body and mind and purpose could not be deflected lightly. It had a quietude, too, that was impressive.

The talk drifted through the reasons for his own social engagement. He smiled as he drew for Joe's benefit the crowd who would be there, the makers and defenders of capitalism, the real bourgeoisie.

"You'll enjoy it?" Joe asked, nodding his thanks to the barman.

"Most certainly I shall. That's where I belonged, and to me it is just as human and a good deal more pleasant than many another group of human beings. Wouldn't you enjoy it?" Will added water to his whisky.

"I doubt it," said Joe. "However, that's merely a personal reaction. I might find it difficult to divorce from my mind what they stood for. But I realize that's beside the point of enjoying a social evening."

"That's where I think you're wrong—deeply wrong."

"Oh?" The broad face with its pale fair skin, clear forehead with light hair brushed neatly, and steady blue eyes, suggested force both in restraint and at peace.

"You make the mistake of mistrusting the personal."

"In what respect?"

"Oh, it's more than in the matter of a social evening. It's a fundamental philosophic cleavage in you, since you have inevitably not only lost touch with the personal but—almost lost belief in it."

"I am afraid that is beyond me," Joe said, after the short thoughtful pause that was characteristic of him.

"You merely mean that I should be less general and more particular. But that implies the personal—and there it is."

"That means nothing—unless it means you merely want to be personal," said Joe. "If you do—go ahead. I think I'll be able to stand it."

"I know you will. The more difficult point for me is will you be able to understand it?"

"That remains to be discovered, as always, in *praxis*."

"Good!" said Will, enjoying the dry Marxian thrust. "Stating the case broadly, then, to begin with, so that we may get our principles—for personal application in due course—I'd say that you are obsessed with the importance of social relations to such an extent that the individual tends to become an element in those relations—a mere element rather than a free individual. In this way——"

"I must interrupt because I do not know what you mean by a free individual. No individual is free. He is a product of and is conditioned by his social relations. That is a fact—or is it not?"

"It is a fact. I admit that. We may take it for granted that we both know the accepted philosophic basis of our creed. It's the amount of acceptance, its application, and where it may land us, I'm concerned about. I am quite well aware that I am talking like this because I am a social product. Society has given me speech, learning, the arts, even whisky, bless it! Had I been cast at birth into the wilderness I should have been a jibbering savage. I grant all that. But at the end of the day, that's just obvious. It's like employer and employee, where the employer says, It is I who have given you work, and you should be grateful, for if I hadn't, where would you and your wife and children have been? Now the fact, as you and I know, is that the employee gives as much to the employer as he gets—and a bit over or there would be no profit. So, we get our stuff from society all right, but we give back as much as we get—and a bit over, or there would be no evolution. But we do that in the last analysis by individual personal contribution; by the individual freely developing, by being allowed freely to develop within himself, something that will be a personal contribution. Without that personal contribution, society, however perfectly you arrange it, will become static, and as we cannot by our very natures remain static but must either go forward or back, then society will go back.

"Granted. But the whole aim of our socialist creed is so to run society, so to eliminate its shocking miseries and tyrannies and botched economics, that the individual in the socialist society will be in a far better position to contribute the maximum that's in him and so help society forward to a degree that's never been seen before."

"Granted. So we establish the validity of the personal contribution. Now this is what I want to suggest: that it is possible, by our over-concentration on the importance of social relations, on the importance of a society functioning in a certain 'perfect' way, it is possible that meantime, in the process, we may so forget the need for the intimate personal life and development of the individual, so relegate it to the machine-like function of achieving the perfect state, that it will tend to atrophy in itself, tend to the perpetuation accordingly and in due course of the machine-like state."

"You can postulate any possibility. But what you say is, I think, a bit thin. Where we have to deal with such terrible realities as war and the possible destruction of humanity because of capitalist relations, your fear is, if not fantastic, at least academic. Take a great desire like peace, world peace. It is an emotion, intimate and personal to each one of us. Can you in the process of achieving the perfect state see that emotion, that emotion that is part of our socialist inspiration, possibly becoming atrophied?"

"That's a shrewd one! But I daren't dodge it, I suppose. So let us have a look at it. The first thing I notice is that you say peace, and then immediately, automatically, say world peace. That is, the peace—which is an absence of war. The very conception of peace in your mind has become *negative*. It is no longer an individual possession: it is something beyond you, it is something that belongs to that amorphous thing called society and it is placed in the future. It has ceased to be a reality, and has become, of all terrifying things, an ideal. It's not the peace that passeth understanding. It's not the peace that—that makes you feel —that lifts you on its wings, not that lovely exquisite moment of understanding when you know, beyond all telling, that life is good; deeper than that—that life is creation. It's not that *positive* peace."

"But in the permanent absence of war, surely that *positive* peace—as you call it—would have a better chance of thriving?"

"No doubt," said Will.

"I would seem to have missed the point?"

"Which is perhaps the whole point." Will smiled. "It would be the usual endless discussion anyhow. And probably, as you say, the point is merely a fine one."

Joe's face grew a trifle stern. "As you like—but you should play fair, even in discussion. Either you had a point to make or you hadn't."

"The point, I had hoped, was made. *If* that conception of positive peace is not in your mind, is not in the minds of all those striving for an absence of war in the ideal state, then I cannot see logically how it is to be in the ideal state. Individuals cannot contribute to any form of society what it is not in them to contribute. If you talk peace, but do not know positive peace in your own mind, you are talking a lie. It happens to be a historic fact that those who did know this peace and wanted to contribute it to society, were crucified by society, or made to drink poison out of a bowl, or similarly liquidated."

"I see what you are getting at. But again I think you are being fantastic. You are shrouding the appalling facts of social life, and therefore of individual life, in a mere metaphysical argument. That takes us nowhere. It's not talk now: it's action we need. Looking at things sanely, with a sense of balance, surely that is clear?"

"Quite clear. Remember that I agree with all your fundamental propositions; that I have worked, after my fashion, and will go on working, for the cause. That is why it is all the more imperative that you and I see quite clearly what we are doing. Very well. All that I'm trying to say is that it is you—not me—who are shrouding the issue in metaphysics. That's my point. I want peace, real, vivid, now, as a personal possession. You say we can't have it now because we have to fight to have it in another form of society in the future. My realist mind sees that as a form of dangerous idealism, based on an illogicality. If I am not quick with life inside myself then the belief that I can bring life to others is a fake. It's this *life* I have to find, and meantime I see us making for death. In our minds, peace talk is already thrilled through with the sensationalism of death. In our own leaders is this sensationalism of revolution and death, in our most austere and heroic men. The mood induced by the mass emotion, the mood of heroism and death. But death."

"They die—so that we may have life more abundantly."

"And after two thousand years—where are we? Being crucified, not individually, but in batches. Why? Because we have failed to understand that it is the individual who must have life more abundantly. You and me. Only then can he contribute of the abundance to a common stock. You cannot take whisky out of an empty bottle. All you can do is to go on imagining what the empty bottle will be like when it's full."

"You mean that—you mean that, to put it shortly, all our leaders have been crucified in vain? You mean that they will go on being crucified in vain? You mean that all the purpose, organization, results—all have been in vain? You mean that?"

"I mean something much more profound than that. I mean this: that it is we—you and I—who have crucified our leaders, and who will go on crucifying them. Why? Because we have abdicated life. Because we are empty bottles. Just as there is no true peace in us, so there is no true life in us. When you shift the emphasis from the individual to society, to social relations, you shift it from the vivid springing core of life to a windy, if convenient, abstraction. But, and this is the snag: it is *difficult* to be a real individual living from your feet up. It needs grit, and pride, and courage, and power to endure through despair; you need to be quick with beauty, and light, and love, and sex; you must see men, not as social units, but as your individual brothers, full of this magic thing called life. And that is difficult. But—it is *easy* to be a socialist, it is easy to cry for ideal justice and go forward as one in the ranks, shedding this difficult thing that is real life upon the imaginary back of the army. You are then like one committed to a great fate. You have the surge of the crowd emotionalism within you. This surge will carry you over the barricades superbly. But when the surge is spent and you are sitting on your backside with a sore head—you are not then Joe Wilson, the individual, the indomitable, an entity in its own eternal right under heaven —you are merely a unit who has got lost, and you scurry around until you regain the obliterating safety of the army, and then the surge of crowd emotionalism again, and once more the barricades, and—so on, until, of course, you reach your own final fatal barricade. But that army has its leaders, must have its leaders, and its leaders must be individualists. Power is sweet. The temptation is strong. And you can always make it look like a beneficent bureaucracy—to an army of units. But you could never on God's earth make it look like a beneficent anything to an army of individualists."

"Isn't a lot of that pure rhetoric?"

"Ah, but such rhetoric!"

"I could put up a case to prove that the life of the unit, as you call it, may be something a little different from your conception——"

"Listen, Joe. All I am trying to say is you can't *prove* life: you can only *live* it. And living it, it should be a thrill, a joy. If it isn't going to be that, it doesn't seem to me it matters a damn what it is going to be."

"But you know there's another side to all that. You know, for example, that if there is one thing that keeps us back from attaining socialism, it is that very individualism that you boost. To have power against the forces of destruction you must have discipline; to conquer, you must submerge your own petty so-called independence in the greater social purpose that will win real freedom for all, including you. What's wrong with the Scot is this self-same curse of individualism, the anarchy of the individualism that creates schism, for ever and all the time. And I now see it rising in you."

"I know you have wondered why I have been so attracted by Scottish Nationalism, and so far I have given in to your fear that it would merely cause a diversion in *our* fight. I am beginning to doubt your wisdom very profoundly. Look at the history of this nation before it became a herd of lost units in a southern army. When these individualists decided to have their own church, they combined all right—and my God did they put up a fight? And won too, just as long, long before they defended their national independence—they themselves, the common people —against terrific odds. But then, you see, the poorest, most miserable crofter, surprised by the enemy— think of 'the killing times'—was not a lost unit. He faced his enemy; he fought by himself, until he died. Why? Because that poor crofter *was* the Scottish church. He was not merely one of the many. He was *one*, one in himself. The church burned in him. And he respected and trusted his brother like himself. And they combined in that way, and won. And that is the way men should combine, and in that way they must surely win, for they not only bring strength unto death, but they bring in themselves that which they seek."

"We've discussed all that before."

"Doubtless. But you've never answered it."

Joe was silent. Will, looking at him, smiled slowly. Arguments did tend to go on endlessly.

"We seem to have wandered a bit," said Joe.

"From where?"

"You said you were going to apply your findings, if any; something about my having lost faith or belief in the individual."

Will saw he could not avoid the real issue any

longer. "It seems rather absurd, doesn't it? Particularly when we think of that night at Jamie's; what you did —for the individual—there. I know." He grew silent. Then he said quietly: "Not to realize how individual and personal you were is to suggest that you were slumming."

Joe looked at him. Will met his eyes, then stared down thoughtfully at his hand on the table.

"You think—that?" said Joe.

Will shook his head. "No."

"Well?"

"But there may be the suggestion of something in it. Otherwise I am slightly at a loss."

"Go on."

"It's very difficult, Joe," said Will, reluctantly, "because you happen to be one of the great individualists, the born leader. That being so, however, you must, in the final count, be concerned more for your great aim than for any particular individual. Jamie and Ettie. . . ." Will paused, and looked away. "I merely perceive that I am going to make a mess of it. An unpardonable mess. I withdraw—unconditionally— and slightly ashamed."

"You mean that Jamie and Ettie were units to me? Not altogether, of course, but still what I did for them I really did for the cause? In the long run I should be prepared to sacrifice Jamie and Ettie and you and even myself—for the greater glory? That being so I am losing my individual response, losing this vivid personal life you talk of? That's really your point?"

"Well?" said Will, but without any challenge.

"Perhaps there's something in it. There would have to be something in it."

Will's smile twisted slowly. "Rub it in."

"No," said Joe quietly, "for it's a simple issue. Had it not been for the cause, I should not have done what I had done? Possibly. What is certain is that had it not been for the cause I should not have known them at all, and so have done nothing. Though no doubt I should have been trying to make my precious little personal life vivid in some other way."

Will's laugh came in soft gusts through his nostrils.

"The personal now with a vengeance!" he said. "That's me being hoist with mine own criticism. And I have nothing to offer—except sincere acknowledgments."

"And we can't even leave it there—because of the personal. For all this talk has been really about something much more personal."

"Sort of camouflage about my personal conduct that night with the prostitute. I have been trying to criticize you indirectly—for your personal reaction to my behaviour. I—who profess to believe in the personal! You always could make a fool-proof case, Joe."

"I was wrong," said Joe. "That's what's troubled me. And I'm glad we've had this talk. I have no right to be personal. The personal is always sticky and full of misunderstanding. It destroys—what the mind builds up. I had no right——"

"Oh God, you had a right! Otherwise how are

we going to march together? You had—and you must. At this point niceties are drowned. There was just this odd inconsistency, it seemed to me. You could understand not only Jamie and Mary and the policeman and the rest, but you could also understand Ivy, the prostitute. You would work for them in understanding and forgiveness. They are products of their environment. But when it came to me—I was a product of *my* environment. There was no excuse for me. It was not a moral judgement with you—though it was perhaps to some degree, because you, too, are a product of our puritanical background. But actually it was a judgement delivered from the point of view of the betrayal of the cause. By my conduct, I was bringing our crusade into disrepute. And that—got you."

"Roughly, that is so. And by that judgement I still stand. I see no inconsistency."

"Perhaps there is none. And so I may make my small point. Primarily, then, to you, we are all products of our environment. That great social fact brings out the best that's in you. On that basis you have understanding and pity and act with kindness and personal consideration. I wish I could emphasize the greatness of that—but I don't want to embarrass you or myself. Still, at that moment of judgement, I was primarily a product—not Will Montgomery, your friend. That is the matter from this *personal* point of view."

"I admit—that is what has troubled me. But I must be honest and say that, though I might have acted differently, my judgement would not have been affected. And that's the cardinal matter. I do not want to be personal, heaven knows. But let me be done with it. I am sufficiently class conscious to feel that when you want to mess about with prostitutes, you should stick to your own part of the town. That you were in the habit of doing that sort of thing was new to me. Still——" He paused, for feeling had begun to creep into his voice.

"It was an odd night that night," said Will, thinking back on it. "The experience of the night before had been strong enough to keep me from sleeping. Ettie would cry now and then: *I am very tired!* I tried to get hold of you. I felt rather disembodied. And the whisky kept up the illusion—that queer following night when I wandered about alone. Identity with the object they call it in philosophy. And all that's wrong with that is—the absence of life. Particularly when the object is alive itself." He smiled reflectively and went on in the same reminiscent tone: "You see, I have never been with a professional prostitute in my life. That was the first time I ever even stood one a drink. Poor Ivy—she didn't know what to make of me. And she was prepared to comfort me, the dear girl, out of her warm instinctive woman's heart. All wrong, I suppose. But I felt at that moment, in some way I can never make clear, that it was natural and right. And—odder still—that I shall continue to think it was natural and right until I die. The only thing, possibly, that was wrong—though this is supposition or theory—was that I did not go home with her." He moved his eyes and met Joe's. Joe held the look, then dropped his head.

Will saw the small knob of flesh gather above each eyebrow. A gentleness suffused his own mind. They understood each other now better than they had ever done.

CHAPTER SIX

★

Felicity surprised him. Here was Paris all right with London thrown in! She had walked right out of her old self and did not yet seem to have got over the surprise of it. Her dress, of dull shimmering green and gold, with full skirt, threw up her bare shoulders with a positive suggestion of plumpness, and set her brown head with an air of challenge upon her rather thin neck. After he had watched her dancing with Sir Norman, "the iron magnet", whose reputation as a roué moved gossip's head sideways, he asked her: "Do you think that was fair, exciting the old boy like that?"

"He loved it!"

"I know. Did you?"

"Well—it was a temptation to pull out all the stops." She laughed, a gleam in her eyes. "All the same, I could do with one."

The Mansons' home, at one time a country mansion house, was now within the city boundary. It was really too big for them, according to Philip's mother, too unnecessarily costly to run, but she had discovered in one of the depressions that it was unsaleable, because of its size and excessive feu-duty, not to mention rates and taxes. But it had the compensation, fully appreciated by all her guests, of being a splendid place for a party. One spacious public room led to another, and the party had the crowning virtue of being large enough to make it a matter of little consequence whether one was dancing, drinking, at ease on down cushions, or youthfully sitting on the stairs.

"I must admit they do it pretty well," said Felicity who, having started on gin and French, declared she would stick to gin and French.

"And I must say I'm enjoying it more than I ever thought I should," said Will, who, having started with cocktails, declared he would stick to whisky.

"I say, we *have* grown up!"

"Grown up? You've grown up and flown open."

"Flown open?"

"Full flower."

Her eyes grew wicked in enjoyment. "And to think how dumb you were! Clever always—but oh, so reticent!"

"And you so tentative—and coy."

"Not coy! Oh, *not* coy!"

They went into their youthful past, into earnest and not so earnest college adventures, quoted Swinburne murmurously, and roared with laughter.

A young man came and asked her for a dance.

"Must I dance?" she begged him.

"You must," he said. He was just turned twenty, with black, well-brushed, oiled hair, and was full of assurance and youthful party mannerisms. He had played for The Rest in the rugby trials last season and had nearly been picked as a reserve. So he now bowed exaggeratedly and crooked his arm, for he had a reputation to keep up before his fellows. Felicity came from Paris.

Will got hold of Philip's sister, Maisie. She was in her last year at the university and said she would like to go in for literature.

"You mean honours and specialize?"

"No. I just mean writing."

The gravity of her face, her shy spirit, almost hurt him. Why did gravity in a girl's face always affect him?

"It's difficult for me to advise you," he said simply. "You might have genius. I don't know. I'm just a working journalist."

After the dance, he stood talking to Maisie's mother, who was so gracious a woman that her smile was more than most women's deepest comment. From her, very obviously, Philip had received his physical endowments and the grace to use them.

"You ought to know that old Scots folk don't dance, except once or twice, ritually," she said. "But wait—Nancy, do you know William Montgomery?" Nancy's father was the senior partner of a firm of stockbrokers. She danced close up and silently and very well. He caught sight of Felicity. Her eyes threw him a swift agonized request for a lifeline, while she revolved and side-stepped and chattered to her black-haired cavalier. Will was so amused that he inadvertently clasped his companion more firmly. She accepted the pressure. "I say, you are a lovely dancer," he murmured. She gave him a languid gleam: "Don't chatter." When the dance was over, he led her away. How could he, unless properly relieved, go to the assistance of Felicity?

But he reckoned without Felicity, who now appeared, crying: "Will, have you forgotten?"

"How could I?" he replied. Felicity guided the black cavalier to Nancy.

"It was bliss to know you wouldn't stare and say 'What?'," remarked Felicity, as they went towards the music.

"What was I supposed to have forgotten? That this was Johann Strauss and we were booked to celebrate?"

She paused involuntarily. "That's uncanny!" Then she gave him a happy little tug forward. "Oooh! The agony of that knowing youth. He was being a man, you know. He was knowing all about it, what what. With the limping gait of a socially constipated young elephant. Not but that he dances", she added, with the driest malice, "quite well."

"I thought he had been to Paris?"

"He has. He went to the *Folies Bergères*. He told me."

He laughed. "I don't know quite what that means," he said, "but it sounds delicious."

"You have never been to Paris?"

"No."

"What a waste!" She looked at him. "Will, why

don't you? You cannot possibly live here. This is money-making, this is success, this is—oh, this is death. Don't you see that they live for their—for their power and position—that they live to hold it—that they'll kill what opposes them? Don't you feel that it's—terrible?"

"I only feel that it's rather pleasant. I must be getting deeply infected."

"You are, a bit. You hold me, for example, too close. At every turn round, when, you understand, it mightn't be noticed, that young sportsman squeezed me—like this. Snatching his sex on the sly."

"Did he, the young rascal!"

"You are clever enough not even to be hurt in your vanity."

"Not to show it, you mean. Tell me how I should dance."

"Like this. A little apart. So." Presently she added: "Isn't that—more subtle?"

"Ah," he said with Swinburnian rhythm, "to remain thus exquisitely for ever poised in tension!"

"There's a time", said Felicity, intoning clerically and with a fair mimicry of their old minister, "for all things, and the time for one thing is not the time for another thing, and the time for another thing is not the time for one thing. World without end."

Will gave the response and, while they were negotiating the dead corner of the room, saluted her very lightly on the forehead, as his head turned apparently to find the way.

"Will, that *was* a risk!"

"How calmly you keep countenance—so that even the dowagers may see it didn't happen. Tell me this. See the covey of them we are now advancing towards. They seem to me to have been sitting there for hours. Just sitting and looking. What's passing in their minds?"

"They have no minds."

"Come! That's too easy. For the one most certain thing about them is that they have minds of their own. They have sized you up pretty completely, I bet! And me—they'll have said: 'Just a journalist. Not even an editor. And after eight years at it, too!' Then they'll go into that strange mystery of my father having put so much into America and, in the crash, lost the lot. Had he put it into gilt-edged in London—like so many of the others! Those fellows, you know, who sold out to the south, sold out the great businesses their fighting fathers had built up, for gilt-edged security and a public school. But no, he was hanged if he was going to do that and sit pretty. So he adventured into the American quicksands, and they opened, and swallowed him up. Nineteen shillings in the pound! If they're blaming me it is as my father's ghost. It would round off the story if I became an absolute down and out. It would be poetic justice softer than a sad sigh. I'll have to think it over."

"Will, I'm sorry but I must brutally compliment you. I never really thought you would be like this. I could not see how you could outgrow—I mean all this repression—more than that. Even I would be vindictive against these dowagers."

"I haven't started to compliment you yet, Felicity.

217

But one thing at a time. What do you think is really passing deep down in the minds of these grey-haired, stout and thin, ladies, while their men are away having a few and discussing armament profits?"

"Will!" she exclaimed, with a chuckle, "are you being romantic? How deliciously provincial! For you are liberated enough to have the provincial upon you, but rather—don't you know—with a slight distinction; like a brilliant speaker with the charm of a slight, oh, a very slight, stutter!" The last word came out in a drawled staccato, while she arched her brows; her lips closed in a dismissive pout.

He embraced her, murmuring: "But still I wonder —if they wonder about life at last—and vaguely question and wonder why?"

Looking up at him, she shook her head. "They are just watching the coming generation, the fruit of their loins, anxious that the right marriages be made and that they themselves accordingly be justified and pass with sad honour to the grave."

"Felicity, you are cleverer than I thought you would be and profounder by half."

"Is that a relief?"

"And a joy."

"Will, I should like to kiss you."

"Well?"

Her lids lowered, and her eyes gleamed wickedly. The dance became more exciting. "Ah, Johann Strauss!" she murmured slowly, pronouncing the name like a Viennese girl, for Felicity had always been brilliant at modern languages.

More than anything she had said, this brought the Continent before him.

"You really like Paris?"

"I love it. Ah, the excitement of that time of the crisis!" The gleam in her eyes grew soft. "I could not tell you. You would not understand. It was—terrific."

"Standing on the barricades?"

"And the nights—the nights—what a time! I could not tell you; quite hopeless to try." She sighed.

"Perhaps your escort helped?"

"That, dear Will," said Felicity, "is the provincial coming out in you. I don't mind. Really, I don't. I still want to kiss you, but don't—don't—destroy it too much. One escort didn't matter. A hundred escorts didn't matter. I had my escort, as you call him and as it happens. He was an Embassy youth; English, with the intense emotion of that time coming through his Sassenach self-restraint. The English are far more sentimental than the Scots, once they break through. But they have manners and can behave, and they are —ah, he was very ver-y charming. But, that apart, if I may say so"—— she paused to smile at him—"it was something quite beyond, a feeling that you were living intensely in an atmosphere like quicksilver. It was *living*, all the time; living on the edge of—I don't know what."

"I'm glad you didn't say the edge of a volcano."

She gave a soft chuckle, then looked at him shrewdly. "On what edge then?"

"Wasn't an edge at all. Not even a brink. You

know how civilization stood on the brink of the precipice, I hope?"

"Will, you ravish me! Tell me, where did I stand?"

"Alas, Felicity, it's not that you really want to know where you stood, because you think you know that better than any one could ever tell you. As indeed you do. But you're curious, you wicked woman, to know where I think you stood, so that, in the process of telling, my innocent provincial self may be exposed to the merciless lens of your rather lovely dark blue eye. And why should I play?"

She gave him a little shake. "How true! So you have to tell me now, or I shall pass away in your arms. Quick! Where did I stand?"

"It was really a dance——"

"Oh, that's good!"

"——and your partner held you, at a little distance. So. And he is quite the most impressive of all partners. We use the word sensational loosely. But he is, in the magnificent sense, sensational. And you never knew when he was going to lean forward, to bridge the gap between you. No wonder you were thrilled."

"And his name?"

"Death."

She took a moment. "That's splendid, but—not—quite true." She was looking at him. "It was *living*: not death."

"When the girl jumps on the barricade and waves the boys on, that's living, that's not death; it's not death until the next moment."

"But I wasn't on a barricade."

"No. But your experience was heightened in the same intense way; only it was not heightened by fighting: it was heightened by—by I don't know what."

"Why did you hesitate? By what?"

"By sex," said Will, and looked at her.

For one moment her whole face seemed to shrink in dismay. She stared at him penetratingly, about to protest, but was held back by something she couldn't be dishonest about.

His smile broke into a soft teasing laugh. "Surely you are not grudging me one thrust of green jealousy at the Embassy man?"

But she could not respond and danced silently, gazing over his shoulder. He rallied her. The music stopped with a final rumble.

"This has been a frightful shock to me. For heaven's sake protect me from that young crew. The doctors I don't mind so much, but——"

"But how can I protect you, if one of them comes and asks?"

"Very well. I'll protect myself. Put me there—and fetch some drinks. No, I'll stick to you—and we'll take the drinks across."

"I'm sorry, Felicity," he began, as they sat down, "but really I didn't mean to suggest seriously——"

"Please do shut up," she said. "Will you never learn to understand when the perfect effect has been created? I know men who would give half their fortune for your gift—or, at least, for what your gift could be. It's been a frightful shock."

She suddenly met his puzzled look and smiled maliciously. "I've got you guessing, haven't I? And such innocence! You're like something come out of a wood. Yes, a squirrel! You have eyes like hazelnuts. And your hair is exactly the colour of a bat's. Only your teeth don't look as if they were made to nibble. Though they are a trifle shy behind so intriguing a mouth. And your smile dawns on your face! Positively like wind coming on a pool. You really would be too good to spoil. If you could be in Paris —and do everything—and still be yourself, ah!"

"You had just better mind your eye! And fancy you, the emancipated, the Parisian lady, with complete knowledge of the world, of life, of *living*, being shocked at the introduction of an idea, hardly even that, a fanciful conception, because it's based on sex! I mean to say——"

"Oh, go on," she said, gloating. "This is too delicious."

He regarded her doubtfully.

"I can't keep it in any longer," she said. "I was shocked, shattered, to discover—that in this matter of life——"

"Of *living*. Yes?"

"——you are cleverer than I am. Can you possibly understand what a blow it was?"

He looked at her. Then—she was quite right—his smile dawned, and darkened, while his eyes caught a gleam deeper than any squirrel's.

"Felicity," he said softly, "you are very ver-y clever. I admit your mastery."

"Will," she said, "that is very ver-y superb of you." Her eyes were alive; softly hot. She was moved. The music started. A rising young surgeon stood before her.

"Jim," she begged him, "would you mind if I didn't this time? There's something gone wrong with my heel. I must get it put right. Perhaps then? Oh, there's Philip. Philip!"

Philip excused himself to a tall dark girl and two others, and came across.

"There's something gone wrong with the heel of my slipper, something coming through and hurting a bit. Could you flatten it some way?"

"Why, yes. Let me see. It'll mean the garage. You wait here, and if you give me the slipper——"

"I'll come with you," she said, "and mak siccar."

"Very well. We can go out the back way." Philip turned to Will. "Perhaps you could come and hold it while I bump?"

"Lead on," said Will.

It was a large garage, with electric light and a work bench. Philip was very careful that Felicity should not soil her dress. Will watched Philip's face as he felt for the defect inside the slipper, but Philip's face remained perfectly solemn.

"There's a distinct lump there," he said.

"Let me see." Will took the slipper. "Yes. But it's not a nail. It's a lump. It will have to be hammered very gently. Do you mind if I try?"

"Do," said Philip.

"I am sorry," said Felicity to Philip, "taking you

away like this. I called to you, with my usual reck-lessness!"

"Not at all," said Philip, looking at her closely. "But if Will could manage alone——"

"Leave it to me," said Will. "I'll put this clean piece of waste round the heel and fix it in the vice, then tap tap away."

When Philip had gone, Will asked: "Who exactly is the tall dark lady to whom I've noticed Philip being particularly, almost proprietorially, attentive?" He closed the vice gently.

"One of the Clive-Smeatons."

"Phew!" whistled Will softly. "Anything really doing?"

"Philip is reticent, of course. But, far as I can gather, she's the anointed."

"Philip has the unlucky habit of blundering into money, hasn't he?"

"Malice deep and dyed?"

"No. Truth does sometimes slip out in a forgetful way. But that wasn't truth really. What do you think of her?"

"I think she's quite all right. A bit stiff, perhaps."

"But you think she'd make a very good official wife? Feel that."

"Oh, it's gone!"

Will stooped, put her slipper on, and arose beside her. "Thank you, Will."

He smiled to her, and she put her arms swiftly round his neck. Will responded. . . . She broke from him. "Ooh! You're rough."

"And the light, too," he observed, his breath disordered.

The switch was at the door and when he had turned the light off, she said: "How glorious to find you again, Will!" and got into his arms. Then she began to whisper to him, to teach him a few small things in love's gentler art.

When the experience got a little too much for Will, she restrained him strictly, saying there's a time for all things and this is one thing, and a sweet stinging gentleness is the tide on which it's borne, and tried to make him understand the wisdom thereof and succeeded as well as she wanted to.

"And now," she sighed—"we must go."

"Why? I shan't see you alone again."

"Why not?"

"How can I?"

"And us sleeping in the same house?"

"But—when?"

"After the ball is over."

"Felicity."

"My door", said Felicity, in a whisper, "is just before yours."

He kissed her, for he could not answer.

She pulled him by the hand out of the open garage, and found a mirror and a wash basin, before they reappeared. "We must", said Felicity, "do a little more of our duty now. I am even prepared for the dark cavalier." She saw Jim and hailed him and they went off gaily together, talking about heels and blisters and a doctor's lapsed opportunity.

The night now took on for Will a tension and strangeness behind all his overt acts. He got talking to some of the older men, too, who had known his father; for one like fat jolly Mr. Calder, the fruit importer, with the small shrewd kindly eyes, he felt an affection; there were oranges in his skin and a half-tumbler of whisky was "a small one". Will laughed at the size of the drink he accepted from him. Others, too, whose names stood for shipbuilding and overseas trade, spoke to him in a friendly way as the son of his father. There was a reticence about a few of these men that touched him. Most were full of social manners, with hearty voices and a proper importance.

But whisky seemed to have no effect on the quiver and tension at his heart. And he wanted it to have an effect. He wanted to move swiftly away from the tension, to subdue the quiver. For there was something about it all that was scarcely credible. Then he would see Felicity's head, and the sensation of intimacy with it became for one swift moment overpowering. During the moment, his muscles flexed rigidly, and on one occasion he in this involuntary manner embraced the calm Maisie, but at once said: "Ah, that was nearly a bump!" and guided her sideways.

With Felicity he did not dance again. Some of the older guests began to take their departure and at two o'clock came the end. Dark coats and white mufflers and hats in hand; fur coats and satin shoes and bare sleek heads. Thanks were offered for a perfectly lovely evening, while, outside, cars were started up and young men strode hither and thither with commanding vigour.

"Can you tell me", Felicity whispered to him as they stood in the hall, "why so many of the faces of the fully middle-aged ladies of this city are little noses on blobs of water?"

They happened to be looking towards two or three women rather small in stature, but rotund, whose red slightly blown watery faces rose out of the rich collars of their furs in a way that gave Felicity's question an impressionistic warrant.

He did not turn and look at her. He could not look at her. He laughed instead. All his cool assurance was gone. He had to say something equally wild, anything but meet her eyes.

"Do you know what I was thinking just now?" he asked.

"No."

One of the ladies sat down, her richly tinted face heaving a sigh from the depths of her two-hundred guinea coat. "Ah," she said, "I am very tired."

"Well?" prompted Felicity, and looked up at him —when her glance immediately concentrated on his expression. He was staring at the woman as if she were an apparition. In a moment, he blinked, and began vaguely: "Ah——"

"Will? Tell me."

"A ghost walked over my grave," he said, and his smile twisted drily. "Let's watch them go." She went with him to the door.

But here was Sir Norman. He shook hands with

her and said: "Now, remember!" in a playful mean-
ingful voice and departed.

"Let's watch, if we must, from a window," said
Felicity. "This is too cold."

"Imagine the old boy staying right to the end!"

"He's an old rip," she answered. "Let's sit here.
We've said our good-byes—or enough of 'em." Her
gay manner was reckless still, but a trifle more down-
right. "Now, tell me your story."

"About the ghost?"

"Not about that—unless you like."

"It's not really personal. It was about a poor married girl who died in the slums—a case I was dealing
with lately. But, by an odd chance, the stout lady ..."

"Mrs. Dobson. Yes?"

"... said something which coincided oddly enough
with what I was going to say to you. Have you ever
imagined yourself looking down on a city and seeing
it like a clay model of itself? Just a queer vision I
sometimes have of it. You know my politics from
of old. Well—here we have the spacious residential
quarter on the Hills; and down there we have the tall
dark slums of the River. That isn't strictly true, of
course, because you can get the worst slums off a
main thoroughfare, but it clarifies the picture, if you
see what I mean."

"Perfectly."

"When I saw the guests making for their cars, the
fantastic thought arose in me—of the revolution
swelling up from the River to the Hills and the folk
of the Hills preparing to meet it. Have you ever

thought of something like that happening in our city?"

"It couldn't," she said. "There isn't the fire in us."

"It wouldn't be fire. It would be something much more grim and bloody and unyielding."

"What a thought!"

"Assuming it happened, Felicity of the Left: what side would you be on?"

She looked at him. He met her eyes with a calm smile. She searched his eyes.

"It's a thought, isn't it?" he said.

"Will, tell me—feeling all right?"

"Naturally a bit excited."

"Dear Will," she murmured and pressed his hand. "Come. Let's go. We'll talk—and talk—alone." She jumped up. Outside the cars were whining, one after another, into the distance. "I hate starting something and being interrupted by inquisitive faces. Here's Philip, his dark lady gone."

The house party was small, and after they had sat for half an hour discussing the evening, the ladies retired. The men sat on for a little, then Mr. Manson, a personable man, bald on the crown, rather quiet, with an easy-going nature, threw his cigar in the fire and got up. He yawned and knuckled his eyes audibly. "Well, it's bed for me. Good night."

Philip suggested to Will that there was no particular hurry for a few minutes, unless he was tired.

Will found himself gladly accepting the idea. He must have drunk far too much whisky, for in recent minutes, while sitting still, he had experienced a queasy feeling of insecurity and had had to move restlessly on his chair in order to ensure command of his body. It would have been rather a dreadful thing if the room had tilted and slid his body sideways before them all!

Not that he was really drunk. It was a light-headed feeling from an odd sickly excitement in the stomach.

"What about a last drink?" Without waiting for Will's response, Philip went away and fetched two whiskies well charged with soda.

Will, after a mouthful, felt himself again, and they lit cigarettes.

"Enjoyed yourself?" Philip asked.

"To be quite candid, much more than I expected."

Philip smiled. "Good. I could see Felicity and you were hitting it off. And that's often a gamble—renewing youthful fellowships, I mean."

Will grew quickly animated, talking about Paris and barricades, and soon Philip and himself were on the friendliest terms.

"Have you fixed up about seeing her any time?" Philip asked.

"No," said Will. "Somehow—it . . . didn't think about it, really. Why?" He finished his whisky.

"I'm not being inquisitive," said Philip with a smile. "It's simply that if you had fixed up anything with her, then I shouldn't feel the responsibilities of a host so much. And she's the girl who will *have* to be doing something—probably wild. She is really very charming."

"That's true," said Will. "Yes."

"And you'll be off before she's up in the morning and you won't see her."

"Hadn't thought of that," said Will.

"Oh, it's nothing, but I mean you could have come to my aid, so to speak, and, well—it mightn't be doing you, I had hoped, a disservice either, what?"

Will smiled in response and moved restlessly. "But I will, of course! I mean—certainly. I'll—I'll get in touch. Somehow the evening just finished—you know—and——"

"It's only really one point," said Philip negligently. "I'm getting a new car next week and I was thinking of having the week-end off—a week to-morrow—or, I suppose I should say to-day, for it's Saturday now. A fellow needs occasionally to get away from his home crowd." He slowly finished his drink and, as he was setting his glass down, added: "If you fixed up somewhat early in the week with Felicity for the Saturday evening, then—that would be that. She has really an uncanny gift of getting at you!" He lit a fresh cigarette.

Will stretched to the floor and lifted his empty glass automatically.

"Oh, have a last spot!" Philip got up.

"Thanks." Will handed him his glass and, when Philip had gone, got to his feet. His whole body underwent a slow rigor, the head tilting back, eyes shut, teeth showing, and the right hand coming up breast high and clenching into a fist. Christ's name came through his teeth in a hiss. It looked like the reaction to an intense knot of physical pain. It passed, as it came, and his palm went up and across his forehead. He sat down, as Philip returned, but he could not command his hand, which shook a little as it took the glass.

"Feeling all right?" Philip looked at him, brow wrinkling in concern.

Will slowly smiled. "The truth is, Philip, I've already had, I'm afraid, just a wee drop too much."

Philip's brow cleared. "Perhaps you'd better not have this, then?"

"If you put plenty of soda in it?"

"Just the usual."

"Oh. Uhm." Will considered the glass with thoughtful humour. "What's one more amongst so many? Here's how!" He drank it all right off. "Ah-h," he exclaimed and went on, "it's a strange thing that the more alcohol you take, the drier you get. It's the alcohol probably does the drying. I wouldn't put it past the stuff."

Philip began to chuckle. "Look here, old boy, you're well on!"

"Think so? Suppose I am a bit."

"Come on! It's bed. And thanks for—being so helpful."

"Don't mention it. But why bed? There's a stage you reach when bed appears an unwelcome irrelevance. You don't feel like making a night of it?"

"No. And you won't." Philip was amused at this unusual manifestation of Will and, finishing his own drink, got up. "Come on!" He took Will's arm. Not since they were adolescents, confessing some shy ideal, had Philip felt so near, so tender, to his oldest friend.

"Well, if we must, I suppose we must. There's an end to all things—even to things that, in the inscrutable wisdom of God, never had a beginning."

Philip's laugh was soft and warm, in acknowledgment of a humour dry enough to be nearly bitter. He led Will to his bedroom, opened the door, wheeled him round and pointed out the bathroom: "Just in case you make a mistake," he whispered, "and go in by the wrong door!" Then his expression cleared. "Good night, Will! Good night, old boy!"

"Good night, Philip." Will nodded, as if he had not heard Philip's final friendly inflection, and went into his room. He stood on the floor for a little time, filling his lungs with air. Then he methodically undressed, to the extent of folding his trousers along the creases. The slight tremor in his flesh was troublesome, and, in his pyjamas, he sat down on his bed, but got up almost at once and into his dressing-gown. He filled his lungs again as if his blood were poisoned and needed a lot of oxygen. Then he walked out of his room and into the bathroom. Returning from the bathroom, he had to pass Felicity's door. He came to her door. There was no one in the corridor. This was the moment. He paused. A weakening sensation mounted from his chest to his head. He went in blindly at his own door and with an exhausting waste of energy tried to close it quietly; then quickly, in a staggering little run, reached his bed and stretched himself out.

Bitterness. Black deep bitterness. Nothing else. Not

drink. No excuses. Black obliterating self-bitterness. He sank into it; his consciousness dwindled, losing its brightness of pain; it became small in the smothering darkness, was lost for a little, then became small again, and slowly grew. He opened his eyes. From between the narrowing lids, they glittered as if the light hurt them. He pushed himself up, took off his dressing-gown, switched off the light and got into bed.

Felicity was waiting for him.

Why should he have to endure this torture of humiliation? Out of what did it come? Why? Why? Why?

Why should the poor bloody body be tortured like this? Jenny had nothing to do with this. That was sheer fantasy. That she should be having her first week-end with Philip, what was that to him? What in the name of God had that got to do with anything? Let him be honest at least about that.

Felicity was waiting for him, wondering.

And he had no desire for Felicity. Extraordinary, unaccountable, unimaginable! Bitter humiliation. Most bitter! His humour grew coarse. With the sexual oaths of the slums, he taunted his spirit and its impotent slave, the body. The humour became more vile than vomit.

Felicity was waiting for him, wondering, and beginning to be hurt in her woman's pride.

But he could find no answer to his Why? For he knew the fault did not lie with his body, which, like all healthy bodies, could be too lusty too often. It was none of the excuses he paraded before himself. It was not even drink—and he knew what drink could do! Genuinely, profoundly, he could not understand this appalling, this insuperable *reluctance* that had him in its grip. It was like an intangible octopus, holding him. The only thing that might have overcome it, he thought, in one of the washes of bitter humour that went over him, was—if he had been used to sleeping with women. But in the instant the thought was born, beneath it was the certainty, as if spoken out of some alien mouth inside him, that even then he could not have overcome it *now*.

It is a most terrible, damning, dreadful thing, that a man's mental side should be so developed that it interferes with the potent body. And, said the alien mouth, at once and with a leer, *It isn't even that!*

He smothered that mouth which, in its leer, had become like the mouth of a mud fish.

His head rolled on the pillow. Would he go? Would he get up and go? Mounting with the thought came that weakening excitement and its horrible feeling of nausea. He would have to go! The feeling receded and left him without any thought—until it began to come again. Mounting wave and slow recession, until exhaustion brought another wave across his brain, a wave of darkness, of the beginning of dissolution.

He fought that back with a slight fear—and with a cunning gratitude that shamed him, shamed him to the last secret recess of his spirit. Running away from a decision! Glad to take refuge behind the body's humiliating weakness!

How deep went the root of his manhood into a man! What froth the spiritual was, compared with this dark deep root, and the thin roots that went out from it, gripping flesh and bone and marrow in their wire mesh!

And all the time he knew the decision was being made, slowly, irrevocably, the decision that he was not going into Felicity's room. As in its tortuous torturing course it approached finality, the shame of its acceptance lost its half-liberating spirts of feelings and rebellions and became still and dark and more bitter than any self-shame he had ever known. *At last!* said the mouth. *At last! But this is only the beginning! Before the night is over, you may in fact know something of the dark night of the soul!* . . .

A faint scratching, like the scratching of a mouse at the door. His heart stood still. Then the click of the knob, and the silent invisible swing inward of the door, solid with movement. Once more, he had reckoned without Felicity.

When the light went on, she was standing against the closed door, one arm still outstretched to the switch. Light blue dressing-gown, bare throat, poised head with its dark brown hair, and eyes that steadied and gleamed against the light.

He stirred, getting up on an elbow, and tried to smile. She came over slowly, sat on the edge of his bed, and looked down at him. There was pride in her look, and a certain calm ironic assessment.

"Sorry, Felicity," he muttered. "I'm not feeling very good." His bitter smile looked sick.

236

"What's wrong?"

"Too much whisky."

She kept looking at him, nodded to herself, while her lips moved in their own humour.

"You are as pale as death," she said in a whisper that sounded loud.

"I feel like death."

She nodded again, the gleam of assessment in her eyes.

He turned his head to avoid her eyes, pushed himself up against the back of the bed, and brought movement and stress upon the body, for a new horror was mounting in him. The intense excitement of her appearance was deepening the feeling of nausea and he realized that, unless he could fight it down, he might very easily be physically sick.

Balancing the horror of this was the cunning that sickness *might* help him, might help to show Felicity that it was nothing more than whisky. In degradation, there is still a lower deep, still . . . O God, he was going to be sick! He swung his legs out and staggered over to the wash basin. . . .

As he turned the taps on to wash the stuff away, Felicity withdrew her warm hand from his cold forehead. "Hush!" she said, supporting him under the arms, for his gasping spluttering cough could be heard more than one room away, and it was not exactly the moment for Philip or his father or mother to appear. . . . Taking one arm, she supported him back to bed.

"You are *really* feeling very bad now," she

whispered, as he stretched himself and his head fell back. "Poor Will."

"On the contrary," he said, "I am feeling much better." He tried to keep his lips from trembling, for his body was icy cold.

"You'll soon be all right." She tucked the clothes about him.

His eyes winced; he drew a deep quivering breath.

"Now," she said. "Go to sleep, like a good boy."

He turned his eyes on her, glittering points steady and piercing. She regarded them with her slight smile.

"Good night," she said, and gave a playful snuggle to the clothes over his chest; then she got up and tip-toed to the door. There she paused, her right hand on the switch, and half-turned, her head rising poised and bright out of the blue dressing-gown. Like a perfect actress, she held the look for a time, the friendly faintly mocking smile on her face, then with the finger-tips of her left hand, she blew him a kiss. Click! went the switch, and the darkness came down upon him.

CHAPTER SEVEN

★

I

His case, though it contained no more than dress suit, shirt and slippers, brought cold sweat to his forehead, and by the time he reached the spot where he had seen the wild geese, he was glad to sit down.

It was a calm lovely April evening, with white cloud here and there in a light blue sky, and peace, charged with singing promise, in the world. The last peewit he had disturbed, ceased its crying. A robin, on a switch of brown birch across the road, began to sing, not with the loud confidence that had so astonished him recently when he had first heard it, but with a reflective warbling, as if the faint chill of the evening were the chill of autumn.

How exquisite the evening, with its foreshadow of night and promise of all the days of summer! The promise went forward into summer as if it were going back into youth. There was a slight quivering ecstasy in this illogical, yet clear, timeless apprehension.

For it was a good thing to be rid of the body's humours. It was a good thing to go through that ultimate humiliation, that final defeat, beyond which there can only be either death or freedom. Or was it death *and* freedom? Anyway, not a matter of solemn debate now! As the robin flew off, he smiled and looked slowly about him and up at the sky. Some pigeons winging to the wood. And one pigeon, shooting upward suddenly, balancing on the peak of its curve a moment with exquisite suspension, then stooping with half-closed wings—to rise again. And all for no ostensible reason in the world. In fact, very un-pigeonlike! An airy grace of swift movement and exquisite poise, taking the wind on its enamel-bright feathers, on its unwinking swift-seeking eyes, on its breast—in soundless ecstasy.

Pretty good at it! he decided, and his eyes rested on the wrinkled bark of an old fir-tree. A suggestion of red, coming through the wrinkles, the red of dead suns and ancient Caledonian forests. And the eyes stare—upon wraith-grey evocations.

The wild geese would be making their nests in the far north. Pairing! He watched them for a moment in a clear vision of landscape and sea, then got up—and went down to the farm.

And here was Mrs. Armstrong, with her husky-laughing welcoming face, full of stout comfort and hospitable manners. The dear woman!

Yes, he admitted he hadn't had much sleep and was going to bed whenever he had got something to eat.

"You had a good night, then?" she asked, lifting her tray and having a last look at the prepared table.

"Yes, very good. Dancing and that, you know—and the refreshments, they were excellent. Perhaps just a little too good for simple fellows not used to strong waters."

"Ah! Hah-ha!" She nodded. "So there was a late licence?"

He laughed. "There was," he admitted. "Very much so, I'm afraid—and very late."

"Ah! And were the ladies very nice?"

"Whisht!" he said. "Sure it's a marvel that I'm in it at all. I had the feet taken from under me so often, that if it hadn't been for the late licence, it would have gone hard with me. It's a dreadful thing—when you don't know how to go about it."

She laughed. "You needn't try to tell me that! I know how the girls would—I know." She nodded.

"Perhaps you do," he said. "For I'm beginning to think that women have some mysterious knowledge or other. However, they didn't tell it to me, and, fortunately, there was always, as I say——"

"The late licence." Her whole generous body shook with husky laughter. "Was it a nice-looking licence?"

"Oh, very nice. About as attractive a licence as I have ever seen."

"What did—what——"

"What did it wear? Now, let me see. It was all a shimmering glory of dim green and gold. It sort of fitted tightish up here, with a couple of slim shoulder bands and then down below a full flowing skirt that—

241

that, as it swayed and draped itself, just put the heart clean across you."

"Oh, my word!"

He started eating, and, after a little further talk, she went out.

His expression grew bleak. He had gone a bit too far. Not quite so completely freed as he had hoped. "You bloody fool," he said to himself calmly. The food lost its savour and, tired of the physical act of eating, he got up and stood looking out the window.

He stared at the elm-tree, until the stress passed away. I am getting used to the trick of it! he thought. But though he had thus banished the stress of memory, he could not command the airy freedom he had known coming down the road. But perhaps he would learn that trick, too—given time! The faint irony made him restless and deepened his feeling of absolute weariness. He must stretch himself out. Mounting the stairs slowly was like mounting step by step out of himself. He was walking towards his own door, when Jenny's door opened and she appeared. She was clearly taken aback and he stood quite still, looking at her, his face very pale.

Her hesitation was only momentary, but as she came on past him, out of her surprise, she said, the gravity of her face breaking into a smile: "Good evening."

"Good evening," he answered.

She was out of sight, going down the stairs, before he got his door open.

He threw himself on his bed. "Lord, I am tired!" he muttered. His heart was beating in a way that made his weariness almost intolerable. A long day's work, following on no sleep and too much whisky....

He closed his eyes and slowly the pulsations subsided.

The twilight deepened, and he got up presently and looked out of the side window. Jenny was in the garden, not working, but moving slowly from one place to another. Sometimes her head rose, and she appeared to look at something in the distance. He saw that she had the power to stand quite still, lost in what she was looking at or thinking. She moved in the grey twilight naturally.

He came away from the window and, sitting on the bed, his eyes to the front window, upon the still twigs of the elm-tree, he thought to himself how fantastic was that conviction of certainty which had come upon him when Philip had spoken of his week-end. There was absolutely nothing to connect it with Jenny—apart from the fact that Philip appeared to be friendly with her. But, after all, there was Philip's own girl. And Philip might be wanting a quiet week-end for a score of reasons. A cruise, a man's party, and a bit of a gamble—for Philip and his friends were all yachtsmen. A week-end's golf . . . Philip would not want to appear too selfish. And Saturday and Sunday were his only really free days in which either to take Felicity about or go off on his own. And his dark lady might not like him to float about too much with Felicity, even if Felicity was only staying for a week or two. But Philip would never lose his head over a girl like Felicity, even if she hadn't been his first cousin. As it was, there was a little too much of the same blood in both of them. Felicity would see through his most charming vanities. There wouldn't be a sufficient contrast for savour. And though Felicity, failing something more exciting, would flirt with Philip all right, she would also restlessly want him to "take her around". So Philip was trying to do the escape act. . . .

But his reasoning did not convince. And this astonished Will: that he should be so certain of what could be, after all, no more than a matter of intuition. Yet it was exactly the sort of thing that had been happening to him since that time, so long ago, when the birds used to torture him in the morning! It was not Philip's words that had spoken to him; it was Philip's secret mind through his eyes, his imperceptible gestures, his negligence, through the blood and lack of blood in the skin of his face. It was uncanny—and quite certain.

More than once lately—he had to admit it to himself—Jenny's face had developed the trick of appearing before his mind's eye. Grave face, with clear steady eyes. Sometimes the face seemed larger than life. The texture of the skin was very clear, not pale, but warm with life, as if there was light in it, yet smooth and grave. It seemed to be waiting. . . .

He got up and looked out into the garden. Jenny was gone, but in the dim light he got a very strong impression that she was still there. The sort of feeling one might have about a woman who had loved her garden and was now dead.

Only Jenny was not dead. She was very much alive. Yet she was in the garden, though he could not see her. And he knew that she would always be. . . .

Was he really going mad? Was he creating "another world" of shadows, of desires? . . .

Jenny, moving through the grey light, watching the springing life from her labours in sun and wind and rain. Her secret passion—deeper, he could swear, than her passion for Philip!

Which, anyway, was certainly quite mad!

That a few little flowers, pushing up through the earth, could affect her more than—than—Philip and herself burning together! He banished the absurdity upon a sudden deep beat from his heart.

He turned away from the window and an inner voice, ironically casual, said to him: "Looks as if you're falling for Jenny, my boy!"

He stood quite still, mid floor, while his face narrowed vindictively. Then a swift destructive impulse possessed him and he looked around, fists clenched, for something to grapple and destroy. It landed him on the bed, whose coverlet he clawed and twisted, until the black fury of unreason passed and he lay flat out on his back, exhausted.

The ironic voice was still speaking, but he would not hear it. Presently, however, in a lull the mouth said: "*The dark night of the soul? Last night was only the dark night of the body's vanity. You wait!*"

He got up. Really he must keep some control of

these destructive forces. He must. Giving into them was just an indulgence, like giving in to drink. He began to undress calmly, though his flesh trembled weakly. But the cool contact of the sheets thinned the body, dissipated its humours. He lay looking at the still branches in the deep dusk now passing into night, until his mind grew calm, and apprehensions came upon it with a remarkable clarity. . . .

There, for the first time in his life, he realized the existence of pure evil. Not a negative force, like the absence of good, the absence of ethics, of morals, the destruction of custom; but a *positive* force functioning in its own law and right. His apprehension of it became so acute that it touched his senses, touched them in a darkling way, and the bones behind his nostrils grew dry as in a rank crushed-gourd effluence of some unholy hemlock. . . .

Out there in the night, in that grey light, passing into final dark, in that appalling stillness. The grey of the window panes dazed his forehead, left his breast open. When he could no longer bear the horror, he turned slowly over, crying inwardly: "Oh God, I am very tired!" He repeated the cry so that all his senses be deafened by it, his mouth grabbing at the pillow. "Ettie!" cried his smothered mouth. "Ettie!" But his brain did not hear. He began to drown in that smother of warmth, for there was little energy left in his body; and, in fact, as if his body had been dealt a final blow, it gave one slow last wriggle and lay still.

Lying in bed, after a long glorious sleep, watching the shadows of the twigs against the blind, and, the blind raised, the twigs themselves against the sky, was very pleasant. His landlady had brought his breakfast up, and it was nearly noon before he dressed, got downstairs and walked out bareheaded upon the lawn. Such a divine day! He strolled round the corner of the house and up into the garden without allowing himself a conscious thought. From one bunch of shoots or flowers he went to another, until he came close by Jenny and said in a casually friendly voice: "Good morning." She returned his greeting, half lifting her head, and then resuming her task of weeding out coarse grass from among the pink spikes of a large clump of peony.

"Your garden is looking very well. Things are coming on."

"Yes." Her voice was calm but not unfriendly.

"That's a lovely blue. What is it?"

"These are scillas," she said. "They're just about past."

"Yes, I can see that lot there have opened very wide."

"That's glory-of-the-snow. Not the same."

He found the difference. "What lovely delicacy of colouring against the old dead earth!" His eyes lit up at the sight of slim stalks bearing balls of blue-purple flowers.

They were primulas, she told him. *Denticulata.*

"And these?"

"Wandas."

"What's the colour?"

"A deep maroon, I suppose."

"Not a very good sound for it!"

But she answered simply: "They've been in bloom quite a long time. They, too, are going."

Looking at them, he could see that dissolution had touched the edges of the petals.

He must have seen spring flowers often enough, but never certainly had been moved by this sensation of vivid colouring, this note of the incredible in the living purity of colours against a ground still largely wintry and dead. A sheer miracle, each little bloom.

"Oh, look!"

She glanced up at his face and followed his gaze. "These are daffodils."

"I know," he said. "I know daffodils. But these are——" He stopped.

"I had them in my rooms last year in a pot," she said. "They are not so good this year."

"They're like butterflies," he cried, "about to take off! I never saw anything like them. Never!" And they did rather look like butterflies, tilted to the sun, shallow trumpets, and petals outspread like wings.

"I liked them—but couldn't afford them."

"So you bought them?"

"Yes."

He laughed. "How lucky you were! I mean, to have that experience." He glanced at her and saw the gravity of her face dissolve in a faint humour. But she did not answer him.

"You don't really mind if I walk around, do you?" he asked lightly.

"No. I don't mind. It's not my garden."

"You can't keep me from walking around, so to speak?"

Reserve came back to her face and she concentrated on the weeds.

"Sorry," he said. "But, after all, you brought it on yourself. For it *is* your garden."

"No, it's not," she remarked indifferently.

"I beg your pardon," he murmured and moved on up to the top of the garden. The bishopweed was mustering in full invasion on the bank to the left, and was deep in ambush amongst the roots of the currant bushes now in delicate green leaf. As he came back, she was trying to lever out the clump of peony, but could not break the hold of the roots.

"Please, let me have a try." He took the four-pronged fork from her and, after a struggle, got the clump free.

She thanked him. "There is often no other way", she explained simply, "of getting weeds out. Besides, I want that over there."

"Where?" And when she had pointed to the spot, he carried the weighty mass across. He saw that so long as he remained completely impersonal, she might not mind his presence.

"Anything else I can do for you?"

"Nothing, thank you."

"If there is anything—for goodness' sake, ask me. I can always navvy. If I may be allowed to enjoy the beauty of this garden by looking at it now and then, surely I can pay for the pleasure by doing a little donkey work?"

"There is nothing really you can do."

"What about that bank of bishopweed?"

She looked at him directly, her eyes wide and calm, then changing in their depths to an impersonal humour.

"I'm not asking you to do *that*."

"You mean, you won't ask me to do anything. You would not like me to intrude even on your garden. I see." He shrugged, smiling.

"I am glad you see," she replied coolly.

"All the same, when you aren't here I'll steal the beauty."

She was tempted, and said: "You can't. For you can only carry away what you bring."

He laughed, and a suggestion of warmth came into her fair skin. She turned away from him and started working. This time, wisely, he took his dismissal.

But that afternoon, returning by a path that came round a little wood on the high ground above the farm, he saw her at a short distance coming out of the wood. He was first to reach the point where their paths converged and, after moving on hesitantly, at last waited for her. She came in that cool upright way that was untouchable. There was no suggestion now of the pavement, perhaps because her heels were low or her head high or heaven alone knew what, but he felt very awkward. He saw that her body, in its carriage, was beautiful and free, that it advanced upon him out of a wood, the uplands behind, and the horizon, and the sky.

He greeted her with shy politeness. "Getting home from your walk?"

"Yes," she answered, and he knew he should not have waited. She offered no other comment, and walked calmly on at her own pace.

He did not speak until the silence became impossible to maintain. "It will happen now and then, I suppose," he said drily, with a touch of spite, "that we find ourselves in each other's company. It is no doubt very unfortunate, but it seems a trifle ludicrous to—to dodge it."

"Dodge it?" Her voice sounded as if she had raised her eyebrows, but he kept his eyes in front.

"Not the best verb possibly, but 'twill serve."

She said nothing.

"I had heard", he proceeded, "of the gift of silence. It had never struck me that it could be a tyranny."

"The remedy is simple."

They went on for fifty yards without a word. She was quite merciless, walking as if he did not exist. He was beginning to feel nervous and resented it. Analysis was his only help. He would be damned if he would stand still and let her go on!

"I realize the position quite clearly," he said. "You resent my intrusion here. You want to have this place for yourself. I did not know you were here. Had I known, I should certainly not have come. I came myself for the very thing you came for. I resented your being here. That's how I presume to know your feeling on the matter. Fortunately it's not beyond remedy." In speaking, his voice had grown cold. He felt pale with anger.

"If you knew all that, why do you intrude?"

"It's a fair question and puts me in the wrong. My human nature was weak. Possibly also we have developed the trick of trying to be civilized after our fashion."

"We have to perform that trick so often that I am not impressed by your sarcasm about being civilized."

"No?"

"No. If you really understood what you have been saying, you——" she shrugged.

"What? You mean I do not understand what it means to get away, to get where personal entanglements and nonsense cease from troubling, where——" He shrugged. "You doubtless feel yourself the unique individual who could pass an examination on the final meaning of peace."

"I had never thought of it," she said calmly. "The trouble about a man is that he must have a theory, even if he has to imagine it. You are quite wrong."

"And you are not prepared to enlighten me?"

"Why should I?"

"No reason, of course. I see my mistake." He stopped abruptly. She carried on a couple of paces before she, in her surprise, also stopped. And it was she who spoke.

"You had no right to intrude," she said, with a strange stormy flash in her eyes. To his amazement, he saw she was not calm and detached: she was angry.

At which spectacle, his own anger cooled.

"I know." He nodded. "I apologize. I'm sorry." He looked past her, into the distance. "The city gallant who must bring his appalling ways with him. I can only assure you that I understand. You are right." He tried to smile, but, not making a great success of it, turned on his heels and walked up the way they had come before he knew what he was doing. She stood a little while looking after him, then went on down to the farm.

That evening about eleven, when Mrs. Armstrong was locking the front door, he appeared, declaring he must have a last breath of air to help him sleep. They chatted for a little, and then he went out, Mrs. Armstrong crying after him: "Watch your feet in the dark."

That caution made him smile as he crossed over towards the steading, where the roadway was broad, and stood for a little breathing deeply in the star-lit night. Friendly, the dark, he thought, and listened. There was the occasional sound of a chain round a cow's neck, the clump of a horse's hoof. Sleeping on its feet, head down! There was a pervasive smell of manure . . . generation and growth! In those used to this from their childhood, what would it evoke, coming back to it? How little he yet knew of this farm life going on around him. But he would find out. For here were life, growth, food . . . not the sensationalism of newspapers, politics, death, that sterile. . . .

A sudden light—yes, in Jenny's bedroom. And there

she was herself putting her candle down, its light on her hair, defining her profile. Her features vanished as she came forward to the window and stood looking out.

He got lost, watching her, until, mounting the fence at the top of the garden, he found himself walking down the dimly defined path. He came slowly. She probably could not see him. She could withdraw whenever she liked. He could walk where he liked. He stood under her window, said "Hallo!" in a restrained voice, and gestured her to open the window.

No, she could not have heard, could not have seen him. And now the reckless impulse began to subside. He would walk away. The window went up.

"I'm sorry I was rude," he said.

She did not answer, her head and shoulders leaning out, her face invisible.

"Do you forgive me?"

"More personal."

Her calm slighting voice did not help him. "I suppose it is," he answered.

"And what a lovely night." It was a murmur out over his head and startled him like an electric shock.

"Won't you come down—and let us talk about it sensibly? Please do. I feel miserable about it. Then it would be all over. Please do."

She leaned out there, silent as any sphinx; then she withdrew her head, quietly shut the window, and pulled down the blind.

She's coming! he thought. She's coming! His excitement became intense. She would come out at the front door, of course. He went down the garden with light feet and stole quickly round to the lawn. He felt gay, happy. They would now put the whole thing right. They would walk along like friends, laughing at silly little follies. The sheer friendliness would be cool and delicious. . . .

She was taking a long time. He went round to the garden. Her light was still on. He came back. Presently when he went round her light was out. He waited for nearly an hour, leaning against the elm-tree, but she did not come.

And he knew she had never intended to come. His personal intrusions were like the slimy marks that snails make among the flowers. Odd, too, because it was the sort of thing that he never did, that his own sensitive rather impersonal nature recoiled from. His mouth was dry with bitterness.

3

On Tuesday Felicity rang him up. "You're a fine one!" she said. "At least you might have had the decency to ring *me* up."

"It was not for lack of thinking about you. But—well—I mean to say—what!"

She laughed. "I'm dying to see you. What about to-night?"

So they met for supper. Felicity was in her usual gay spirits, and, after Will had got over his initial discomfort, he responded fully.

She was so irresponsible, laughed so merrily, not

caring who looked or stared, that he felt himself shaken free, like a branch in the wind.

And she was clever enough not to ignore the contretemps of the bedroom. She had the sliest digs at it, until he could laugh quite freely at that, too.

"You seem to have a pretty wide experience, Felicity, of life—I mean, of understanding."

"Now what exactly do you mean?"

"Are you exhibiting—a provincial sore point?"

"Are you implying I am completely free of all morals?"

"The puritan background—still?"

She laughed. "I got your puritan background all right anyhow!"

"Faith you did, and characteristically sodden in whisky, too. But you were—very charming."

"Was I? How nice of you!" Her eyes brimmed with mischief. "Go on!" she said. "Look awkward a bit! Dear Will, I must really take you in hand. Otherwise some straight-faced female will land you as sure as eggs. And what a tragedy to have you solemnly roped in, dumb, and nowhere to go! It just doesn't bear thinking about. I would almost rather you ran off with me to Paris."

"Almost? Why not entirely?"

"Well?" She raised her eyebrows.

"Why not?"

Regarding him with the humour of assessment, she nodded. "But you're frightened to say you'll come. You'd have such a good time, too. Did I tell you I had a tiny flat of my own?"

"No. Very tiny?"

"Oh, not so tiny as all that. Only one bedroom, but I could always make up the couch in the sitting-room for—uh—a stranger from the land of my fathers. I mean, he would not require to be troubled in his mind."

"Felicity."

"Yes?"

"You're running on it!"

She shook the laughter from her mouth.

They finished the bottle of wine; had coffee and liqueurs. Time passed very rapidly.

"And where now?"

"That's the worst of this benighted city. There's nowhere to go. *Mon Dieu*, aren't we civilized!" declared Felicity. "Enough to make you shudder."

"I agree."

"So it's home. And I can't ask you in there either. I mean it would be no use. But, listen. There's a delightful sun-house in the grounds. I can get the key. We could slip in there quietly and talk away. Even got electric radiators and every reclining comfort. Very civilized."

"Really! I say!"

She looked into his eyes. He looked back into hers, and asked: "Find anything?"

"Not much. Still a faint stress, a subtle reluctance." She smiled slowly. "I know."

"You went through it?"

She nodded. "You're very clever. But you're very very young."

He smiled. "You could make anything very easy for anybody, I think, Felicity."

She nodded again. "Come, I must go home. You must stand me a taxi."

So they started off. She took his hand. "It's really lovely seeing you, Will. You are a darling boy."

He kissed her; but then she pushed him back gently —tilted her head sideways, looked at him, and laughed softly.

"Are we going right to the front door?" he asked, sitting up suddenly.

"Yes," she answered.

"But——"

"No." She shook her head slowly at his consternation. "Not to-night. I don't want you to-night. You see," she added, with a sad expression, lifting her palms, "I had forgotten to take the key of the summer-house."

His expression broke and he smiled at her adorable little piece of acting. "Felicity," he said, "you are very ver-y civilized."

"And you do not even ask, When?"

"You are too much for me."

"Saturday—hardly, alas! before Saturday." And she trailed her fingers across his face.

4

The experiences he had had of rising into freedom began to seem very remote to Will, indeed as if they had not happened in this life and were in the nature of a delusion or the carry-over of a dream memory. Nor did he make any effort to re-establish the attitude of mind conducive to further experiment. Such an effort would, in any case, be heavy and tedious and now beyond him. At moments, the thought of it was repugnant.

For it was not unpleasant to be completely root-less, with Felicity in the offing. Felicity had achieved complete rootlessness. Delightful state, with its delicate personal understandings and corresponding manners. Reminding him vaguely of Pater's effort "to discriminate every moment some passionate attitude in those about us. . . ." Something like that.

Mac looked sideways at him with a sarcastic grin as they came together on the stairs. "How's the farm?"

"Good lambing season—without snow, for a wonder," replied Will gravely; "and the spring ploughing is practically done."

Mac grunted his derision as they stepped downstairs, and at the door said: "You don't feel like having one, I suppose?"

"Well, as a matter of fact, I don't mind," Will answered lightly.

The deep enmity between them might never be resolved, but it had its attraction. Will realized he could make a myth about Mac, but about no other of his male friends—except, perhaps, about Joe. But then Joe had not so much the potency of myth as the individual appeal, the apartness, of religion. That sight of Mac going down the arches of the streets was in the very nature of myth. The city itself became a dark mythological city; a city of tall dark walls, a prison-city, wherein man wandered, seeking escape and yet not seeking escape, desiring it and yet afraid of it, appearing for a moment and then disappearing in the shadows of the dark walls, entrapped by the dark walls, trapped and for ever committed. Without even any conscious effort of the imagination, Will could see Mac striding down the arches of the poet's poem with the intolerance, sardonic and bitter, of the damned. Myth is a potent power when it deals with the gargantuan forces of frustration, generating in shadow and darkness.

"Our viewpoints are simply irreconcilable," said Will, when they had finished their snack and were starting to drink. "Granted our civilization is not much of a show, but civilization is a vague word."

"You think so? You think that the office, the sensational dope, the scare-mongering and war-mongering, the round-round-round day by bloody day, is all vague, in the air, a product of our imaginations?"

"No. It happens."

"Don't be rash—or the pretty dream you wrap around your precious self will bust." Some of the hairs on Mac's neck were turning grey. His face, with its ruddy skin, sandy eyebrows and ice-blue, rather small, penetrating eyes, was becoming fleshy, and, at the same time, more impatiently intolerant in its mass effect.

"We all probably wrap dreams about ourselves. And yours, after all, is the dream of frustration,"

replied Will. "Now the important thing in frustration——"

"I never used the word frustration. That's the worst
of fellows like you: you jump to conclusions, you
manufacture evidence to suit your own theories,
your own pretty little philosophies at two a penny;
in your case, sheer escapism."

"You can't head me off like that. Your description
of our lives, in sensational dope and so on, implied
the existence, if not of a better way of living, at least
of a standard of judgement that condemns the way
we do live. You must have that standard within yourself, otherwise there would be no point in your
spitting."

"And to the extent I cannot realize that standard—I
am frustrated?"

"Exactly."

Mac laughed. "God, you're an innocent!"

Will smiled. "Possibly. And very very young.
Haven't you noticed that the country is giving me
a lamb-like grace? However, it's logic with me or
nothing. So let us take it a step further. After all,
roughly, you and I work an eight-hour day. We get
paid to that point, where, if all was divided out in
pure socialism, we wouldn't get much more. Apart
from the fact that the work may not be work we'd
like ideally to be engaged upon, still, humanity will
always have to work, in a great measure uncon-
genially, producing what we, as animals, need.
There's no getting away from that general scheme.
Tell me, then, precisely, what is your grouse?"

"Who said I had a grouse?"

"Why, then, the criticism?"

"It wasn't criticism: it was description."

"True, but your description implied——"

"Jumping to conclusions again! My description described things as they are. It was realist."

"But, by implication, it condemned——"

"Implication be damned! Stick to reality. The office, the sensational dope, the war-mongering, the humanity that feed on the dope, all that is the reality; there it is, and you can't escape from it—unless, of course, you deliberately escape. But I'm based on the reality; I stick to it, even if I stick in its bloody mud. I refuse to blind myself, to hoodwink myself. And all your talk about implications and condemning is just theoretic fluff."

"Curious how you're haunted by this idea of escape. I carry on the same day's work as you do, but just because I change my lodgings, I escape. If I sat in the mud and drank whisky and guzzled and jeered at the whole fantastic show, I'd be a realist. Seems easy. Anyway, it's not much use to me."

"No, because you want to escape to save your soul. I happen to think that my soul, if I may use so august a word, is not worth saving; I think that the totality of souls is not worth saving. I consider that one cow will produce more manure in a night than all the souls of the world smashed to pulp would. Souls!" He ordered another round.

"Souls and escape and salvation—you can't leave the religious stuff alone! You'll be getting psychoanalysed next. However, if you like sitting in the mud, why not? But in heaven's name why delude yourself into believing you're doing something sensible—particularly when, in actual fact, you prefer to rest your backside on a dry chair, preferably upholstered?"

Mac laughed. "Now you're coming on! That's more like talk. Let us stick to our backsides and we can't go far wrong.'

"I'm agreeable," said Will. "But don't introduce terms like dope, escape, freedom, the soul, and so on, and then dodge facing up to them. I don't mind sinking with you into the deepest mud you can find, but I'm not going to hoodwink myself about what's happening."

"So you think I hoodwink myself?"

"More than that. You would like to take these words, like escape and freedom and the soul, and draw them down into the mud, too, and smother the dam' things."

"Are they, as poisonous illusions, fit for anything else?"

"I do not judge: I merely describe."

"Hmff!" The hairs in Mac's nostrils quivered in the gust of expelled air,

"Even your conception of the mud", said Will, "is singularly unfertile."

"Really! Singularly unfertile? You will now doubtless proceed to describe the miracles that emanate from the mud?"

"Yes." Will nodded, "Wheat, barley, oats, grass,

sheep, cows, trees (out of which orchestras are made), birds and all living things, Francis Thompson, Mary Queen of Scots, Shakespeare, Newton, aeroplanes, the universes, Helen of Troy, Beethoven, and Christ."

It was a long argument, direct enough in expression but intricate in design, full of doublings and twistings, but however Will appeared to give in here, to ignore there, he was conscious all the time of a clear purpose, of searching out the design of Mac's mind, until it be finally pinned down and spread out and encompassed.

And a queer remorseless necessity compelled him to this. Occasionally he could not look at Mac directly, could not look at him dodging the profounder issues, using evasive expressions, with a jerk of the head, a fleshy twist of the lips, using a harsh blasting intolerance when he foresaw himself about to be cornered. At moments Will's insight became almost intolerable to himself.

From the brooding half-nightmare of frustration to at least consideration of the conception of freedom, freedom for the individual in social relations; and freedom—let it be agreed—was a myth, an abstraction, a piece of damned rubbish—agreed, agreed—unless it was a path, a street, an alleyway leading to a plane, a state of mind, where integration of all the parts took place, where harmony was achieved. . . . Harmony? Good God! . . . Well, there was the harmony of music, the harmony of natural law, the harmony of revolving planets and swinging suns. . . .

Pinning down Mac in the pub, in the office, on Mars, on Venus, throughout space, through life and death and blasphemy, and generations, and light years, following him visibly, invisibly, remorselessly . . . until he nodded, silent at last, over the full design on the table.

"You see, you can't answer!" cried Mac harshly. "I have got you at last, you b——r!"

"You have," said Will. "I am rootless."

The barman shouted: "Time, gentlemen! Time! Time!"

"That", said Mac, "is what time means. Listen to it! By God, listen to it!"

"Time, gentleman! Time! Time!"

Mac laughed. The lights were flicked warningly off and on. "And that's what light means. All that light will ever mean to you and to me and to the rest of the crawling horde of humanity!" His voice was thick with the lust of triumph.

Mac's design would never now be altered. He was committed to destruction. He desired destruction. In the very thought of "the whole show" being sucked into destruction was a profound satisfaction, as bitter-sweet as a personal revenge. For that's what it was—a personal revenge against the pursuing God. He knew Mac's uneasiness whenever he encountered something that he could not pull within his design. His uneasiness over Will's independence of him, for example. And his secret desire to draw Will into his orbit, to dominate him, to make him submit to the mud.

265

"Please, gentlemen. The police. . . ."

"We know the police," said Mac. "Come on, Will. You're not going home. I know a place."

"I'm going home."

"Not you. Come on."

There was no particular hurry for a little while. But he was going home.

"Well, let's get some fresh air," he said. "Let's walk about for a bit. I've had too much blasted drink."

Mac laughed. "I'll make a real man of you yet!"

And as Will walked along, he had a second and extraordinarily clear apprehension that night, cool and clear as night air and sky above the chasm of the street.

Out of humanity in the reaches of time appear figures like Christ the saviour, Nero the destroyer. But they could never have appeared, or would have had no significance, no meaning, unless in his own little circle walked Joe the saviour and Mac the destroyer. In every little circle, in every village, town, country walked the individual saviour, the individual destroyer.

Helen of Troy . . . Felicity!

Perhaps not only in every circle but in every heart; and there finally and irreducibly.

He took his hat off and cooled his forehead.

"We've had enough of this. Come on!" cried Mac.

"I'm going home."

They walked on, disputing. They got mixed up in a crowd coming out of a theatre. And suddenly, quite close, the glaring entrance lights on their faces, Will saw Jenny.

It was a moment of such complete unexpectedness that he stared at her as at a figure he had known for an eternity and now met on this strange shore. There was the leap of the spirit in his eyes and the astonished cry of his silent white face, before she followed Philip to the kerbstone, having forgotten in that moment to do anything but stare back herself.

"Who is she?" asked Mac.

"She is Primavera," said Will, "the Lady Spring who comes with the flowers."

At this grave humour, Mac burst into rich laughter.

"It's this way," he said, guiding Will, for Mac generally knew of some obscure club up a side-street.

As they went on, Mac half a pace in front, Will suddenly had the feeling of following him, of being led. The last bus was going home without him. He glanced sideways at Mac's figure, assured of itself, lit up, committed to its kingdom. And all at once he saw Mac steering life into the darkest core of night with a pleasure that was voluptuous.

Neither of them spoke until Mac pulled up in a quiet cobbled street. "Here's our howff." He looked at Will. "Things encroach on you and eat you up like lice."

Involuntarily Will spat.

Mac swayed with laughter, then went up the three steps to the discreet door.

The following afternoon was Will's half day off and he made straight for the farm and a bath. He luxuriated in the bath, gargled his throat with disinfectant, and washed his head. Then he came downstairs, picked up the deck-chair that Mrs. Armstrong had hunted out, and went round into the lee of the house, gripping the book that had so long been left unread. He had no sooner stretched himself out than Mrs. Armstrong appeared with a heavy check plaid and cushion.

"Up!" she said, and then she spread the plaid over the canvas and fixed the cushion. "There's a treacherous damp in the ground," she explained, "and it rises up." Her bustling motherly manner was very friendly and he thanked her gratefully. "Now!" she said. "You can put the plaid up over your legs if you feel cold, though it's sheltered here, isn't it?"

"I think the sun is divine."

"That's because you need it," she said, with a minatory nod. He laughed as she withdrew. She was a grand woman!

And oh! the sun was divine. As he sank down into the chair it sank into him. He felt it pressing on his skin, passing in through the pores, through the flesh to the bone and the marrow in the bone, through his lungs and his kidneys, through all the patient internal organs he so badly abused, through the mind. And his mind needed it most of all! . . . What a night! Known colloquially to members as the Blue Club.

Supposedly the place where bawdy stories and vile language could be worked out of the system. Worked out? Worked in, they meant. He would have to be split open and sluiced with sunlight out of a hose, before the stuff could be "worked out". He smiled, closing his eyes, and felt the sun on his eyelids.

Lovely divine sun. Dear God, how lovely! His heart was filled with a gratitude light as laughter, filled with tender worship; filled with a slow abandon as if his body were sinking into an unimagined paradise. He felt sleep coming upon him with a noiseless surge as of waves on a remote shore; faintly, infinitely distant. . . .

He awoke in the cool sunny air, his eyes casting quickly about him.

"I'm so sorry. I didn't know you were asleep." Mrs. Armstrong came back with the tea tray, for she had started quietly retreating.

"I must have been asleep," he said thoughtfully. He looked at his watch. "Not for over two hours?"

She smiled at his amazement. "Well, you haven't moved for over two hours anyway!"

"Really!" He got up, still with wonder upon him. Then he looked at her. "That's been the most wonderful sleep I have had in all my life."

"Just because you needed it! Now a cup of tea will freshen you up."

"You are kind to me. I don't deserve it."

"Perhaps that's why you're getting it," she said, making her joke, but flushing a little with pleasure.

He finished his tea and saw the last of the cigarette smoke float away on the air.

This was life, and there was this always behind everything, this sun and air, this warmth, this light. It was no vision. It was simple reality. It was where the deeper self rose up and took the air. Not an escape from reality. On the contrary, an escape from the sensational, the phenomenal, the changing irritating surface, back to calm certainty, to this surprising fact that here, at last, is myself. Here is Will Montgomery, this simple living animal with the sun on its skin, and with the cunning sunny mind inside, this is his native place, whence he sallies forth to Mac's mud and Joe's faith. . . .

How far away had he got from his solemn reading? What could it mean to him now? Particularly that bit about—where was it? Yes, here; in the "Conclusion" to *The Use of Poetry and the Use of Criticism* by T. S. Eliot. He became excited as he read it: "I know, for instance, that some forms of ill-health, debility, or anaemia, may (if other circumstances are favourable) produce an efflux of poetry in a way approaching the condition of automatic writing. . . . To me it seems at these moments, which are characterized by the sudden lifting of the burden of anxiety and fear which presses upon our daily life so steadily that we are unaware of it, what happens is something *negative*: that is to say, not 'inspiration' as we commonly think of it, but the breaking down of strong habitual barriers—which tend to reform very quickly."

270

There followed a reference to a footnote "in confirmation of my own experience". The footnote was a quotation from the poet Housman's *Name and Nature of Poetry* and Will consumed it eagerly: "In short I think that the production of poetry, in its first stage, is less an active than a passive and involuntary process; and if I were obliged, not to define poetry, but to name the class of things to which it belongs, I should call it a secretion; whether a natural secretion, like turpentine in the fir, or a morbid secretion, like the pearl in the oyster. I think that my own case, though I may not deal so cleverly with the matter as the oyster, is the latter; because I have seldom written poetry unless I was rather out of health, and the experience, though pleasurable, was generally agitating and exhausting."

And Mr. Eliot's comment: "I take added satisfaction in the fact that I only read Mr. Housman's essay some time after my own lines were written."

So manifestly—for the scholarship of these men was enough—the implications behind their fascinating confessions had not been worked out by any one, much less co-ordinated. *There* was a subject for a fellow who had vaguely hoped to write a book called *Definitions*!

Will smiled, and when Mr. Eliot went on to find his experience "a very different thing from mystical illumination" he immediately doubted that "very different". What did he mean by "mystical illumination" anyhow? When was illumination in the mind "mystical"? When one thought of God or something high and mighty? But nonsense, because the final feat of the mystic was to realize his deeper self, to apprehend it calmly in a condition of light. It was this light or illumination that mattered. Into this light might come an apprehension of the nature of God, but also, and equally, an apprehension of the nature of the world or of the strange crawling movement of a man's bowels. Unless they were seen in the same quality of vision, in the same tempo of apprehension, they were not seen or illuminated at all.

And in any case, the very essence of the mystical movement, that uprising of the deeper self into freedom, was characterized precisely by "the sudden lifting of the burden of anxiety and fear. . . ." The envelope opened out and he was freed. Yes, yes, he saw Eliot's point in a way. To call this experience *negative* was no doubt understandable enough in the context, with its implications, under illness, of bodily passivity and automatic acceptance; but surely to goodness than the "breaking down of habitual barriers" there could hardly in fact be anything more *positive*? Clearly Housman's "the experience, though pleasurable, was generally agitating and exhausting" was a better recorded memory of the reality, a more graphic description. The experience itself was pleasurable despite the illness, and the agitation and exhaustion that followed on the effort to record the essence of the experience (the poetry) were natural.

Will had had typhoid fever in his 'teens, and he knew that this curious experience in illness, noted by these two poets, was common enough (if not, of course, its recording in "automatic writing"!). It generally happened when the illness had burnt out the clotted physical pains that thickened the head or sickened the vitals, and the body, thus purged by its fevers, entered upon convalescence. Often a most delightful time, cool and pleasant and full of long thoughts. The note of a bird beyond the window went over the gardens, and over the fields, and over the mountains. "Far away" had something added to it as a flower has scent and memories. Quite naturally you could listen to silence, not merely to the different kinds of silence in the sick-room, in the house, and outside the house, but to other remoter silences that these led to. Your mind could have the most intimate times with itself. It could hear the voice of a child, or the voice of a saint. And when a vision, particularly a dramatized vision with, of course, oneself as principal actor, became a trifle too intense, then the head fell back, a cold dew on the forehead, and one let the vision drown in a complete passivity.

All that was commonplace; and Will's first impious thought was that Housman, waiting to get ill before he could write poetry, was like the Chinaman burning down a house to get roast pig. The illness burnt down "the habitual barriers". But why wait for illness? Presumably because the barriers were too much for him in health. Will smiled. Acquiring an illness seemed an expensive way of writing a poem! Not only that, but manifestly illness reduced vitality, and poetry-making is a creative act, and every such act needs concentration and pith (whence the "agitating and exhausting"). Illness might well reduce the vitality to so low a pitch that the remembered sensation was *negative*!

Eliot said that the poetry he wrote at such times could not be distinguished by others from the poetry he wrote in health. (Roast pig being roast pig however contrived?) But—for a chance shot!—how perilous then the use of the word *negative* by him, because a critic with a penchant for school logic might be tempted to apply it in a description of all his poetry. Which was absurd; ergo his *negative* was inexact, italics an' all!

What did seem to emerge was this: if it were possible to break down the barriers in a state of health, then with the maximum vitality available for creation, the negative should fade in the glow of the positive and the whole conception and performance be "enlarged in a wonderful manner".

Was Shakespeare able to break down the barriers almost at will? What the normal man so graphically calls the "flatness" of life—could Shakespeare, at will, see it with a stereoscopic eye? Had he developed the technique for this? (leaving alone for the moment the question of a descriptive "gift").

Develop a "technique of sincerity", said Richards.

Why not?

Why not develop a technique for any experience that had already proved real and that depended for its repetition solely on the individual mind? If thorn-trees and a bird sufficed for stage properties to-night, then almost anything in nature should suffice for to-morrow—or, anyway, for next time.

The trouble would be in overcoming the terrific inertia that Will now saw was so powerful in life. We would almost do anything rather than do that. Write poetry, even! Or go in for the most difficult analysis! Because so often—nearly always—in both occupations we are writing or working *on* something, executing a task, not *breaking through*.

Which began to cast a new light on *Man's loneliness* (*the isolation of the human situation*). Literally to cast *light* on what was sombre or sunless there!

From this simple point, his thought went on to quite intricate argument, which, like Mr. Eliot's "automatic writing", seemed to produce itself. And the ease in this intricate thought, its subtlety and power, the way in which, so to speak, he kept up with it, gave him a pure delight, somewhat like the delight a man must get moving amid the higher mathematics. There was in it, too, something of the physical sensation of flight. And though he had to think in words and sentences—there being no other way—yet his mind did not have to complete its sentences, or, rather, it used sentences, a turn of thought, as he himself used grammalogues in short-hand. The very swiftness of the movement, as in skating, permitted the making of intricate figures or arabesques with certainty and poise. You must have speed before you can loop the loop!

Until he suddenly thought: What about getting some of this down on paper? When at once he breathed heavily and lay back, for the experience had been "agitating and exhausting"! He wasn't just in the pink of condition. But that would come!

He got up, and strolled slowly into Jenny's garden, and at once experienced the feeling of her being both present and absent. Even more so than if he had come on her clothes in a room. Sly devil that he was! for he had found out a few hours ago from Mrs. Armstrong, very inadvertently of course, that she was expecting Jenny as usual on Saturday. And this was Thursday. Quite clearly from Mrs. Armstrong's tone, Jenny would have told her before this had she not been coming, had she been going away for the week-end.

Whence all the mystical illuminations!

He laughed softly at himself and eyed the bishop-weed. If Jenny did not come after all, that should prove a fair test of the illumination? You watch your eyes! he said to the bishopweed, and, taking the four-pronged fork from its small dilapidated shelter, he started to dig the weed up. He could always arrange with Mrs. Armstrong to let it be understood that one of the farm hands had had a free hour or two!

Working slowly, he became absorbed in the job, and when his back ached too much, he would squat down on his heels, following the endless white roots with his bare hands through the loosened earth. He liked the resistance of the earth, the choked feeling in his nails. His hands burrowed like moles.

Jenny came into his mind. Then suddenly he had a strong feeling that she was in the garden, so strong that he could not turn round. He fumbled after a white root, pulled it out, straightened up, and slowly faced about with the wary "innocent" action of one who did not want to precipitate a blow. And Jenny was there.

He felt the blood rush to his face and stood awkward and helpless, trying to smile. After one swift glance at his face, she looked at what he had been doing. She seemed not at all awkward, except for a calmly suppressed annoyance or anger.

"Fine evening," he suggested.

"Yes," she answered shortly, glancing around at her various blossoms and clumps.

He looked down at his heap of white weed. Dammit, he wasn't stealing her garden from her!

"Sorry," he said drily, his face going pale. "I'm not trying to help you. I'm working for Mrs. Armstrong, who can't meantime put one of her men on the job." He couldn't stick the fork in the earth and walk away. That would be too dramatic. So he turned his back to her and started working again unhurriedly.

After a little, half-turning to throw weeds on his clump, he saw her wandering down the garden, looking at her possessions, one by one, as if she had come to say good-bye to them. A slow sinking sensation beset him, following an instantaneous intuitive conviction that she *was* saying good-bye to them. Not good-bye for ever, but good-bye to a life, a relationship, with them, now about to be broken. It would be a different Jenny who would come back after the week-end was over. For the moment he had no feeling that he was being absurdly romantic, even fantastic. On the contrary, the sweetness, the wholeness, of her secret virginal girl's life broke over him with a fragrance that drained the life out of him. He half-turned in his work so that he could dimly see her. At the bottom of the garden, by the gate, she stood quite still. Her face, out of focus, was blurred and pale. She stood so long that he could hardly bear it, but he kept on working stolidly. She could not go! She came back and started working with her bare hands in the earth.

In a little while Mrs. Armstrong's voice called them to supper. "Coming!" Jenny answered, in a clear assured voice. He waited until she had gone, then went slowly down.

Mrs. Armstrong would have rallied him about his work in the garden if Jenny had mentioned it. Obviously Jenny hadn't. "Jenny turned up all of a sudden. She's full of excitement."

"I thought I noticed her."

"Yes. Came back for her heavy country shoes. Apparently we're not going to see her this week-end."

"Oh. Going away?" asked Will negligently.

"Yes. Some of them are going hill-climbing. The break, I told her, would do her no harm. Though I must say I'll miss her. She's such good company."

For one moment Will was tempted to ask if his presence here annoyed Jenny, and, if so. . . . But he suppressed the temptation. For suddenly he realized that he would leave this place, and it would be mean to put the blame on Jenny.

After supper, he tried to go on with his reading, but dropped the book with a dry smile. The glory had departed from it and the illumination! He went walking up the avenue of trees, where, in the dusk, the birds were singing. He felt quite drained of any feeling, almost pleasantly lifeless. Well, that was that! There was no more to it! His face was pale, his eyes bright and inclined to stare. He would be sorry leaving this place. He had grown genuinely fond of Mrs. Armstrong. There was a deep generous woman-warmth in her.

The interesting thing about women was that they had no morals at all; did not, at least, subscribe to any ethical code. They had their own sort of morals, of course, based on their instinct, and they would break any code to satisfy such instinct. Which was profoundly right. When code and instinct coincided they were, of course, superb moralists! Uhm.

Jenny was right. He was glad she had the courage— to be right.

Felicity, now—the trouble with Felicity was that she had half sterilized the root of her instinct. She did not know this or admit it to herself, but she felt uneasy. That time when he had brought it to a point and called her excitement in the crisis the sensationalism of sex, it had suddenly pierced her like a knife. She had very cleverly turned it off by saying that she had been upset by finding him cleverer than herself. But her woman's instinct had been hit. And for a woman to lose the potency of her instinct is her first and last sin to herself, whether she can admit it or not.

All this was clear to Will and seemed to be produced in his mind without any effort, without any stress, in that inner light of the mind that was rather like the gloaming about him.

And he saw Felicity, as he had seen her already, her head poised above her blue dressing-gown, a flame over the barricade, a flower springing out of the sensationalism of sex. A vivid bright flower. *All* flower.

Whisky had something to do with his behaviour, yes. Puritanism, no doubt. Lack of use and wont, possibly. But—there should be more than the sensationalism of sex, that lovely and exciting fun; there should also be the fulfilment and peace of sex, deep and silent as the gloaming, with the singing of birds that you hardly hear.

Had it been Jenny?

Had it been Jenny—he would have crawled to Jenny.

His head drooped, he stood still, and even thinking ceased in him. When he lifted his head, he saw Jenny coming up the road towards him, a brown-paper parcel under her arm, her shoes. He wondered what he would do and remembered he had seen some nests being built in the hedge on his right. He studied the hedge, and, while Jenny was yet a few yards from him, he calmly, unostentatiously, turned and stepped over the ditch and began separating small branches. He thought he heard her footsteps pause, but he did not look round until he was sure she was gone.

When he faced the road, he hung on to a branch. The sederunt in the Blue Club had taken the guts out of him all right! He blew a slow deep breath, and, feeling very exhausted, sat down and lay back and closed his eyes.

6

The following afternoon, Friday, he had promised to ring up Felicity. This worried him while he was working in the office but only vaguely. It had been her final instruction. He had said he had a meeting to go to, but had agreed that he would ring up anyway and, if they could not meet, they could at least arrange for the Saturday. I can ring her up later, or even to-morrow morning, he thought. At the moment he did not feel in the mood, but later on he might want to see her, might want to see her quite urgently.

The dull drained mood was still upon him. It was not unpleasant, and pervaded him with an almost extreme feeling of tolerance or good nature. He did not want to break it. Let it carry him along. He could always make an excuse. Could say—let him see—that he had been trying to get a fellow who would let him off going to the meeting, and did not want to ring her up until he had got him. Something like that. But it worried him slightly, for not to meet an obligation was against his nature.

He hung behind talking to Don until Mac had gone. Then they went out and had a couple of drinks.

"And how are things in Europe?"

"Pretty bad," said Don. "It seems to be coming all right. And I'm beginning to doubt if the only thing I was vaguely banking on can stop it."

"What was that?"

"The fact that the peoples themselves don't want war, and that they know that all of them don't want war."

"They don't want war. Do they want peace?"

Don looked at him. "What do you mean?"

"The women are beginning to have fashions in gas perambulators. Quite a lark getting fitted on with that pig's-snout of a gasmask. Of course it has got to be done. Quite."

"I don't get you."

"There's nothing much to get," said Will, "except perhaps the simple point that there's no peace in our hearts. *Au fond*, it's a spiritual affair."

"Good God! You're not joining the crowd who say that we must have a change of heart!"

Will couldn't help laughing. "Hadn't thought of it," he admitted, "and shouldn't join anything anyway. All the same, the heart is basic. At least, the spirit or the soul. However, it's a dull topic."

"You mean humanity is not interested in it?"

"You have the subtle Highland mind!"

"The point is obvious, I agree. But you have to take humanity as you find it, and, that being so——"

"It's a poor show for Kirkcaldy? So it would seem."

"I disagree. Humanity does want peace."

"Of course. It's merely forgotten what it is and therefore how to get it. Though the use of that 'it', of 'humanity', is pretty bad. Vague. Instead of saying you and me, we say humanity. We're getting diseased with that spewing of our individual responsibilities and emotions upon some vague collective-mass. Same everywhere and in everything. For the most thrilling allurements of sex you go to the pictures, not to bed."

Don laughed. "You for a socialist!"

"I'm a socialist all right, and a nationalist."

"But not a bigoted one?"

"Sea-green and incorruptible to the end. But I cannot close my eyes to what's happening, even on the pictures."

"There is something in what you said there about sex." Don smiled, in a half personal way, looking at his glass. "It's all the trimmings that matter. I mean in all this hectic jazz-dancing business and so on. After all that glittering swimmy-oozy stuff, the actual act itself is an anticlimax. Rather nasty. Disillusionment of the sweet young thing. Ugh!"

Will laughed. "Have a cigarette."

They discussed sex and peace and similar public affairs for a time, then Don had to go.

Will went round to a pub-restaurant and ordered a steak. "Thick and underdone," he said, "with chips."

As eight o'clock drew near, he found he did not want to go to the meeting, did not want to talk to Joe or the rest of them. He decided, quite calmly, that he would not go. So he went out and began walking through the streets of the city.

The feed had given him ballast, and he walked with ease, looking at things and people with the detached eyes of an outcast or stranger. He felt the city about him, apprehended it again in that odd mythological way, which the newly lit lamps and coloured street signs made half gay and half terrifying—the giant story with the inner beat of panic. Felicity came into his mind and he smiled. "Sorry, Felicity," he said, "but that's the way it is!" Then he thought of her more particularly and knew that it would be all right to-morrow night; it would be gay and splendid. For Felicity was civilized. And it was all very nice and large talking about sensationalism, but, after all, Felicity had been pierced that time. The root was still there! And oh she would know how to do it! The delicacy of her art! Dear Felicity!

He was walking towards the river now. He knew he had been heading for the river all the time. He wanted to get lost for a while, to lose his personal identity, or, at least, all personal urgency, in the human forest, in the jungle, in the swamps, where all sorts of odd creatures prowled, tarts and touts and bookies' runners and cut-throats and gangsters and razor-slashers, where the unemployed were as grey wilting trees but where the main forest itself was yet green, dark green, sombre. Night-fires in the darkness, pubs, warmth . . . and the river, the river, quietly flowing past, flowing on.

If there was any one anywhere he would like to

meet this night it was Ivy. The thought of her was comforting. It would be no effort speaking to Ivy. His hand went up to his breast pocket and felt the bulk of his pocket-book. She would enjoy a generous hand. No haggling over half a dollar. A change for her! They could buy some grub—fruit, say, bright oranges, lashings of fruit—and some gin—and some whisky! Then he could lie back in that room and talk to her and see where her instinct had gone, and his own. They would discuss her professional life. She would see that there was no condescension, no prying, on his part. Only a deep fellow interest. And she was not a sentimentalist. She would not use the fake sentimental self-pity stuff. A tough root in Ivy. Strange how the prostitute had been sentimentalized in the world's literature. Some deep reason for that. Because mostly, of course, they were blowzy and weak and self-indulgent and vicious. How the strong clear-headed decent women despised them, not so much for trading their sex, as for being flabby vicious weaklings. Nice girl, Ivy! he thought, with a smile, and hoped for her company.

Penetrating the worst slum-tenement part he knew, he was suddenly taken by a desire to go in through a dark narrow close, to stand in the inner narrow court and stare up. This he did. The midden smouldered. The acrid smell of garbage dried his nostrils. His whole body became extremely sensitive to attack. He was also shamed a little by the feeling that he was prying, and this shame seeped deeply into him with an occult sense of personal guilt. Then he became

285

aware of the thin figure of a young man coming towards him, not directly, but cautiously, sideways. He turned at once and left, certain that the figure was following him.

He went into a pub two streets away, for he did not care to stand in a door to see if he were being followed. In any case, he wanted no trouble; he wanted to forget himself. He was not the fighting kind. But he stood sideways at the counter and saw a youth come in, slim, pale-faced, with the snout of his cap a little over his left temple. "Eight," said the barman. Will's total change was fivepence, so he took out his pocket-book and tendered a pound note.

When he had put the change away, he lifted his glass, drank half of it, and as he was taking out a cigarette, glanced around. "A glass of bitter," said the youth. He did not look at Will. There were quite a few in the pub, and when Will had smoked his cigarette and finished his drink, he turned and went out. The youth was talking to another of his own kind in a corner. They did not look at Will, who felt he had been a trifle over-sensitive.

All the same, he would go into another pub, for it was an odd sensation, this of being stalked. There was the recent case he had sub-edited of the fellow about his own age who had murdered the little girl he had lured from a close. And, anyway, he needed a drink or two to make him comfortably sober before he tried to get hold of Ivy. He got talking to a boilermaker, who had been on the dole for a month, and now was celebrating because he was starting on Monday. A decent kindly fellow, "hellish glad" over the new job. Will liked him and stood him a drink, and then the boilermaker insisted on standing Will one.

Will was moved by the quiet human pith of the man. He had found recently—another inheritance from the wild geese!—that he could be moved too easily by evidence of the fundamental or primordial human goodness in man. It affected him like a cry. It moved him to tenderness, urged him to a swift lavish generosity. He controlled the emotion, but he loved it, too, for show, or ostentation, was not of its nature. He forgot all about the two youths whom he had left drinking their bitter; and, in fact, they did not come in.

Presently he found himself by the river, moving past the spot where Ivy had first spoken to him. She was not there, and he realized it had been a bit foolish of him to expect that she would be.

There were no stars in the sky. There seemed indeed to be no sky, only a uniform lowering darkness. The river affected him in a sombre way, for he suddenly saw the glitter of its water through an iron railing about the size of the spiked railing in the tenement stairs. It provided the obvious parallel of life flowing inevitably, until it reached its sea, which is nirvana or death. Slowly, soundlessly, impure, confined within its prison walls, made to twist here, to deepen there, hammered at by myriads of human hands, overcoming the obstacles of mighty ships by floating them, crossed by bridges, traversed by ferries, dredged and banked and piled, this river, that was the destiny of generations of men, persisted in flowing slowly, dourly, invincibly, until it felt the first slow pulse of the sea.

The pulse of the sea; for the sea itself, what was it but a new kind of river, an endless river, taking its pulse from the sun and moon; the sun and moon that flowed themselves in a mighty river. . . .

Hardly worth man's while to bother with his bootless little savageries. The cry of his savageries would hardly carry as far as the ping of a gnat. But his understanding carried a long way, and was borne on the great rivers. . . .

Ettie came into his mind. And then Jamie, and he wondered about him. Would he still show that insensate hatred towards him? Strange bitter hurt you could do a man by recoiling instinctively from him. You cut deep at the root of his instinctive being, and that is a wound not readily forgotten or forgiven.

A small shiver of apprehension made him turn round. At a few yards a woman was approaching. Behind her were two young men, and overtaking them, with a hurried limp, an old ragged man. Some distance beyond, a group of people were interested or arguing about something. Beyond them, the lights were bright over the roar of a main thoroughfare.

The woman came straight towards him, stopping and enticing him in a wheedling voice. At once he side-stepped, saying: "Sorry." But she wasn't letting him pass so easily: "Ah, duckie, you darlin', come now! What's all your hurry?" His voice hardened:

"No, nothing doing." But she had him by the lapel of his coat, and spoke on in her beseeching wheedling voice. The old man hurried by. The youths stopped. "That's enough!" said Will firmly, grasping her hand to remove it. In a shrill, choked voice, she cried: "Don't! Don't!" as if she were being hurt.

"What's the game, mate?" asked one of the youths.

Will looked at him. The snout of his cap came down over his left eye. The youth who had followed him from the close! At once he saw the whole thing was a "plant". But instead of warily meeting the situation, he got angry; body and brain were caught in a flame of anger.

"What's *your* game?" he rapped out.

"Oh-ho! So that's the way is it? Caught you red-handed."

"You damned tout!" Will took a step forward and was immediately tripped up from behind by the other youth, whom he had forgotten, and fell full length. But it was only four years since he had played his last rugby game, and before he had quite hit the ground his body was gathering and preparing to roll free. He rolled over so swiftly that the boot that was launched at his stomach did no more than graze his ribs. He had picked himself up and was almost upright before the second blow got him, but already he had been staggering away from it, and he kept his feet.

Now he had them! By God, he had them now! With his left, he caught the second youth smash in the face, as he came in. To Will, school boxing had always been an exciting game, and though he lacked

289

weight, the explosive force, he had been agile, had shown a nimble swaying pliancy that was extremely tough and could be backed to do its best in the last round—if it got that length. But it had always been a game (he had refused to go in for championships), a keen singing laughing game of the flesh.

He saw something gleam in the first youth's hand. At sight of the steel, the girl cried out genuinely: "Help! Help!" Will retreated as the youth came for him. The second youth, on his feet, was coming in on his left side. Will pretended not to see him, but whirled round and ducked at the final moment, swinging his right to the pit of the stomach. The youth doubled up and sat down with an astonished grunt. Then Will bolted, the fellow with the razor on his heels. At fifteen yards, when they were stretching towards top speed, Will flopped, and the youth shot clean over him. Instantly Will picked himself up, and dived, grabbing at the right arm and twisting it round, his knee between the shoulders. The razor was not in the hand. He wanted the razor. But now others were closing in. He had to watch himself. The girl came forward crying. He was being surrounded. He got up, with half an eye on the lad on the ground.

"What's this?"

Will looked up swiftly. It was Jamie.

"He tried to do me dirty!" whined the girl.

The youth got up. "The—bastard," he said, "trying to get something from her for nothing."

Jamie's face was white and the eyes small, black, and shut in by the gathered eyebrows. He came slowly forward, his mouth puckering tensely. "You bloody swine!" he said. Will saw the hand coming, but it raised no physical response, and the smash of the blow on his face was heard beyond the ring of on-lookers. Will staggered, dropped his head, and stood still.

There was a commotion; a girl was pushing herself through, crying shrilly. But no one paid attention to her, for now they were jeering at Will's cowardice.

Jamie was waiting for him with his one hand. And when Will stood, beaten, he said: "Even a rat has some guts. Keep to your own end of the town, you filthy swine!"

But the girl had won through. "You shut up!" she cried to Jamie. "You bloody well shut your mouth!"

"Here—here—what's the row?" asked the fellow she had been with, his burly body barging in.

She swung round on him. "You shut up, too, Jake," she cried. "This is a dirty plant! I know this chap. It's a dirty plant!"

"Oh, you know him?" said Jake, taking Will's measure. "Hmff! Gode!" His tone implied that there wasn't much to know, but then Jake had been a human punch ball in a boxing camp in his day, had punched and been punched by names in the sporting news, and, though he was forty, the scars on his flattened face still made his companions think twice.

"Yes!" cried Ivy. "I know him! And he's a damned sight decenter than you or the whole pack of you put together. And that's flat!"

"Is he, begod?" said Jake, advancing upon her. "Is

291

he—you black bitch!" He drew up his open hand as if to slap her. The action released Will and before the hand could fall, he stepped forward, caught Jake's uplifted wrist, twisted it swiftly backward over the elbow, and, before any one quite knew how it had happened, Jake was on his back.

A gasp went up from the crowd, of astonishment, of fear, of wild expectation.

"Get out!" said Ivy to Will. "Run!" He smiled to her. "For God's sake," she cried, "clear out!" In her desperate anxiety, she pushed at him. Jake's hand caught her by the shoulder and whirled her aside. Will landed with all his might between Jake's eyes. Jake staggered back a step, shook his head, and, lowering his forehead, regarded Will with the killer's look.

Instinctively the crowd pushed back out of harm's way and formed a fair-sized ring.

Will was now feeling intensely happy. His blood was singing in him. Three rounds, he knew, would drain away the last ounce of his strength; but for about that time he could go all out. His body and toes had never felt so light. He had never fought with bare fists before, and the jar on his knuckles when he had hit Jake had jangled with joyous pain. For the best of it was, he did not mind what happened. He had no fear of the burly battering-ram of a figure. As he danced around at first, the crowd jeered, and cried to Jake, who was following him like a wary bulldog, head between shoulders, to chassis. But when Jake did step aside and forward and Will, after a duck and a sidestep, lashed in a swift one and danced back, the mob's stupid jeering ceased. Jake's main trouble was too much beer. Even in that poor light, and though he could not read Jake's eyes, Will could see the intention to let out gather in Jake's shoulders like a public announcement. So long as he kept Jake from cornering him, Jake should not hit him. And he must not let Jake rush him to a clinch. Once or twice Will's escape was narrow enough, for the crowd was wildly in Jake's favour, and he had distinctly felt a boot trying to trip him as he dodged back. If they got him down, he was done for. And—gee!—if that one had got him it would have killed him! The missed blow swung Jake almost off his feet, and Will took the opportunity of clipping the right ear with all his pith. Will was scoring steadily, but not damaging Jake so much as his load of beer was doing. Then Jake landed one by a clever feint that was quite a brilliant touch of the old ring days. It sent Will staggering back against the human ropes. A yell went up as Jake went in for the kill, but there was Will dancing away again, spitting blood from his gums, and smiling. If Jake managed the same punch again but with a little more shoulder behind it, Will knew he would be out for the count.

And Jake very nearly did, lashing out with both hands and exposing his face to Will's longer reach in an effort to get near enough to feint, draw Will's counter, and smash. But Will saw the whole thing coming and just saved himself. He knew now that with his bare hands he could never hurt Jake's face—

however he might hurt his own knuckles! Jake was panting and the only hope was a body blow to knock the last of the wind out of him. Will was manoeuvring for this when Jake hit him over the heart. He staggered away, for the instant not seeing Jake very well; something soft came swishing about his feet and tripped him and he fell. At the same moment there was a sharp cry of: "The peelers! The peelers!" and feet came surging against his body. Will doubled up, shielding face and vital parts in the scrimmage. The feet kicked him in the back severely and in the groin. Hands came thrusting at his breast-pocket. He bit them. There was a terrific smash on his chest, followed by a kick in the head that sent a thin tongue of flame across a world that vanished in darkness.

CHAPTER EIGHT

*

Will lay in a bed near the end of a long ward in the City infirmary. His bed was against the inner wall, and whenever his eyes opened they gazed at a square of sky, sometimes grey, sometimes blue. He lay on his back so that it was no effort to look at the sky, framed by the top part of the tall window. Its colour seemed to have something to do with his mood. When he was weary and sleepy, it was grey, but when he felt a bit brighter it was blue, and then the stiff dull aches of his body were not so tiresome. At first it was more comforting to be weary and sleepy; but by degrees the blue became less bright, more tender, and he could gaze at it for long periods, forgetting his weariness, forgetting even to blink his eyes.

He was glad when the doctor moved on or the nurse was finished with him, for then he could lie back and, after the turmoil of the visitation had subsided, could open his eyes and gaze at the sky with an added ease. He had not even to think of it as sky;

in fact, he did not think of it at all: it was colour and light, far away and high up. Sometimes he so lost himself in this piece of sky that he became the piece of sky himself. It would come down to him, daze him slightly by its near presence, then take him away back with it through the air. He never saw anything on those trips; never wanted to see anything; he just became one with the piece of sky. Now and then it was a lovely airy feeling, and he fell asleep with a smile on his face, like a child in a cradle.

His nurse did not like this habit of childlike gazing. She was a well set-up, buxom girl from the Lews, with plenty of energy, but with dark soft eyes. Her voice, too, was soft and pleasant, even when she made it cheerfully peremptory. But he did not want to bother with her very much, and was always glad to be left alone. Often he pretended not to be aware of her presence, particularly if the sister was with her; and one day he heard her say: "I don't like the way he lies there gazing for hours at the sky."

"Why?" asked Sister coolly.

"I don't know," said Nurse, with discomfort in her voice.

"Have you a superstition that he is to be taken away?" asked Sister, with light but penetrating irony.

"Oh no," said Nurse, obviously sorry now she had spoken.

"Forget it then," said Sister.

For the first time, a faint humour spread through Will, and that evening, as Nurse was going off, he beckoned to her.

"Do you think", he asked in a solemn, if weak, whisper, "that I am to be taken away?"

Her eyes opened wide in dismay. "Oh no! What nonsense! You——" Then she looked at him more closely. "Are you trying to have me on?"

He wrinkled his brows as in vague lack of understanding, but could not keep the humour from welling in his eyes.

"You are!" she said. "You overheard me talking to Sister?"

He smiled at her, and a blush went right over her face. She nodded with business-like decision. "My lad," she murmured, putting the sheets unnecessarily straight, "you watch if I won't sort you for this!" But her decisive tone did not seem at all vindictive.

"You have a soft way with you, Nurse."

"Soft, did you say? I'll soft you before you leave here."

"And——"

"Yes?"

"You are rather charming."

She regarded him sternly. "None of your impertinence, young man, or I'll report you to Sister."

"That's one thing you won't do anyway," said Will, and closed his eyes. He opened them as she moved off and gave her the ghost of a wink. She looked very indignant.

The effect of this humour, the surprise of it, came back into his mind now and then. It was an odd new experience, like something softer to lie on, and his back was often painful enough. He did not care so much for the night nurse. She was too practical, too competent, and had no soft colour or light about her. During the night, however, when the sky was shut out, his eyes would roam occasionally over the other beds in the long ward.

His early reluctance to know anything about those beds, or the people in them, or what went on around him, was partly a desire to be left alone, to be left alone, for example, with the sky. This reluctance began to be pierced, not so much with human curiosity, as with the strange night pattern the ward made, the passage between the double row of beds up which the white-clad figure came, the dim light; everywhere whiteness and straight lines. It had provided him with an austere satisfaction, unearthly as his mood, but sometimes now when a voice moaned in its sleep or in pain, the mood was touched with an unearthly sadness.

Then one day Sister came up the ward with a tall broad man, and said to Will brightly: "I have brought a friend to see you."

Will looked at the man and murmured: "Nice of you." He did not want to be intruded upon by strangers.

"He says he has met you once or twice, but probably you have forgotten him," Sister explained, watching Will.

The man was looking at him with a friendly steady smile. "We met at political meetings. My name is Joe, Joe Wilson."

Will's brows troubled for a moment. "I seem to know your face," he said politely.

"The Labour Rooms committee meeting," Joe explained. "And once down by the river. I had to see a fellow called Jamie, who had lost an arm in an accident." He spoke slowly. "You may not remember the circumstances. Jamie came for me the night you had your accident and told me all about it, so I thought I'd come along and see how you were getting on."

"Thank you," said Will. "I am getting along very well. They are quite good to me here." He acknowledged Sister with a vague smile.

"He's quite a good patient," she said to Joe pleasantly. "But he doesn't seem to remember anything about the accident. It must have come upon him very suddenly, for it's a complete blank. No wonder, in a way, because he got a bad smashing."

"Did he?" said Joe. "Was there much damage?"

"You would think a herd of cattle had gone over him. But only two ribs broken. Wasn't he lucky?"

"He was indeed." Joe smiled to Will. "You don't remember much about it?"

"No," muttered Will, with a certain uneasiness, as if the conversation were already tiring him.

"You don't remember Mr. Wilson?" Sister asked Will.

"No," he replied and let his head fall inertly back.

Sister gave Joe a significant look, and then said: "I have never got the right story about it. What exactly were the details?"

Joe spoke quietly to her, as if his remarks were meant for her alone. Will had closed his eyes. He went over the main incidents of the scene and fight as Jamie had described them to him.

"And who was this girl, Ivy?" Sister asked.

"Just a girl of the streets," said Joe.

"She knew him?"

"Yes."

Will had opened his eyes again and was staring at the patch of sky.

"Well," said Sister, "wasn't it nice of Mr. Wilson to come and see you?"

"Yes. Thanks very much," muttered Will.

"Good-bye," said Joe. "I'll look in again to see how you're getting along."

Will moved restlessly, but when they had gone he was relieved, and in a very short time had forgotten all about Joe's visit.

When he saw his day nurse coming towards him, he closed his eyes.

"So you've had a visitor, I hear," she said cheerfully.

He did not open his eyes. She was going to add something, but thought better of it and left him.

When he saw the usual stately procession approaching of surgeon, house surgeon, sister, and, this time, two nurses, he felt himself getting stupidly tired, and what responses he gave were dull and automatic.

The surgeon was obviously puzzled. "I wonder now?" he said. "His symptoms don't seem to fit a simple case of concussion and exhaustion. Could there be a psychological factor involved also, do you think? A defence mechanism of some sort? Probably quite unconnected with what we have heard about him so far."

"The scene", replied the houseman, "was certainly rather extraordinary for a fellow in his position. Before he landed himself in it, I can't help thinking there must have been some unusual urge. I have talked to one or two of his friends. They were amazed. Sister here. . . ."

There came a thoughtful muttering from the surgeon to the effect that it seemed outside his province now. ". . . Better ask a psychologist to come up—probably Ross—he is good with this type of case. . . ."

Will caught the drift of the talk but without much real interest. There was a barrier made out of mist, behind his mind. And they had no idea of the energy it was going to take to tear it away.

A man trying to see the earth through a floor of white cloud. Well, he just couldn't see it. . . . And there was no great point in seeing it anyway, so long as he could see the blue sky and fly in light. Effort and stress would come soon enough. . . .

On the next visiting day, Joe came back. Will did not know him, and, to get over the discomfort of worrying over why he did not know him—for his loss of memory had now been openly discussed and the psychologist had sympathetically tried to get him to co-operate—he let Joe talk.

When Joe's head went up, Will followed the

301

astonished look on his face. Nurse Macleod was bringing a girl visitor, and presently announced her as a friend to see him.

She was dark, with a rather thin face, made up, but not too noticeably. Her eyes were very bright; glittered, in fact, as if they had been washed in a drug. Her defensive manner, slightly, if unnaturally, militant, suffered an awkward moment when she looked at Will's bandaged head. He had been shaved that morning, and his face was death-pale and frail. His eyes gleamed at her from between half-closed lids; then automatically a tired smile came upon his face and it broke her stare.

The nurse tried to put her at ease. "He is getting on very well."

"I'd be all right," said Will, "only I have a difficult time with my nurse. You don't happen to be a nurse?"

"No," she said.

He looked at her. "May I ask your name?"

"Ivy."

His brows gathered for a moment. Then he slowly oscillated his head. "The old mechanism refuses to function."

"It's all right," she said. "I didn't think you would remember me. But I——"

"Please don't be upset because I don't remember."

"I'm not upset—about that," said Ivy, struggling with the emotions that the unusual situation was generating in her. "I only came because I hoped to be able to help you." She looked mistrustfully at Nurse Macleod and at Joe.

"You may as well say it to me, too," said Joe. "I'm looking after the case, as you know."

Nurse Macleod withdrew, a little against her inclination, for she had heard about Ivy and had been taking long side looks at her.

"I know who did it," Ivy said to Joe quickly. "I've got his pocket-book back. There's no money in it, but—I know. And I'll swear it. I'll go into court."

"That's plucky of you," said Joe. "That *is* plucky. But don't get that lot against you. You haven't told any one?"

"What do you think? How was I going to get the pocket-book back, unless I tore it out of the bas——, out of the fellow? I frightened him a whole lot," concluded Ivy, correctly.

Joe smiled. "All right, Ivy. If you come and have tea with me when we go out, we'll get down to the business. We must be very careful what we say, and for goodness' sake don't let the police know what you know. Not any one."

"Not likely! . . . But—why?"

"Well, you see, you know him." He nodded towards Will. "Tell me, do you think he's capable of squashing the whole thing in order to save any one, even the young bastard who did it on him?"

Ivy looked at Will, then she looked away. "He is," she had to acknowledge, nervously twisting the handle of her black bag.

"So what can we do? By the way, have you his pocket-book?"

"Yes. Will I take it out here?"

Joe nodded and Ivy produced a brown leather pocket-book. Joe opened it and then handed it to Will. "You don't happen to know this?"

Will slowly examined it. It was quite empty; money, visiting cards, stamps and odds and ends, all gone. "Can't say I know it," he replied.

"Will I stick to it?" Joe asked Ivy.

She looked at him keenly, and then decided to trust him.

"This is simply a piece of evidence for the accident you were in," Joe explained to Will.

Will smiled, but now a trifle wearily.

Joe looked at Ivy. "Well, I'll have to go. Would you care to come now or——"

Ivy glanced at Will, and found him staring down the ward with a terrible intensity. The nurse was walking towards them, accompanied by a tall golden girl carrying a small bunch of long-stemmed daffodils.

They came right to the bedside, but Nurse Macleod's cheerful words about another visitor were left unspoken in her amazement at the concentration of Will's gaze on the visitor's face. The concentration was so naked, so burningly intense in the eyes, that it was extremely painful even to look at. Then his body caught the concentration and strained upward a few inches, the head actually leaving the pillow, and hung there a moment, before it dropped back in a dead slump.

The nurse immediately went to him, and, turning round after a few seconds, said with an audible expulsion of breath. "It's only a faint, I think. Please go."

As Jenny turned from the death-pale face and bandaged head, she met Ivy's eyes. For a few moments the two women looked at each other. Automatically Jenny's small social smile came to her face and, passing Ivy, she walked up the ward carrying her daffodils.

Though Jenny's advent "shocked" the memory into him, Will could see that the doctor or house surgeon was more worried than ever about him. He was sorry in a way, for he liked the doctor. Obviously he had been a country lad, not because his speech was without trace of the characteristic rhythm of the City speech, but because of the way he looked and held his head. Will could feel the country wind blowing about the head and shoulders, smoothing and shaping them, knitting the eyebrows over the sea-coloured eyes, that concentrated and stared. He was truly concerned about Will, but also he did not like to be beaten. More than that, he had contrived to make it plain that if a person in Will's condition had made up his mind to die, then nothing could stop his dying, and yet he wanted to make Will live despite himself. Had they been boys in the country they would have had a fight over it and the doctor would probably have walloped him!

What the doctor could not understand was that, in the personal sense, it really was no concern of his whether Will lived or died. How much less then could he understand that it was a matter of no concern to Will?

Which was all interesting enough to Will, even had he not been able—as he was—to appreciate the lingering thought at the back of the doctor's country-bred mind that any one who did not want to live, who would not put up a fight, was fundamentally a weakling.

The doctor questioned him and probed him. "Now it all rests with yourself. You're all right. Say to yourself, get it into your mind: I want to get better. I know how weak you feel. But don't give into that weak feeling." He smiled with the kindest expression. "Pull yourself together!"

"Right," said Will quietly, smiling back.

The doctor concentrated on Will's eyes, searched them as deeply as he could, but all he found was a pleasant baffling.

As they moved away, he said to Sister: "I can make nothing of him. Frankly, he is dying on our hands." It annoyed him.

But Will had the pleasure of being left to himself.

For one thing he had now conquered entirely was the fear of death. Sometimes, lying there, with his mind working in its clear detached effortless way, he would have liked to be able to tell them how important this conquering of the fear of death was, important because it gave the mind a feeling not only of freedom but also of force and—he had to suppose —of dignity. For once you conquer the fear of death, you conquer the last fear of all, you surmount the last barricade. But the calm assurance of this he could never hope to convey. Certainly not to the doctor who wanted him to fight on his feet until death walloped life out of him, until it left him dead and defeated! Yet it was so obvious that that was the wrong way to fight death, entirely the wrong technique!

This had a humour of its own, too, for he felt completely calm.

Who would imagine, looking down on his white sickly face, with its weak voice, looking down on this patient who had not the energy to bite his thumb, who had so palpably given in and was "sinking", that he was yet capable of this clarity of thought?

What did people think about when they were dying, when at last the mind was coming away from the sickly humours and obscurities of the body and was free to make its own clear patterns of thought? What was important *then*?

That was a teaser! Money? Status? War? Equality? ... Will smiled.

He thought of Joe and would not have minded laying a few considerations before him, on the purely personal aspect of death!

But first of all, if only he could have laid a few things before them (those whom it might concern) regarding what he had found important in life! Not the horrors and tragedies and social savageries and razor-slashings and bomb smashings, not that welter of emotional sensation by which humanity was glutted, and horribly fascinated, and glutted again, not all that, which was the unresolved desperation of the human mind, but—and this would be extremely difficult to do because it was so simple, so incredibly simple—

Nurse Macleod stood beside him.

"Ah," he murmured, "was I sky-gazing again?"

"You were."

"It's beginning to look", he suggested, "as if you were right about that!"

"Nonsense," she said. "You made me ashamed of myself. I am disappointed with you."

"I made you blush anyway."

"What's that?" She stooped over him. His voice was weak. "Well," she replied, "you at least won't have the satisfaction of making me blush again."

How subtle her woman's instinct, "shocking" him into being interested!

"I could make you blush now."

"You?"

He nodded.

She smiled satirically.

"What you bet?" he asked.

"Sixpence."

His head moved negatively.

"Well?" she demanded.

"A small one. On forehead, if you're frightened of proper place."

"Well?" she demanded.

He looked at her, an eerie gleam gathering in his eyes. "You should be ashamed", he said slowly, "of way you carried on with *him* last night. You went a bit too far."

308

"What do you mean?"

"Do you deny it?"

"Certainly I do." Her eyes were wide on him, with a touch of superstitious fear, as if he had "the sight".

"Nurse!" His voice strengthened. His face became unearthly calm, his eyes large. "Do you understand what you have done?"

"What?"

"You have denied the true love you have for each other."

"I didn't deny it," she said swiftly. Then she saw the glimmer come back into his eyes, the small smile of mockery and triumph, and right over her face and neck went a deep lovely blush.

"You!" she said, bending her head and putting the straight clothes as straight as they were.

"The forehead—if you're frightened of my poor dry mouth."

"I wouldn't touch you", she said, "with the handle of a broom. Besides," she added, "how could I do it here?"

"True," he said. "I'll let you off—if you promise to do it when I'm dead."

That dismissed the blush, but she faced up with spirit. "You dead? You're too wicked to die before ninety." All the same she glanced at him uneasily and glanced away. "How did you know . . . ?"

"About last night? I'll tell you. And this is simple truth. Three times to-day I saw you—gazing at sky. Yesterday I saw you gaze once, but excited, restless. To-day, you got lost in sky—and came back with a small shiver of delight, and then you looked about you quickly."

"I hope you're not exciting him too much," said Sister.

Nurse Macleod started guiltily. Will smiled: "No, Sister. She is my only tonic."

"Do you feel equal to a visitor?" Sister asked.

"I'd rather not, if you don't mind."

"It's a Mrs. Armstrong, who says she wants particularly to see you. Your landlady, I gather, from the country."

Will's brows wrinkled. "All right," he said. "But give me a few minutes."

He closed his eyes at once and let his body get its "suspended" feeling. The little business with Nurse had drained him a bit. But he knew exactly how to get rid of the physical stress, and in fact within three minutes he was feeling completely "free" again.

Mrs. Armstrong must be having a long conversation with Sister, he thought, after ten minutes. They would be going into his history and wondering what could be done about him!

But when at last he saw her coming up the ward, her broad embosomed figure "of Flora and the country green", her glowing face shy a little, and when she drew near and he saw the smile inhabiting the very texture of her skin and gleaming in her kind eyes, he experienced the sharp poignant stab of an emotion very like dismay.

He saw, too, the quick stab of dismay his appearance gave her, though she hid it in a moment.

"This is a fine way to frighten us!" she said, taking his hand.

He smiled, unable to speak. Lord, he had hardly realized how weak he was!

"And when are you coming out to the farm so that I can feed you up?" Her eyes were growing unnaturally bright. He turned his head away. Oh, God, he was going to weep! He felt the disgrace coming upon him, the sickening impulse to weep like a bairn. He shut his teeth as hard as he could and kept his eyes closed.

Mrs. Armstrong took the opportunity to wipe her own eyes. "I'm just an auld wife," she said to the sister, smiling, trying to excuse herself. The two women spoke to each other, until the spasm had subsided in Will. He had not wept, but his eyes were wet, and while he took his handkerchief from under his pillow, Mrs. Armstrong continued to tell the sister about her farm.

"Kind of you to come," said Will, with an uncertain smile.

"I've just been longing to come. What a shock you gave us!"

The sister said she would be back in a minute or two.

"Are they good to you here?" Mrs. Armstrong asked in a quick whisper.

Will smiled, feeling light-hearted. "Would you like to have me under your eye?"

"Faith, I would," said Mrs. Armstrong. "Wouldn't you like to come?"

"Yes."

"Well, why not get better as quick as you can—I mean, well enough so that you can be shifted?"

She looked so innocent—as if she hadn't just been told that he was going under!

"What a bother I'd be to you."

"Bother? How can you say that?" Her eagerness was almost hurt. What a genuine woman this was! Her whole nature, to give, to give. Not to take, not to demand her dues, but to give. And a landlady at that!

"Thank you very much," he murmured.

"It's not thanks I'm wanting."

"I know."

"Well—will you promise me you'll come—as soon as you can?"

"All right."

"That's settled." She nodded firmly, ignoring his unconvincing tone. "That's fine. Well, well, now. What a steer you put us into!"

"Did I?"

"When you didn't come on the Saturday night, I thought you would just have been up to one of your ploys! But when you didn't come by Sunday afternoon, I felt sure there was something wrong. Jenny just laughed at me. She said I didn't understand the present generation. As if I was an old wife!"

But Will was looking at her as though his earthly mind were finding slight difficulty in following all this. "I thought", he said, at last, "that Jenny was away for the week-end?"

"Her? Not she! I gave her a good scolding when she trooped in on the Saturday, large as life. 'Och!' says she, 'when it came to the bit I couldn't leave my garden.' Did you ever hear the like?" Will had turned his gaze to the window. Mrs. Armstrong studied his expression now with shrewd penetrating eyes and rambled on: "By the Monday I was quite convinced something had gone wrong, so I asked her to find out from your office. She phoned, it seems, and you hadn't turned up. Then she got a bit anxious, and in some way or other found out you were in the infirmary. She came out late at night to give me the news. We were in a gey state about you, I can tell you!"

"Were you?" said Will smiling, but with scepticism deep in his eyes.

"We were that. She phoned the infirmary every day and either came out or wrote me."

"Nice of her."

"Ah, but you don't know how nice Jenny can be until you get behind her reserve. And that's mostly shyness! She's one of the finest lassies in the world. If Jenny was on your side, she'd die for you as natural as—as—eat her porridge. But I'm wearying you out?"

"No. I just get little tired. Don't mind that." His eyes slowly closed and his breath came out in small open-mouthed gusts. She sat quietly beside him. Was she going too far too quickly? Her shrewd expression grew soft and she was manifestly threatened by emotion again. He looked so frail, she could have taken him in her arms and carried him away.

He opened his eyes. "Thank you for coming."

"Is there anything I can get for you, anything you would like?"

"No, thanks."

His smile twisted the heart in her. "Is there any one you would like to see?" she asked gently. "Jenny would like to come and see you, but she's frightened to—to trouble you."

A touch of the old mocking humour came to his face. "I'd rather have yourself."

"Me? An auld wife? Tut! Tut!"

"No one has been so kind to me."

"Oh, now, now! Promise me", she pleaded suddenly, her reserves down, "that you will get well."

He looked at her steadily, but did not speak. For the first time she felt clearly that he was removed from her, from every one, and that he was going to die. Awe and compassion overwhelmed her. They spoke to each other with their eyes. The intimacy was dear and, in her case, terrible, but, in his case, calm.

"Well?" said Sister. "When is he going to be well enough to go out to see you?"

Will lifted his eyes and stared at her, too. "Soon, I hope," he said with deadly calm.

"Now, that's the way to talk!" Sister nodded.

Mrs. Armstrong had some last words for him. He did not hear them properly, because he apprehended more clearly the message of her eyes, and her eyes did not ask anything; they gave without measure out of the store of her loving kindness.

After she had gone, he found that he had lost the flawless calm of his assurance. He became restless and much more conscious of his physical aches. He stared at the sky, but could not get its remote calmness. This vexed him and he began to feel the prickling sensation of fever. His thought, too, became erratic. He tried to clarify his thought by deliberately thinking of Jenny. Assuming Mrs. Armstrong had come specially to tell him Jenny hadn't gone away for the week-end, what then? He saw the implication—that his loss of Jenny had subconsciously inhibited any eager desire for life and accordingly a "defence mechanism" had been raised up. . . . But how humanly trivial, how absurd—as if men and women did not die without such romantic excuse! It was an indignity heaped upon a man's integrity and loneliness. The next thing they would be doing would be bringing Jenny to see him, as their last trump card! That would finally be unbearable.

Clearly, too, if Jenny had not gone away for her week-end there was some hitch in their programme. She would not back out of an arrangement like that at the last minute. She was not that kind of girl; and, anyway, he would despise her if she did.

Damn them, why couldn't they leave him alone!

When, later, Nurse Macleod came and took his temperature, he did not speak to her or observe the astonished look on her face. She stuck down the black dot on his chart and went hurriedly away.

House surgeon and Sister appeared on the scene. He didn't mind. Visitors were forbidden. Philip

Manson was denied for the second time. Mac and Don went away silent.

Oh, he knew all right what was happening; he knew the paraphernalia of the business, but presently his mind lost interest even in that, for it entered the confused but at times intensely vivid world of delirium.

In this world there came upon him a compelling conviction. The straight lines, the whiteness, the dim night light, the high-up window showing but shutting out the sky (night and daylight at the same time) became a prison, and not a stable prison, for sometimes the white lines, the solid edges of the rectangular beds, could tilt up threateningly against his desire to escape.

The more he was defeated in this way the fiercer his conviction became. And his conviction was simply this: that if he could get to the place where he saw the wild geese, all would be well with him again. He did not think of being bodily well in life. He thought of bright ease and peace and light, kindly light, glistening with the singing of birds, and an air cool, cool, cool on his face and along the skin of his body and cool to the sky. A divine loveliness of being, slyly and laughingly aware, and free.

Now he realized, in his delirium, that his resources were slight, that the prison was strong, and that his only chance lay in cunning. Once or twice, however, his conviction grew so overpowering that he threw caution aside and started up swiftly . . . but at once the forces in the prison gripped him and pushed him back.

As with a sea-anemone that has been roughly

touched, his resources drew inward, to protect the core of his being. For he realized quite clearly that it was a very small core, about the size of a nut, and now he had to defend it lest, of itself, it should pass into nothingness.

The extremities of his physical body, left unprotected, were growing cold. He could hardly feel the doctor's hands on his feet. The doctor was deeply interested in his case, because it baffled him and he did not like to be baffled.

But now he could not afford to think of the doctor, for the core of his being was losing its stability, its central assurance, was wanting to float away . . .

And presently Will did in fact have the perfectly clear and delightful feeling of floating out of his body, floating above it, and looking down on it. He saw the doctor's tense puzzled attitude, his bluff shoulders, as he stood upright staring down at Will's face. Sister drew back from the bed. It was all over. Nurse Macleod was silently affected. As the death-screen was set up, the doctor turned away.

And now Nurse Macleod approached to pull the sheet up over his face. Will gathered all his resources and sent them to his face, but he could not move a muscle. With an energy that to him was herculean, blinding, he tried to move an eyelid. And faintly, but yet perceptibly, to the tender human eyes of the girl from Lewis, the right eyelid quivered. The sheet dropped from her hand and she involuntarily called out: "Doctor!"

The doctor came back.

An hour later the doctor was able to inform Mrs. Montgomery that her nephew had got over the crisis and that there was a fair chance now of a complete recovery. "Although", he added, "I can guarantee nothing, for the case is a very complicated one."

She was moved in a way that made her look heavy and stupid.

"I hope you will consider, doctor, that this is your private case. As for the infirmary, I hope that I know my duty."

He glanced at her closely, for she had spoken with dignity; then he accompanied her to the outer door.

When he came back, he said lightly to the sister: "The human mind is a profound mystery."

The sister answered: "She wouldn't miss an odd thousand anyway."

The doctor smiled. He was feeling tired.

CHAPTER NINE

*

Will lay in his deck-chair, "floated" by rugs and cushions from the deft hands of Mrs. Armstrong, and looked at the elm-tree.

Was there anything in the world as lovely as a tree? A yacht in full sail? A woman walking down the world? The silence of a mountain? A symphony? A host of golden daffodils? The essence of Leonardo's mind smiling through paint? . . .

Lovely was the wrong adjective, but it served, for it had something in it of light and grace. . . .

And a tree was grace and ease, deep-rooted, deep- and wide-rooted in the earth, the black earth, under the vivid grass, and wide-branched above the earth, under the sky. It gave a voice to the invisible wind from regions behind the world, from desolate sea inlets, from prairies awaiting in grey silver the rising of the sun, from wastes of seas that know no land horizons, from the down-rush of mountains, from beleaguered cities, from battlefields, from the back courts of tenements where it whirled the children's pagan fires. . . .

There in the branches it sighed more gently than any woman's mouth; or shrieked in the night like all the lost souls in hell.

But now—the calm, the dignity, the poise, that incomparable effect of ease, of breadth, of balance. In the gloaming its myriad twigs and branches, gone black, were a necromantic etching against the sky. In the sunlight they lifted the light up, lifted it up on the air, as they lifted the singing of birds.

Wise and ancient and wrinkled, with a listening silence, like the silence in the heart of a harp—ah, more than that. . . .

The twigs bowed and rose again. . . .

Dear lovely elm-tree!

This was the time of convalescence, when he should outdo the poets! And the poets were right; not the poets who thought, but the poets who, having thought, listened.

This, this was at the back of *everything*.

He had tried to make Joe understand something of this on the way hither. He had insisted on dismissing the taxi at the spot where he had seen the wild geese, and there had told Joe smilingly of the incident of the geese, had explained to him how he believed that the incident had saved his life. "You know how difficult it is to kill a cat or a weasel. Have you ever tried to drown kittens?" Joe hadn't. "Well, you've got to drown them a very long time. Once, as a boy, I helped at the drowning. It was in the country. We put them in a pail of water. You have to keep poking them down. At last we held them down with our hands. I hated doing it. So I made sure that there wasn't a single move left in them. I wanted them to be drowned utterly. Well, when it was all over we poured them out on the refuse heap. I wanted to bury them, but that was voted soft. An hour later I sneaked round to see them—and there was one, with its blind head, moving . . . I was that kitten, and the impulse to move was provided by the wild geese."

Joe's eyes grew thoughtful.

Then Will told him, as they walked down to the farm, about the incident of the bird-singing in the dawn. He told it with the air of one telling an amusing fairy story, otherwise Joe might be embarrassed. And even as it was, Joe said little.

"An odd delusion, wasn't it?" Will remarked.

"It was," said Joe.

Will laughed, and explained to Joe why he laughed, slyly pulling Joe's leg.

"You mistrust anything in the nature of the mystical! Anything that savours of the irrational, the religious, you at once are up against. You see it as the insidious enemy, the social dope?"

"Don't you think there's reason?" asked Joe.

"Of course! Yes!" But Will's laugh was full of gaiety.

He had tried to tell Joe that an experience of that sort did not make a man an apostle of its theory or creed or philosophy; what it did was to bring him into harmony with himself, to integrate him, and so make him a stronger force than ever for—well, for the help, say, he would now give to Joe.

But Joe was not too sure. Yet he was troubled also.

As if there was something that Joe had denied himself, a memory of an old childish indulgence, a private weakness not for the grim world of modern social relations!

It was going to require courage to be gay! Easy enough to be gay in company, laughing and drinking to all hours, in a positive orgy of escape. Escape from what? From oneself, of course. But it was another matter being gay *in oneself*. To look at a bunch of grass, a tree, the sky, to feel the wind, the rain, the light . . . ah, light, not only outside, in the air, on the body, but inside, behind the mind . . . to see, to feel, in the final core of oneself, and so to be whole—and therefore all the more game to break the fell clutch of circumstance, individual or social!

Hail, Felicity! Philip had told him she had very nearly chucked up her Paris job when she had learned the full details of his misadventures. In a long letter she had rallied him, asked him a score of questions, and begged him to come and see her. It was a thought! Why not? His convalescence would certainly run to three weeks. His eyelids quivered in a primordial humour. And this sun did stir the sluggish blood with snake-like thrills!

A voice called inside the house. The voice of Jenny. She had arrived!

Will's head fell back and he breathed heavily. It was going to take him a little while to get all his pith back.

Presently she appeared at the inner end of the house on the way to the garden, raised her hand in greeting, hesitated a moment, and then came walking along the grass towards him.

"Please!" she exclaimed, stopping him from getting up. "I'm just going into the garden. Mrs. Armstrong says you are getting on?"

They were now on easy speaking terms. Yet when she smiled, there was still that calm reserve of the features, mixture of reserve and wonder, that had affected him from the very beginning. She could look at a flower as if she were seeing it for the first time, he thought.

"You were longing to get at the garden?"

"I was," she confessed.

"It's a great hobby."

"Hobby?" She opened her eyes in a half-startled expression, half-assumed. Then she smiled as he smiled.

The trouble about her smile to Will, who was in a rather weak and therefore more readily excitable condition, was its contrast to her gravity. He withdrew his eyes.

He watched her move about the garden for a time and then closed his eyes. There was all this afternoon. But to-morrow, Sunday, Philip was coming, and perhaps some of the boys from the office.

He listened to the wind's quiet sigh in the elm; felt the sun; and slowly his mind lifted and floated. Delicious feeling. He was learning the trick of it all right! Nothing would ever deny it to him again. It

was pagan and primordial. Or were these just words
—for the earth-old inner rhythm of life itself?

Mrs. Armstrong brought out his tea-tray. "It's a
poor old bachelor," he said, "who has to feed by
himself."

She laughed and brought out a tray for Jenny and
called her from the garden. "I have to see the grieve,"
Will heard her shout. "You can pour the tea."

And Jenny came and poured the tea, sitting on a
rug in a friendly way.

"This is very kind of you," Will acknowledged.
"If I move too suddenly I still feel some of my
bruises."

She looked at him with troubled eyebrows, the
clarity of her eyes hurt a little.

"Would you like to hear the real story?" he asked
with quiet humour.

"I would," she said naturally.

"I don't know if you know much about our slum
regions? It's a long story. If I'm going to make it
intelligible I'll have to tell you about Joe, and socialism, and Jamie Melvin, and his wife Ettie who died
in childbirth, and Ivy, and that last strange night—
when a bruiser and myself fought on the street and
I was knocked down and trampled upon and success-
fully robbed. You wouldn't understand it otherwise;
and I'm afraid it's too long a story."

"No, I should like to hear it, but—just as you like."

"I should like, frankly, to tell it to you," said Will
simply.

"Please do, then."

He told it calmly, describing the characters and the places and the incidents with an interest that now and then drew her into the recital by such indirect questions as "But perhaps you don't know that . . . ?" until the whole thing lived for her. His description of his meeting with Ivy had a cool detachment that made it very real.

"I don't regret any of it," he concluded. "I blame no one—hardly even myself—for what happened to me. And I am very glad of one thing—that Jamie came to see me just before I left the infirmary. He had been greatly struck apparently by the way I did not hit back at him and yet let out at the boxer! Of course Joe told him a few things, too. He was also on edge that night, poor devil, because he knew that the decision about his compensation was just about due."

"Did he get it?"

"Yes. About thirty shillings a week. Mary and he are hitting it off quite well, Joe says, and he's on the lookout for any sort of light job."

"Must be dreadful—living down there in the slums."

"No earth, no flowers . . . ?" Will smiled. "But it's not really as bad as it sounds to us or as it is written about. Their reactions are not our reactions. Your garden here would bore them stiff. And the overwhelming mass of them are extraordinarily decent; the women caring for their room and kitchen, or even single end, their home, keeping it clean and tidy, concerned about the menfolk and children, putting up a magnificently stoic fight against a real or

325

ever-threatening economic famine that is hellish because it shouldn't be. It's that awful greyness, gloom, that got me. Their lives are not dramatic. They are grey. But they don't feel that greyness as we would. To them the street noises and the grinding trams are their singing-birds. Well, all right. But for God's sake, keep them from fear, fear of want; let us—oh!" Will dropped his head back.

"I am glad you spoke to me like this," said Jenny quietly.

Will lifted his head and shook it with a wry smile. "I did not tell it to you for nothing. You see, I feel guilty about having intruded on you personally."

"Please, let us forget that."

"It's not that: it's this. Philip Manson and I are old schoolboy friends. He wanted to come and see me to-morrow. How could I keep him back? I have never told him, of course, that you were here. I have always respected your—your obvious desire to have some corner all your own. Oh, I know. Please understand me. And perhaps", concluded Will, who had not looked at Jenny, "he will bring my aunt."

Upon his ears came a small, suppressed, and infectious laugh. It startled him like a blow, and he glanced at Jenny with an astonishment that in a moment became confused.

"It was—the lugubrious way—you mentioned your aunt," she tried to explain, trembling on the verge of complete laughter.

Will looked away. "Oh Lord, that's divine of you," he murmured, tremendously excited, because in the instant he saw what she would be like when she came from behind her reserve and spilled over in golden fun. Primavera might be solemn in the picture, but once on her toes in the wind. . . .

They were both awkward for a little, a trifle nervous, and suddenly Jenny asked solemnly:

"Why do you think I should mind about Philip Manson so much?"

Will gathered all his resources and looked at her. "Don't you?"

"Well," she said, "I certainly like him very much."

Will glanced away and wet his lips with his tongue.

"What have you on your mind?" she asked.

"That *would* be personal!"

"You have been very personal to me about yourself—in that story. That was nice of you. I liked your frankness."

"And you would be frank in return?"

She looked away. "Yes."

They were silent. At last he said: "He's coming about three to-morrow. If you're not in, I shan't mention that you're here."

She turned her eyes on him, and, with that curious expression of troubled hurt, they accused him of being trivially evasive, of not saying what was really in his mind.

"How can I say it?" he asked.

"Is it about——" she paused.

"That week-end? Yes."

"Did Philip tell you?"

"Oh no! Philip would never tell."

"Who told you?"

"No one. I just—knew."

She removed her eyes from his face and looked into the distance. "I felt that you knew," she said.

"You didn't go?"

"No."

"Why?"

"I don't know. I—it was dreadful."

"Was it?"

"Yes. I found I didn't want to go—and felt horrible about it, and mean."

He looked at her. "Why didn't you want to go?"

She shook her head. "I don't know."

"Did you hate yourself for not going? Did you cry out inside yourself: 'I must go! I must go!' and yet could not drag your feet to go?"

Her eyes came full upon him. "Why couldn't I go?"

"It's difficult. It goes pretty deep, I think."

She was now all alive, sitting perfectly erect, her startled yet calm head rising up out of the earth.

The gate from the steading clicked and Mrs. Armstrong cried to them cheerfully as she approached.

Will lay in bed watching the shadows of the twigs of the elm-tree floating on the blind, and, thinking of last night, floated with them, and beyond them.

Jenny had said it would be a sunny morning, because of the slight touch of frost as they came down through the twilight and the red haze on the horizon. It was the most magical walk he had ever had. They were extremely friendly and full of quick laughing talk, but still shy and reserved. They did not carry on the conversation interrupted by Mrs. Armstrong. They made no effort to "explain" anything. There had been the living moment, each sensitively aware of the other, of bird-singing, the darkening trees, each finding out about the other in a thousand impersonal personal ways, and Jenny—he could see it in her—frightened that he might come too close too soon.

But he hadn't—not with the whole summer ahead! At thought of the whole summer, the weeks and the months, the early birches, the warmth in the earth, the uplands, the June nights, the long enchanted June nights, his mind swooned away under the sun, carrying the June twilight of its thought with it, wherein Jenny walked bareheaded.

He was still a bit weak probably! Silently he laughed and looked with slanting eyes at the shadows on the blind.

What a change had come upon his spirit since he had come to this farm! Yet all that had happened had really been the simplest thing in the world. By a lucky chance, he had broken through the integument of fear and hatred and grey concern that wrap the daily life around, and risen above it. There was nothing mysterious at all in the performance, though the effect was magical. Any simple person lying on his back in the sun, with closed eyes, listening to the wind in a tree or the sea on a shore, would experience the effect to a certain degree. And any one who has so experienced it for a moment opens his eyes with a smile, a smile of goodness and beneficence, and an inclination to hum with wind or sea.

After that, thought Will, it is entirely a matter of degree. Personal trouble or social tragedy may supervene ... but always cunningly at the back of the mind will be the *memory* of the release, like an effect of light.

And what works for the individual must also work —let it come!—for humanity.

Noble thought! It charged Will with happy laughter. Most of the solemnity and ideals that infect the world should be stuffed into a bag and drowned in mid-Atlantic!

Oh Lord, was Jenny never going to get up? Was she lying awake thinking—what? He could see her grave face turned towards the window, the eyes brimming with light. There was a picture for a poor fellow! He groaned—and came alive like a squirrel as her door opened and closed.

He leapt out of bed, and then sat heavily down again. The body was not quite so strong as all that yet! Its weakness was a joke. Perhaps it never had even had concussion. Defence mechanism only! You watch it! said Will. It's as full of tricks as a bag of monkeys.

They breakfasted apart, but set off immediately afterwards on the walk which Jenny had promised to take him. But first the tour of the garden. She so loved the garden that in a moment she was all alive. And Will saw that this was something which no one could ever take from her. It was her elm-tree and her sun!

And he was glad, profoundly glad, that she had something she loved, apart from himself or any one else.

"Behold the hole I made in the bishopweed!" he said ruefully.

She looked at the wreck of his labour and turned away at once.

He glanced after her and followed. "I suppose it was very wrong of me, but I didn't——"

"I was horrid," she interrupted him shortly.

As they were going up the farm road above the steading, he said: "I'll tell you an odd experience I had. I was once walking along a street and I saw a girl walking in front of me with quite the most perfect figure you ever saw. So I thought to myself what a pity it is that in life you rarely see a body like that with a face to match. So I hurried up a bit and had a side glance at the face and lo! it did match. That so took my breath away that I swerved and found myself in front of a bookseller's shop; and staring at me was a book, entitled *How to Make a Rock Garden*. So as I didn't want to overtake the girl, I went in and bought the book. An odd experience, wasn't it?"

"Very."

"Though to give life its due, it's full of these odd experiences. But I never had the courage to give the girl the book."

"Why?"

"Well," said Will, "you gave me every chance to present it to you, didn't you?"

She stopped and looked at him with that troubling

of surprise and wonder that he would never get used to. She read the truth of the story in his eyes and went on at once.

They were silent for a little time.

"It's a very good book," he said, in cheerful practical tones. "I have it down there. And that bank is a grand place for it. I'll have to do a little work to toughen me up, and a little harmless weeding—if you're sure I wouldn't be intruding?"

She stopped abruptly. "Would you?" she asked, her face kindling. "I have longed for rock plants. Plants that come up every year. I cannot tell you about them." She thought for a moment and then went on: "If we plan that out—I might come out one or two evenings during the week—to see how it's going on. The bus fares would ruin me, but—I'd come."

"Would you?"

"Yes. And we'll have to get stones. And not ordinary stones but bits of rocks, and not just sticking them in the ground like little dogs' graves, but making ledges of them and building them up."

She walked away with this exciting thought until they came to the place where she had overtaken him as she came down from the wood.

"That's the wood," she said. "Perhaps you'll find it a sad wood."

"How have you found it?"

"We'll go this way, by the small burn. . . . Look!"

In every nook and cranny, overhanging the water,

everywhere, the two sides of the little burn were starred with primroses. "These are celandines," she said, "Wordsworth's flower. And that, colts-foot." She was walking on. "This greeny-gold stuff is wood spurge. Of course, the year hasn't started yet. But this spot is a marvel, right up to the wood. To lie here and listen to the humble-bees on a summer day, when it's in full flower, is very pleasant. You don't quite go to sleep, but hover about, like a bee yourself. Do you like it?"

"Yes," he said quietly. Its intimate invisible face ran round the corner.

She walked on calmly, and he had the odd notion that the flowers did not look at her but at him, the intruder, before they turned, and went on with her. Her ankles were firm and her feet moved with a sure grace over the springy turf. With a momentary touch of panic, he saw her in sober truth as Primavera, and he stared at the curves of her body and her golden head. Then he looked down at the grass, at the primroses, with an expression arrested a little in awe.

When they had opened and shut the field gate, she told him to follow her, because for a short distance it was marshy in between the scattered trees. She went quickly from tussock to tussock and he followed. "Now it's all right," she said.

The ground sloped up what looked like the side of a mound, and they had to stoop under branches and dodge round bushes; but within a few yards they emerged on flat ground, on top of what seemed a great circular mound, covered deeply in yellow-green of moss and close-cropped grass. Their footfalls were so noiseless that rabbits sat up before taking to their long hind legs. "Look!" she whispered, and pointed with her eyes to a rabbit couched under the root of a juniper bush a couple of paces to his right. It obviously had been surprised too late and decided to risk lying still. Round eyes, flattened ears, and sensitive nostrils. He followed Jenny at once. But there was a quick beat in his heart now, and looking up he saw the sunlight arrested in this still place. And the trees—had he ever seen that exquisite brown of larches before the délicate green needles come? But what was this? Each larch seemed lit with little upright red globes. He rubbed his eyes, but they did not vanish. He went forward and gazed at the fairy-like lights, at the tender deep red cone flowers. Slowly he looked about him, in the hushed warmth, and softly began to laugh, his eyes alert and his ears. Then he remembered Jenny and looked at her.

She was smiling, her face full of a deeper warmth than sunlight, and an expression in her eyes friendly and tender. "I hoped you would laugh," she said.

He glanced away from her, until the sudden tumult would subside. "So this was your test?"

"No. It wouldn't have mattered anyway. But I'm glad. I love this place."

"You come here often?"

"Yes. Every Sunday. The sun always seems to shine on this ancient mound. No one has ever been here with me before."

He could not look at her. Could not trust himself,

did not know what to say, so he said: "You did not seem happy, coming down from the wood, that day."

"No—because you had destroyed my happiness. You were digging in the garden. You came into the wood in my mind. I think I hated you. I was fond of Philip."

"But what had I done?"

"Nothing. That face of yours just haunted me— like a crime." She tried to smile. "You cannot understand how that made me ashamed of myself, how it drove me—oh, I don't know."

His expression quickened in humour. "Crime! It is an accepted fact that persons with a secret vice know each other when they meet. In a moment they know it, without sign or symbol, as we knew each other." He was finding it difficult to speak. He gazed over the tops of the trees. "The wild geese are nesting in the far north." But his effort at a smile ran cold upon his face. He looked at her and found she was trembling, as he was himself. They came to each other swiftly, and clung strongly together, to keep their parts from flying adrift.

The shadow of a pigeon sped swiftly over the grass. A pair of chaffinches flirted through the air. Bird-notes warbled down through the branches that carried their tiny deep red cones and pin-points of green. Up from the valley fields came the crying of a colony of gulls. Far into the moor above, a cock grouse crew.

The mound lay with its back in the sun, full of

silence, of the past, of sleepy memories of strange rites being dreamed into the present, into the future. A rabbit appeared from behind a juniper bush and, seeing them, sat up on its hind legs, its forelegs drooping against its body, its ears cocked and pink against the sun, like a rabbit in a fairy story. Everywhere the yellow-green moss was patterned with sunlight and shadow. Through a depth of tree-tops came the croodling of a pigeon: *You're* too too *lazy! You're* too too *lazy! You!*

They were sitting now a little apart, he with his legs crossed and she with her heels tucked under her. Because of the strange sweet tension in their hearts, they sat in silence, their minds and bodies open to their environment so that they seemed part of it, diffused through it.

Out of the tranced mood, he smiled and said: "This is an illustration of a theory of mine. At that moment when you are most intensely yourself, you are also most intensely part of everything else—even of some one else." He gave her a sly look. But she did not respond nor yet withdraw her eyes. An amber cup brimful and still. She had the intuition to wait for his deeper meaning. And he suddenly said sharply: "Oh Lord, Jenny, don't look at me like that or I'm lost!" He turned his head away and the rabbit hopped a few steps and sat up again. "So let us talk. How often we'll have to talk!" His voice quivered with mirth. "Are you looking forward to it?"

She nodded, and her smile, deep and glimmering, came outward upon her face.

"Jenny, you are very very lovely," he said quietly.

"I'm waiting!" she replied.

"I think you've been waiting since time began. And—you'll be waiting on some such mound till time is dead." His head moved in restless humour. "Were you conscious of waiting?"

She sat quite still, looking away. "Yes," she said at last. "And yet I don't know," she added. "Or—at least—I know only now."

"That's a lovely one," he murmured.

But she did not let the remark disturb her. "I loved being here alone. There were moments—sheer lovely moments—I did not want any one. The green coming on the grass, on the trees. And the sun. Then, too, down in the garden. Sometimes, in the office, when things were difficult, I could, away at the back of my mind, walk into the garden and look at a primula. I could—get its scent. It—I don't know, I can't tell you."

He sat looking down at his hands, silent.

"I'm sorry", she said, "that I was rude to you, but you came—well——"

"The serpent into the garden, the insinuating city serpent."

She nodded. "It was even worse than that. *That* I might have managed. But your face, against the trees, that first time I saw you: you looked round— I'm not good at explaining—but there was something about that moment that was uncanny. It was as if I had seen your face before in some other land or in a dream—all of a sudden, before I could think, like a heart-beat. I saw at once it was nonsense. I banished you. I laughed calmly at myself. But there were moments when you persisted in coming back, that I hated you. Nothing like it had ever happened to me before. Young girls may fancy they fall in love and so on, but—nothing ever *like that*. I wasn't curious or interested—I think I was afraid—perhaps, too, because of other things that were happening to me. Let me confess one silly thing. I saw you more often than you are aware! I was trying to see you look ordinary and commonplace. And twice—twice—I thought I did. I was glad. And then, one day in the office, when my mind was all in a tumult—you looked at me from the edge of your wood. It was terrible, as if you'd stung me. And it was, oh, it was humiliating!"

"The day you came down the ward, you didn't sting me: you stabbed me with a knife. Think of the utter humiliation of fainting!" They were both smiling, their fingers plucking about the moss. "You came down the ward like Primavera, calm, with the sun in your yellow hair and birds about your head and daffodils in your hands. Dear God, had you no idea of the enormity of what you were doing? Had you no pity?"

"If you had known the effort it took to do that!" He looked away. "There are five rabbits now."

"I have counted eleven," she said.

"Why are they not frightened of our voices?"

"Because we don't mean them any harm."

Her simple words made him breathe deeply, as if they had raised a small tumult of emotion.

338

"Do you think we'll ever get to the end of this story?"

"I hope not," she said.

He looked at her, but she dropped her eyes, leaving the smile on her face.

Her skin was transparent as a film of amber against light. Her eyes were wide-spaced, her brows clear and firm. The sunlight warmed itself in her hair. The stillness, the calm, that was of the essence of her personality, brimmed before him. But as he looked more closely, he saw the calm invaded by a subtle tremoring. Her hand, moving about the moss, quivered ever so slightly. The smile passed, and as she looked up, giving him frankly her eyes, he saw a troubling in their depths so lovely that it was more moving than tragedy.

"We're late for lunch," she said.

"I know."

They made no effort to get up.

"There may be love at first sight and all that," he said. "I don't know. What I am sure of now is that between minds searching for the same thing, there is some mysterious communication. I'll tell you about the wild geese." And, as they sat there, he quietly told her the story.

It interested her very deeply.

"It's like a fairy-tale," she said.

He laughed. "Not quite true! And it isn't—quite true."

She regarded him.

339

"I mean, you can't make it quite true—in the telling."

She nodded. "I have never been carried away like that, yet I know what you mean."

"So you see that's the sort of thing you walked into," he said.

"The city girl, with her insinuating tricks!"

"I called you that at least. You and your flowers! Spring! I scoffed at you. I never hated you. You didn't interfere with my mind enough for that. I didn't even own you in any interesting way to my mind. You had entered it and gone out of sight in it. I shrugged. Hmf! Who are you? Yet the sight of you coming down the ward. . . . And it was enormously complicated by the wild geese, by that queer preoccupation with light. More than that. May I tell you?"

"Please."

He stirred restlessly. She heard the excitement in his voice as it tried to retain its ease. "There is much to tell you. You are like some one who has been a long time away. And it's the queer stuff. But it's very real, Jenny. (I love your name!) It's as real as the slums. It's more real than the slums in a way." His fingers began plucking the grass. His words were light, like froth playing about, half-veiling, this new incredible reality of the nearness and relationship of their two solid bodies. "It's a long difficult subject and has to do with society and socialism and freedom, all the things that are going to be intensely important to the folk of our generation, things we may have to fight for." He gave her a sidelong smile. "You see, they are making all sorts of mechanical theories about the individual, about human nature. The individual is nothing without society, we know. That is the mechanism. But the creative spirit—it is a personal thing, and I have the idea that it comes only out of love and tenderness." He regarded the moss in his hand for a moment. "When you've been wandering through the shadows, the grim facts that seem to have no purpose, and then hit on *that* truth; when you know in yourself that it's as true as anything in science; then—you have a sudden feeling of freedom and happiness. You begin to see things in its light. But I'm not really explaining anything. I'm just talking to pass the time!"

She did not speak for a little. "There are meanings I do not quite follow. But—I'm glad you spoke like that. And—I'll understand yet."

With a slow dawning conviction, he said: "Jenny, you will!"

She gave him a shy flash of his own humour. "You sound like one for whom life is only beginning."

"It is," he said. "And you?"

She could not speak. Looking at her, he was drawn into a swift movement that scattered the rabbits; but a few of them stopped to sit up; whereupon, seeing no further cause for alarm, they went on eating.

NEIL GUNN 1891 – 1973
THE SCOTTISH COLLECTION

THE LOST CHART
A cold war thriller set in the Scottish city of Glasgow shortly after the
Second World War, '*the Lost Chart*' moves on two distinct planes –
the physical and the metaphysical.

THE LOST GLEN
The famous novel on the decline of Highland ways and values
in the 1920s.

THE OTHER LANDSCAPE
'*The Other Landscape*' returns to the familiar setting of the Highlands
but with a new element of dark humour.

THE SILVER BOUGH
Archaeologist Simon Grant comes to the Highlands to investigate an
ancient cairn. A stranger in a strange part of the country, he finds that
there are barriers to understanding between him and the people
of the community.

SECOND SIGHT
The setting is a Highland shooting lodge, whose occupants are depicted
in stark contrast to the local people. A violent death is foreseen.
But whose? How? When? The drama is played out against a
background of strange mists and elemental landscapes.

OFF IN A BOAT
'*Off in a Boat*' logs the adventures of a man, who at a critical point of his
life, throws caution to the wind, and with his wife as Crew, navigates his
way round the West Coast of Scotland.
Whilst Gunn masters the art of sailing and anchorage, the Crew
explores the possibilities of the camera.

AS IT WAS

An Autobiography 1897-1918
Naomi Mitchison

Naomi Mitchison celebrated her ninetieth
birthday in 1987 and is considered one of the
foremost contributors to the literary scene. In
SMALL TALK she plunges us into a child's eye
view of Edwardian life. Girl matures to woman in
ALL CHANGE HERE and Naomi Mitchison
explores her desire for freedom to be and know
herself and her own mind.

CHARLES RENNIE MACKINTOSH

1868-1928
Jocelyn Grigg

An indispensable fully illustrated guide to the
architect, designer and watercolourist who, for his
futuristic vision, was acclaimed father of the
modern movement.

BURRELL: PORTRAIT OF A COLLECTOR

1861-1858
Richard Marks

In 1983 the fabulous collections of *objets d'art* built
up by Sir William Burrell went on show in its
entirety for the first time in a gallery specially
designed and built for it.

This is a unique and lavishly illustrated portrait of
an extraordinary genius.

ROBERT LOUIS STEVENSON 1850 — 1894

RLS: A LIFE STUDY (Jenni Calder)
'In this well-researched and fluently written book
Stevenson emerges as an extraordinary and unusually
gifted Scotsman: delicate, magnanimous, capable of
arousing love in women and devotion in men.'

(Alan Bold, The Scotsman)

'RLS: A LIFE STUDY penetrates the moods and
conflicting desires of a writer who could get and produce
unending excitement from TREASURE ISLAND and, as
well, write masterpieces like THRAWN JANET and
THE MASTER OF BALLANTRAE.'

(Emma Tennant, The Guardian)

ST IVES (R L Stevenson)
This unfinished novel by RLS was written between
January 1893 and October 1894. ST IVES begins in
Edinburgh Castle in 1813, where a French prisoner,
Champdivers (alias St Ives) is being held captive.
A tale of intrigue and suspense unfolds.

Because of RLS's recurrent illnesses this tale was taken
down in dictation by his step-daughter, Bella Strong.
About 6 weeks prior to his death, he laid the story to one
side. Jenni Calder has now, with the prompting of
Bob Storey, written a convincing and colourful new
ending which would have impressed RLS himself.

MEMORIES & PORTRAITS (R L Stevenson)
This book documents aspects of Stevenson's experience of
life and literature, and is full of illumination of his other
works. The essays have a special interest in this wider
context, but they can also be read and enjoyed for their
own sake. They are the product of a meticulous
craftsman, who handled words with scrupulous care, and
wanted to avoid tired images and idea.